Eve's Prescription

by Ewdina Martin-Arnold

Indigo Love Stories
Sensuous
are published by

Genesis Press, Inc.
315 Third Avenue North
Columbus, MS 39701

Eve's Prescription

First Edition

Noah opened the front door to his condo in West Seattle on Saturday, and almost droped his coffee. Some sloshed over the rim and hit his big toe. "Damn!"

"Not the reaction I expected, "Eve said, standing on the landing outside his door.

Noah let her in, "Not you, the coffee." He made a comical picture as he held the cup with one hand, and wiped his toe with the other. He put his foot and the coffee down. Then, he looked at her. His expression went from shock, to disbelief, to guarded. She didn't take her eyes off him as she removed her coat. She boldly looked him up and down, drinking in his brown muscles, which gleamed against the white tank top and boxers he wore. She loved how his immense shoulders tapering into lean hips and long heavily muscled legs. She traveled back up and asked, "Do you live alone?"

Prologue

Eve Garrett opened her eyes, confused and bewildered, because her husband, Todd, was screaming at her.

"We're in the river, Eve! We have to get out of the car!" He kept pushing her shoulder.

The words didn't make sense until she felt cold water tickling her feet, snaking up her legs.

Eve cried out, becoming more hysterical by the second because she couldn't swim. She had meant to learn, but never got around to it. Todd was an excellent swimmer, and he managed to get them out of the car before it sank.

The whole time he kept yelling, "I'm sorry, Eve. I'm sorry I fell asleep." Shock, and the freezing water, immobilized her, and then she panicked.

Eve's arms and legs fought the cold, thick water, holding her limbs like molasses, robbing her of her strength. A hard slap to Eve's face brought her back. She was no longer out of control, but she was so traumatized, she didn't really know what was happening.

Eve coughed and almost vomited when her face slammed into a wall of mud. Later, she figured that Todd managed to get them to an embankment that rested several feet above the surface. She got a face full of dirt as Todd struggled to lift her arm above the embankment, and then he yelled something at her. Although she couldn't understand the words, Eve got the message and groped to find something to pull herself up. She felt a shove to her bottom and realized it was Todd underneath the water helping her. She flopped on the ground face first. Turning over, she barely had the energy to spit the mud from her mouth. Eve didn't even think about Todd. In this situation, he was the strong one and, in her delirium, she assumed he was panting beside her, and maybe, just maybe, somewhere in the back of her mind, she was angry with him.

"Hey, lady, are you okay?" She was lying on her stomach and had to twist her neck to look up. The man continued, "I saw your car drive off the road, but it took me a second to get down the hill. I used my cell phone to dial 911. Here, take my coat." He threw something heavy on her. "I think I have a blanket in the car. Will you be okay while I go to get it?"

The man came back. Eve felt him remove the heaviness and replace it with something that scratched her skin. Then, it hit her with a blast colder than the river water. "Where's Todd?" She threw off the blanket, repeating the question with increasing intensity and hysteria. Ignoring the man, she crawled to the bank's edge yelling Todd's name until she lost her voice. Eve was inconsolable as she walked, and when she fell, she crawled around the riverbank screaming for her husband. A needle to her arm finally calmed her and, for the second time, she woke up not knowing where she was. Her confused brain couldn't understand why she was in a hospital. With comprehension came anguish. Bewilderment was better than remembering the accident and the unknown fate of her husband.

Two days later, Eve's worst suspicions were confirmed when Todd's body surfaced five miles from where their car barreled down a rocky hillside to plunge into the river below. The official assumption was that he was too exhausted to save himself. Eve would always wonder if it were exhaustion, guilt, or some combination that caused his death. Regardless of the cause, the result was the same: She was now a widow with a ten-year-old son to raise.

CHAPTER 1

Apprehension fired down Eve's spine as she approached the front door of her best friend's house. She remembered Ebony's short voice mail, "Girl, we found you a new domino partner. Be at my house by seven o' clock Friday so you can meet him!"

It was the "him" part of the message that made Eve's stomach tense. Ebony was a notoriously unsuccessful matchmaker in Eve's opinion. Ebony claimed it was the subject, Eve Garrett that made her efforts futile. For the past two years, Eve's single status had been on Ebony's hit list. She was on a mission to obliterate it. Her friend was determined to see her in what she called committed bliss.

Ebony answered Eve's knock, and Eve handed

her the bottle of wine she'd been toting. "I always play dominoes better after a couple of glasses."

Ebony took the bottle. "Right, Eve. I've known you for years, girl, and I know that you're a light-weight when it comes to drinking." Ebony read the label. "Oh, this is a good merlot. Even so, I'll be surprised if you drink more than a glass."

Eve laughed and touched Ebony's hair. "I like your braids, E-bone." Ebony, a beautician, changed her hair often.

"Thanks, I thought it was a nice change of pace. When are you going to do something different with your hair?"

"Never. I like it short. You know how often I run. Short hair is so much easier to take care of."

"Oh, Eve, sometimes you lack imagination, girl. Let's dye it blonde."

"No, Ebony! I'm way too practical for white hair. Besides, what would the juries think if I were run-ning around with white hair, trying to tell them to find someone guilty? Defense attorneys can get away with that wildness, but everybody expects the pros-ecutor to be conservative."

Ebony nodded her head, braids shaking. "True dat. That's why you're perfect for your job, as straightlaced as you are." Ebony looked Eve up and down. Calvin Klein jeans and a matching jean shirt covered her lithe form. The two were about the same height, five-foot-four, but the similarities ended there. Eve was small and trim where Ebony was voluptuous. "Why don't you undo one more button?"

Eve slapped Ebony's hand away. "Because I don't want my breasts to show."

Ebony laughed. "It's okay to show a little of the top." Turning from Eve, she headed down the hall. "Come with me to the kitchen, and I'll open this up and pour you a glass. How about auburn hair? You'd still be credible with a little reddish-brown 'fro."

"No, E-bone. Stop harassing me!" Eve chuckled and looked around as she followed Ebony, ignoring the house as she peered around corners. She'd been to Ebony's stylish, yet small three-bedroom house many times and knew what it looked like. She was searching for the mysterious "him."

Despite Ebony's cupid complex, Eve wouldn't miss the weekly domino games for the world. It was a nice break from her obligations and responsibilities. Being a widowed mother of a teenage son at thirty-six, hadn't been in her plans. The domino nights helped though. Eve loved spending the evening with her friends. She enjoyed the friendly competition, laughter, and silliness. Ebony insisted she needed more silliness in her life. Well, she sure got it there; she smiled to herself as she followed

Ebony into the kitchen.

Wow, what a butt, she thought before she caught herself. The Levi-covered rear-end straightened itself into a broad-shouldered, imposing man. He turned from the refrigerator with a beer in his hand.

"Oh, here you are. Eve, meet Noah Russell. You two are partners."

Eve's response surprised her. She felt like a besotted teenager. She had been indifferent to men since Todd's death four years ago, and here she was reacting to this giant of a man. He was at least six-foot-two, very muscular, and had a smile that could light up a room. She actually felt relief she hadn't worn sweats, as she was inclined to do, and her short, curly hair had been recently edged. Smiling politely, she offered her hand. "It's nice to meet you," she said. He shifted the beer to his left hand, leaving his large hand cold when he shook Eve's hand. The coldness startled her, and she jumped a little.

"Oh, I'm sorry. The beer's cold." He put it on the counter.

Noah's rich baritone affected her like a sip of hot cider on a blistery winter day. Her brown eyes gazed curiously at the man before her as he rubbed his hand on a pant leg. One would have to be comatose not to acknowledge that he was gorgeous.

His mocha-colored skin looked so smooth, Eve had the urge to touch it to see if it was as soft as it appeared. Taken alone, Noah's long, straight nose would be labeled ugly. But on his angular face, it was noble, even majestic, and added to his overall handsomeness. He wore a white shirt that was unbuttoned at the collar, exposing an impressive column of brown skin, and his legs were encased in faded jeans that hung low on his hips and fit him comfortably, but snuggly.

"Okay, it's warm now. Let's try it again. It's nice to meet you, and I'm looking forward to playing with you." He stuck out his hand.

Laughing, Eve shook it, and found her palm enclosed in warm snugness. The clasp was longer than politeness dictated. Eve retrieved her hand, feeling lost in the incredible sex appeal, and then it hit her. An avalanche of memories whirled through her head as she remembered where she had heard his name before. It floated around the prosecutor's office creating legend wherever it landed. And after meeting him, she understood why. Here she was mentally panting like a sixteen-year-old after knowing him for about two minutes.

Eve's memory bombarded her with everything she'd heard about Noah Russell. He was rumored to be the red-hot stud of the fire department, the lover of the century, better than Aretha Franklin's Dr.

Feelgood, a fireman with quite a hose. Some of the descriptions were quite base and shamefully disturbing, on the one hand, and a little exciting, on the other hand. Remembering the firmness of his hand, Eve's mind wandered and she wondered, how many bodies had it fondled? How many hearts had it left pounding? She shook her head, marveling at why she was even pondering the question. She wasn't ever going to feel that hand in anything more than a handshake.

Noah and Ebony chatted while Ebony opened the wine. Eve found herself glancing at Noah as she continued to question her reaction to him. He pulled her as no one had before. Eve thought back to when she first met her husband. She remembered thinking Todd was cute, but her pulse certainly didn't skitter as it was doing now. Subconsciously, Eve's hand drifted to her chest, as if to still her heart, while her gaze traveled to Noah's lips. Before she caught her overactive imagination, she wondered, how many women had tasted his lips? How many promises had those lips uttered? Maybe he was so good, he didn't have to promise anything.

He turned and smiled at her. Eve wondered if she'd been caught. His laughing eyes gave her no clue. "I was unbeatable at bones in college, but I haven't played since then. I shouldn't embarrass you as a partner."

"Oh, don't worry." She waved her hand dismissively. "We're playing Ebony and Yoshi; they've been married for years now, yet they still act like newlyweds. Watch, they'll get so involved admiring each other, they won't know what's happening in the game." Sarcasm usually offset her anxiety. She enjoyed Ebony's annoyed expression. So did Noah because he released a beautiful smile.

"You're full of it," Ebony protested. "Here's your wine." She handed her a glass.

"And I thought love had smoothed all your rough edges," Eve continued to tease as she took a sip. Yoshi called to Noah, asking about his beer. Noah grabbed another beer from the fridge and excused himself.

All laughter gone, she whirled to Ebony. "What are you doing? Now I know why you were trying to get me to show my tits! You better not be trying to set me up with Don Juan!"

"Calm down." Ebony poured herself a large glass of wine. She knew Eve must be pretty upset to use the word *tits*, and she could see how the body parts in question were heaving. She didn't point that out to Eve. "He and Yoshi work at the fire station together. Yoshi told Noah that Kate had moved away, and our quartet needed a new domino partner. Noah said he enjoyed playing, so Yoshi asked him to join us. There's no ulterior motive or conspiracy going on here. I think you need to show more cleavage in general." Ebony reached for her shirt again, well aware that her hand would be smacked away. She was trying to make Eve laugh and lighten up.

Eve did as expected and hit her hand, but she stayed angry. She sipped from her glass, "Oh, I know how this goes; isn't it convenient that I needed a partner at the same time? I'll tell you what, I'll be Yoshi's partner, and you take Noah."

"Don't be silly. You know he's gorgeous so flirt with him. Todd's been gone four years now. You gave him a proper mourning. It's okay to move on."

Pain, or was it frustration, radiated through Eve's body. Her emotions were so intertwined with guilt that Eve had a hard time distinguishing her feelings. Usually, the surface-level scab she'd developed kept the memories shielded, but every once in a while, the wounds seeped.

"Ebony, he's a baby!" Eve grumbled at her best friend, attempting to put the emotions back where they belonged--deep inside her. "If I was ready to move on, I wouldn't pick a young pup to make the journey with."

Ebony scoffed at her, "Eve, listening to you, I'd think you were fifty. You're only as old as you feel, and you shouldn't feel like you're too old for Noah."

"Ebony, could you try to make your argument a little more circular? I'm not sure I'm dizzy yet."

"Look, Eve, don't turn into the sarcastic lawyer on me. I've known you too long for that, girl. You're just getting that attitude because you know I'm right."

The two stared at each other, and Eve contemplated that they had been friends for a long time. Their strong bond began when they were children and had survived into adulthood. The link was broken during their teenage years, but they were able to reestablish the connection under unpleasant circumstances. Then later, Eve had shared in Ebony's happiness when she served as matron of honor in Ebony's wedding, and Ebony had been there for Eve when Todd died a year after Ebony's wedding. Eve was alone and shattered after fourteen years of marriage.

Yes, E-bone's loving support was invaluable to Eve, and they'd seen each other through numerous hard times. But damn, Eve thought, she can get on my nerves. "Don't give me that look, Eve Garrett. If I weren't married to a gorgeous hunk, I'd flirt with him. You know I always tell it like it is, and that's why you love me." Ignoring Eve's scowl, she continued, "Look, I'm not trying to make you mad, girl, and I swear I didn't set this up, but I'm not sorry it worked out this way. Loosen up, have fun. There's more to life than work and motherhood." She gave Eve a hug and left the kitchen. After a healthy swallow of wine, Eve followed.

Smiling, Eve took her seat across from her new partner. She prepared herself for Yoshi's standard question. She even had a comeback. "So, Eve, how many brothers you put in jail this week?"

"About ten. They were all named Yoshi. By the way, when was the last time you worked?"

Yoshi laughed heartily, enjoying their ritual teasing. "Ahh, I got ya. I was called into the fire station yesterday. I had to cover for somebody. I even had to respond to a call and put out a pretty fierce garbage-can fire at a high school!"

"Oh, so you worked three days this week. You must be pooped." Eve faced Noah. "I have the utmost respect for firefighters, except Yoshi here. I think he's a slacker. Yoshi, when are you going to get a real job and stop playing hero?"

Yoshi laughed harder. "Never, I like having more time off than on." As a fireman, Yoshi worked a nonconventional schedule. He usually worked twenty-four hours, then he would have two days off, after which, he would work another twenty-four hours, then he would have four days off. So unless Yoshi was called in, he worked two out of every six days. The domino nights were either on Friday or Saturday, depending on which day Yoshi had off.

Eve smiled at Yoshi, and then asked Noah, "Do you understand how this works?"

"Yes, we play to one-fifty, and the first team to win ten games gets taken to dinner by the other two."

Eve nodded. "Pretty simple, huh?"

"I like Thai food. What's your favorite food, Eve?"

Eve smirked at his cockiness. "I love chicken fajitas."

"Aren't we arrogant," Yoshi scoffed. "I'll remind you, Eve, my lovely wife and I have been taken to dinner the last three times."

"Oh, but Kate isn't her partner now. I smell an upset in the air," Noah teased. Eve had no comment. Ebony suggested the games as a way to get Eve to socialize, and Kate had been her partner since the group had begun playing a year ago. Their partnership ended when Kate's job transferred her to Boston. Kate was nice and fun to play with, but she refused to count.

In dominoes, there were seven suits up to the number six. That meant there were seven ones, seven twos, and so on. By paying attention to what had been played, who had played it, and counting, a player could guess what was in the other players' hand. Kate just played. She claimed that counting ruined her luck. Eve figured that playing with Noah could only be an improvement.

"Let's begin," Ebony said as she shuffled the bones.

Eve and Noah struggled to read each other at the beginning of play. Luck was with them, and they were ahead after the first hand. As they continued, Noah focused on Eve without a sign of what was on his mind. Eve's eyes were expressive and quick. They roamed between her bones, her opponents, and the charismatic man across the table. In court, she made it a point to conceal her thoughts and keep her eyes blank. It took a lot of energy, so with friends, she intentionally relaxed and let her guard down. She thought of it as a stress reliever. Besides, when she was playing with Kate, her facial expression didn't matter. Noah was loose, but he maintained his poker face whether he was looking at Eve or contemplating his next play. Somehow, they managed to win the first game.

During the course of the second game, Eve got used to Noah's presence. Surprisingly, their thinking seemed to be on the same page, and once again, she found her eyes drawn to him. Noah's long, thick fingers ended bluntly. There was very little curve to his fingertips. He held the bones gracefully. His long thumbs lay across the top, ends touching, while the other fingers lightly cupped the bottom. He moved his bones efficiently with precision. Focusing on his hands gave Eve a reprieve from facing Noah's eyes and wondering what thoughts lay behind them.

Eve played her turn and went back to her study. Her gaze drifted to Noah's sculptured wrist, which was slightly bent as he cradled the bones. This made the muscles in his forearm stand out. Eve shifted in her chair, and Noah's piercing dark brown eyes caught her, daring her to look directly at him. She avoided the challenge. Her focus was shot. She took a sip of wine, which didn't help her concentration. Twice, she forgot which domino was the spinner, or the lead domino. Ebony and Yoshi looked at her strangely and exchanged knowing glances.

When it was Noah's turn, he delayed, thinking about his options. At least that was what Eve assumed. Again her eyes rested on his fingers. His thumb seemed to be caressing the top of his bones. She felt powerless to stop her eyes from following that beautifully toned forearm up to his broad shoulder. There, the collar of his shirt circled his sleek, muscled neck. Her eyes halted their journey. She felt his knowing gaze, and knew she'd been caught once more. A hasty glance at his laughing eyes confirmed her suspicions.

Embarrassment flowed through her. She sipped her wine.

"Would you like more?" the rich, smooth voice asked. Eve glanced up to see him pointing at her glass. "I'd be happy to fill it for you." Eve disregarded the possible double meaning his words invoked.

"No, thank you." She looked at the wall behind his head.

She vowed not to look directly at him again. Her reaction to him was completely foreign to Eve. She'd never felt so drawn to someone before, and the fact that he knew it, humiliated her. So instead of looking at his face, she looked above him or at his chest when she had to look his way. Exactly how they won three out of five games was a mystery to Eve. Noah must have played well. Maybe there was a full moon making the bones fall right. Eve was in the twilight zone. Her ability to focus had vanished and was replaced by an unsettling disorientation. Her mind kept creating excuses to justify the unexplainable, completely irrational attraction she felt.

The night couldn't end soon enough for Eve. Finally, it was time to leave, and Ebony handed Eve her purse and coat, which she'd retrieved from the closet. Eve was turning to go when Noah's voice stopped her.

"See you next week, Eve. I've enjoyed playing with you."

Again his tone suggested a double meaning. Eve's eyes flew to him. She expected the same teasing look she'd seen before; instead, his expression was serious and warm. Their eyes held. She was mesmerized, caught up in some weird vibe that she didn't understand. He melted her with his eyes, softening her up before he ran her over with his next question.

"Let's go to dinner?"

She knew he wasn't talking about the two of them. "Well, we haven't won ten games yet."

"No, just you and me." He leaned forward, resting his elbows on the table.

"What!" Eve dropped her purse. The contents spilled on the floor. Aghast, she rushed to pick them up. Ebony helped her. Noah also stood to help, but by the time he rounded the corner of the table, the two women were done. He bent to help Eve stand up, his hand at her elbow. Yoshi sat in his chair, taking pleasure in the show. It wasn't every day that the infallible Eve lost her composure.

With his hand lightly touching the back of her arm, Noah asked again, "I said come to dinner with me. I know a great Mexican restaurant that serves the best fajitas."

Eve moved away from his hand. She stalled, putting on her coat and adjusting the purse strap on her shoulder.

Yoshi laughed, and Ebony chastised, "Stop, Noah. You're embarrassing her."

Eve's eyes shifted from Ebony to Yoshi before she confronted the one she wanted to avoid. "No." She emphasized by shaking her head.

"Why not?" He sounded genuinely puzzled.

Many reasons ran through her head: because you're a player, a womanizer; I'm a widow, a mother, I have standing in the community, and I have self-respect. She became the ice queen that made defense attorneys think twice about their position and answered, "Because I don't want to. I think that's reason enough."

Noah felt the frost. He stared at her blankly. This clearly wasn't the answer or reaction he expected.

"I'll be damned," Yoshi said. His voice broke the connection between Eve and Noah. "There is someone who can resist your charms, Noah." Then he started giggling like a kid. Ebony tried to resist, but she couldn't, and she joined her husband in laughter. Yoshi massaged his side and wiped tears from his eyes.

Eve's heart started to pound, booming all around her and bouncing off the walls, reverberating at her. She wanted to sink into the floor. Instead, she rushed to the front door.

"Well, if you won't go out with me, at least let me

walk you to your car." He had to walk fast because Eve was already leaving. At the car, he said, "I didn't mean to embarrass you."

Eve was so happy to be escaping and so shocked that she just nodded her head and got into the car and drove away. The dazed feeling stayed with her most of the way home. She was zombie-like; her reactions were so sluggish that she felt like she was drunk with embarrassment. It didn't last long. By the time she got home, her movements were stiff and jerky from anger. The heat coursed through her veins, burning off the lethargy. Her mother had been living with her since the accident, and Eve was relieved that both her mother and her son were asleep when she got there because she didn't want to explain her attitude.

She quietly entered the house and immediately took off her black flats. She placed the shoes inside the hall closet, which was right beside the front door. In stocking feet, Eve made her way upstairs where maternal instincts guided her to the bedroom across from hers. She carefully opened the door and smiled. The anger she felt toward Noah was replaced with a strong surge of love as she looked at her fourteen-year-old son sleeping so soundly. He looked just like his father, except that his hair was darker. Eve pushed back the ache and focused on her son. "Sean, you've always been a wild sleeper," she murmured to him. His boxers exposed most of his skinny frame, as he lay sprawled across the bed on his back. No matter how well the bed was made, it was a complete disaster of untucked, disarrayed sheets by the morning. When he was young, she would put him in a T-shirt, socks, and a zip-up sleeper because she was so worried he would catch a cold during the damp winter.

Eve leaned over and whispered a kiss across his forehead. He stirred a little and rubbed the spot where her lips touched. Eve chuckled. Once Sean turned eight, he declared he was too old for kisses. Eve's opportunities came few and far between. She wasn't surprised he wiped her peck away even in his sleep. Eve retrieved the sheets and blanket from the floor, and placed them gently across his body before leaving the room.

Eve went into her own room and quickly performed her nighttime rituals. After her teeth and face were clean, she donned a blue satin nightgown that hit her mid-thigh and slid beneath the covers. She couldn't believe the audacity of that man, asking her out like that. The anger began to build again once she realized she was offended yet strangely flattered by his offer. This pissed her off more because she knew his interest was momentary at best. She was a mother and way too practical for any one-night-stand nonsense with a player sowing his oats.

How could she be mad and attracted simultaneously? She took deep breaths and tried to imagine Todd's face to calm herself and make her forget that irritating man. The two men looked completely different. Todd had been tall and lanky with skin that was a light golden color reminiscent of the wheat fields that dominated the eastern part of Washington State. The Cascade mountain range divided Washington, leaving the west moist and green and the east dry and tan. Seattle, where Eve grew up, was on the western side, but as a child, her family often traveled to the eastern side of the state. Eve would look at the endless miles of long, tall wheat stalks blowing in the wind and think they were so radiant and elegant. The swaying stalks were hypnotic and watching them usually lulled Eve to sleep. Even Todd's hair had been a beautiful sandy color, instead of black or dark brown. She thought Todd was of mixed heritage when she first met him. In time, she discovered that both of his parents were black; they were just light skinned.

Todd's tone was nothing like Noah's deep brown, coffee-colored skin. His long-limbed form was nothing like Noah's bulk and brawn. "Eve," she whispered to herself, "you're supposed to be thinking of Todd, not Noah." Anger felt like acid dripping in her stomach, dissolving images of Todd. "Who is Noah to disrupt my evening with Ebony and Yoshi?" she complained to the dark room. He callously threatened an evening that refreshed her and allowed her to give more to her family. How dare he violate her space with his shallow intentions!

🍒🍒🍒

"Who is she?" Noah asked as he made himself comfortable on the couch after Eve's departure. He and Yoshi were in the living room watching TV. Ebony was straightening up the few dishes in the kitchen. She told Yoshi to go away and visit with Noah when he offered to help.

Yoshi took his time answering Noah's question. He drank his beer, grabbed the remote, and eased the recliner back. "She's not for you," he stated bluntly. "She's a woman with a kid."

"So, I've been with women with kids before."

"You've been with hoochies with kids." Grinning at Noah's expected frown, Yoshi became serious. "To tell the truth, I don't know a whole lot about her. Ebony claims that she's up close and personal with her pain. It's weird because I've seen her in court, and she's so cold, you would think she poops ice cubes." Yoshi looked directly at Noah. "Her husband died. I knew him. He was a nice guy." Yoshi

20

shrugged. "I don't know the whole story, but apparently she really loved the guy, and Ebony thinks she might have done something crazy if she didn't have a kid. Didn't you notice she still wears her wedding ring?"

Noah was surprised he'd missed that detail. "No, I didn't see it. How long ago did he die?"

"Four years ago. Ebony invented these game nights as a way to get her out. All she does is work and the motherhood thing. Hey, did I tell you she's a prosecutor?"

"No, but I figured she did something with the court system when you asked her how many brothers she put away this week." Noah sat forward, elbows on knees, "How could you forget to tell me that?!"

"It didn't seem important 'til you started lusting after her. I can't believe you just asked her out. Who do you think you are? John Travolta in *Saturday Night Fever*? Snap your finger and the girl comes running."

Noah didn't divulge the eye play he and Eve engaged in. He had experienced too many women not to realize when one was attracted. She may not want to date him, but she wasn't repulsed or indifferent to him.

Ebony breezed through the kitchen door and perched herself on the arm of Yoshi's chair. Yoshi eased his arm around her waist before saying, "Noah's asking me about Eve."

"Oh, is he? You know, Noah, you really embarrassed her."

"That wasn't my intent."

"What are your plans?" Before he could answer, Ebony continued. "Eve is my homegirl, my sister, so if you're not serious, leave it alone."

Yoshi added his two cents. "How can he know that? He just met her." He affectionately squeezed his wife.

Ebony hugged him back. "I know when they met, and I want Noah to promise he's going to be nice before I tell him anything."

Chuckling, Noah nodded. "I promise to treat her honorably. I know better than to get you on my bad side."

"Okay." Ebony slipped into her husband's lap, becoming comfortable before she began her story.

"Ebony, are you going to tell all her business?" Again Yoshi interrupted to add his two cents. "Eve's going to be pissed at you."

"No she won't if she doesn't know. Noah won't tell, right?"

"Correct."

Ebony sat up and looked at him, peering into his eyes like she was searching for something. "I think Noah here might be just what Eve needs. So,

Noah, I'm sharing this with you so you can understand Eve and really be a gentleman. Her life has-
n't been easy. The last thing she needs is more
pain."

Ebony settled against Yoshi's chest and looked
off in the distance. "Eve and I go way back; we
grew up on the same block in South Seattle, and we
were inseparable as kids. It was during our child-
hood that Eve suffered her first big loss." Her focus
came back to Noah. "Eve's lost a lot in her life.
When she was twelve, her dad left and shacked up
with some chick that worked with him. Eve blamed
herself for a long time."

Ebony didn't share how Eve called her on the
phone in near hysterics. Running to her rescue,
Ebony stole a pack of her mom's cigarettes and a
bottle of wine and rushed over. Ebony spent the
night, and Eve's unsuspecting mother let them
sleep in the attic. They smoked and drank while
fussing about the situation long into the night.
Ebony taught Eve more than how to get drunk that
night. She told her that it wasn't normal for parents
to periodically have separate bedrooms. In fact, in
her own colorful way, Ebony told Eve it was quite
strange. She strongly encouraged Eve to stop
blaming herself and believe her parents' claim that
they just "fell" out of love.

Ebony continued with the story. "A year later,

her father and his new wife died in a plane crash. Eve took it hard." She looked pointedly at Noah.

Noah felt like saying, "Hey I didn't make it crash."

"Anyway, our dynamic duo was split up when my dad's job transferred him to Tacoma. I was about fourteen, so Eve was about sixteen. You know, Tacoma's only about forty miles away, but it seemed like the other side of the earth to Eve and me." Ebony chuckled. "We vowed to keep in touch, and we actually did for about a year. Then we both became distracted with school, other activities, and, of course, boys."

Yoshi playfully pinched her.

"Ouch!" Ebony grabbed his hand and kissed his fingers.

"I didn't think you noticed guys 'til you met me!"

"I was just practicing until I met the real thing." Ebony turned in his lap and pecked his lips. Then, she faced forward again and addressed Noah. "Eve and I were reunited under pretty yucky circumstances about six years ago." Ebony paused and looked down. Yoshi gave her a big hug from behind.

Noah had no idea what they were referring to, but obviously it was a painful subject. Noah didn't pry.

Ebony took a deep breath and focused on Noah

once more. "Eve had managed to become a prosecutor, get married, and have a kid by that time. A
couple of years after we were reunited, her husband
died."

"How did he die?" Noah uncrossed his legs and
leaned forward a little.

"He and Eve were driving to a romantic vacation
when Todd fell asleep, and their car ended up in the
river. Todd died saving Eve. Something happened
right before the accident that really affected Eve.
She won't talk about it, but whatever it was, it hurt
her deeply." Ebony stared at Noah intently. "I've
introduced you to Eve, so I'd feel absolutely horrible
if you did something to cause her more anguish.
Leave her alone if all you're looking for is a quickie."

Noah nodded in acknowledgement. Eve
appeared to be too much woman to use up in a
"quickie." No, he planned to take his time and possibly test both of their staying power. Yes indeed,
he was now looking forward to domino nights. He
anticipated that they would be very interesting.

CHAPTER 2

*W*hy did you do that, E-Bone?"

"Whatcha talking 'bout, Eve?" Eve knew Ebony was playing dumb. "Wait a minute, Eve. I have to get my client from the dryer." Eve envisioned Ebony cradling the phone between her ear and shoulder, motioning her client to her station. "Okay, now what were you saying?"

It was Saturday morning, and Eve was in her office taking care of a few details before Monday rolled around. She had been there for a couple of hours and was about to leave. She decided to harass Ebony first. Tapping her pen against her desk, Eve scolded. "You know exactly what I'm talking about. Why is Dr. Feelgood my partner?"

"Eve, we've already had this conversation."
Eve cut her off. "I want a new partner."

"Demanding, aren't we? Noah's perfect
because he and Yoshi are in the same unit. Do you
think it's easy finding someone who plays dominoes
and can fit our schedule?"

Eve made an undignified noise--a sound that
was somewhere between a cough and a snort.

"Girl, you need to loosen up and see if Dr.
Feelgood has a prescription for you."

Eve was incredulous. "I don't believe you. After
all the stories you used to tell me, you want me to
sleep with this guy?"

"See, I didn't say anything about sleeping with
him. Wait a minute, I have to give my client the mirror." Eve could hear the woman telling Ebony what
a great job she'd done. "You've gone too long without sex; you have it on the brain. I've gotten to
know Noah lately, and I may have misjudged him."

"Imagine that," Eve quipped.

"I'm just saying he's clearly interested in you, so
forget everything I said. Try to reserve judgment
because what you see isn't necessarily what you
get."

"So I wouldn't get a gorgeous hunk?" Eve
teased. She couldn't stay angry at E-Bone.

"Well, it's nice to know you're not dead inside,"
Ebony retorted. "There's just more depth in him

than I ever expected. He's a decent guy."

"What makes you think so?" Eve twirled around in her swivel chair. She could hear running water. She knew Ebony was probably rinsing out her combs.

"Well, over the past year or so, he and Yoshi have become quite close, which means I see him all the time. He's real big on community service. Whenever there's a local event, and they want a firefighter, he volunteers. He's always going to grade schools talking to kids, or leading the little ones around the station for a tour. The kids just love him; they climb all over him, and he keeps them laughing. He's great with them. Someone like that can't be all bad."

"Huh, that remains to be seen," Eve was still skeptical.

"Well, Eve, while you're waiting to see, chew on this. If he's such a player, why is he willing to give up his weekend nights to play dominoes?"

Eve did indeed ponder the question after she hung up the phone.

🌸🌸🌸

Eight o'clock Sunday morning. The sun was too bright, the birds sang too loud, and his head hurt too much to be going to breakfast. Only for his sister would Noah get up after three hours of sleep, preceded by a night of clubbing. Sheila wasn't too happy he was leaving her bed to meet another woman, even if that woman was his sister. Although she claimed that wasn't the reason for her bad temper. She said she was upset because he was leaving before she was done with him. Noah chuckled at that. The woman had a voracious appetite. A fact that became very apparent soon after their first meeting.

Sheila Jackson was a realtor Noah met when she helped him buy his condo. There was an instant attraction between them that flourished when she told him she was too busy for a committed, full-time relationship. Noah said, "Great." She followed that by sharing that she wanted a friend, not a keeper. Noah told her he didn't want to keep anyone, so the arrangement sounded ideal to him. When one or the other felt the need, a call was made. Or, when they saw each other out and neither was attached, they felt comfortable enjoying the evening together. That had been the case last night. Noah ended up at her house, in her bed feeling tired, but very relaxed until Sheila started making noise about how well they got along, they were peas in a pod, and maybe they should consider something more serious. Noah wondered how she came to that conclusion when their relationship was so one-dimensional. When he reminded her that their liaison was perfect because there were no strings attached, she caught an attitude, slamming doors and making snide comments.

Oh no, when the attitude starts, it's time to end the association, permanently, he warned himself. Noah hastily pulled on last night's clothes and gave Sheila a peck on the cheek. He considered it to be their last kiss. As he was opening the front door, she boldly asked him why he bothered staying the night. Good question, he thought as he rubbed his tired eyes. Why sleep at all when his sister wanted to meet at this ridiculous hour?

Despite his fussing, Noah knew nothing was too much, when asked by his sister, Dina. Good thing she didn't ask for much. If questioned, it would have been impossible for him to describe the love he had for her. Their bond went beyond the normal sibling relationship because it had been tested. It had been pressed like the earth presses a lump of coal, and the resulting diamond signified the level their relationship had reached. He and Dina shared a love that was mutually protective, everlasting, honest, and deep. They relied on it to form a barrier against life's trials. It was concern and caring without being judgmental. It meant that no matter what, they had always been there for each other and their parents.

Together they had faced his family's biggest challenge. Noah had heard the saying the bigger they are the harder they fall. He must have been pretty big because he sure fell hard his junior year of college at the University of Southern California. That year he got a frantic phone call from his mother, which brought his world to a screeching halt. He remembered her words as if they were uttered yesterday, instead of several years ago.

"Son, Pop has Alzheimer. I came home from shopping today, and he had a gun to his head."

No preamble, no warning. His mother had been too upset to sugarcoat the message, so he suffered the brunt of it full force. Dina received a similar phone call, and they both rushed home. The decision to go home dramatically changed the course of his life. He lost his starting position on the USC football team, he lost his chance to make the NFL, and he lost his girl. But if he had the choice to make again, he wouldn't change a thing. Family was too important to him.

Noah approached the International House of Pancakes and saw his sister sitting at a window seat. When he reached the table, she stood and they hugged. "Hey, handsome," his sister said in her standard greeting. "You look like we should have scheduled a dinner date, instead of breakfast." Dina smiled generously, obviously enjoying his discomfort. Trim and tall, she rose and leaned over to peck his cheek. He hugged her, and playfully ran a hand over her smooth, long hair. "Oh, you need to shave." She rubbed his cheek.

Noah grumbled, reaching for her coffee.

"Still looking for love in all the wrong places?"

"Only on Saturday nights when I'm not on duty."

"By the looks of you, your journey's been successful." Her gaze took in her brother's untucked, wrinkled, white T-shirt underneath a worn brown bomber jacket; red eyes partially covered by half-closed lids. His large hands, cradled the coffee cup as he inhaled the vapors in an attempt to revive himself.

Love and pain coursed through her as she observed her brother. He was such a good person with lots to offer if he would open up again. Being dumped by the gold-digger after he didn't make the NFL and caring for their father for a year until his death from a stroke had changed her brother. Heck, the experience had changed all of them, but he seemed to have walled himself off. He covered it with a playboy, easygoing attitude, yet he rarely let anyone in. Sometimes, it was so thick, she wondered how she slipped through.

Noah placed her empty coffee cup in front of her, drawing her back to the present. "Hey, you met Mr. Wonderful at a club."

"Yeah, but I got it like that!" Dina sat straighter and switched to a haughty tone. "Furthermore, I met Tim, my fiancé, in a jazz club where people are much more refined than in the juke joints you frequent."

The waitress interrupted any reply Noah would have made. Noah ordered blueberry pancakes. Dina ordered strawberry crepes. Handing the menu to the waitress, he caught his sister's look. He'd seen that expression before. He reached across the table and took her hand. "It's not as bad as it looks, so stop pitying me. You know I'm not a morning person, so why do you have me up at the crack of dawn."

She squeezed his hand before she released it. "Eight is hardly sun up. From here, I'm going straight to the airport." Dina was a flight attendant, and Noah knew she liked to touch base with everyone before she began a long tour. "I'll be gone for two weeks. I'll be working for most of it, but Tim's going to join me in Los Angeles for a short vacation. Here's the itinerary in case you need to reach me."

"Couldn't you just have called?"

"No, I haven't seen you in a while; I wanted to see your handsome face before I left." She pinched his cheek.

Noah playfully slapped her hand away. "Do boyfriends of flight attendants fly free?"

"No, not until we're married, and it's still not free, just a very large discount."

"Hey, you're getting married soon, and you'll be going on a honeymoon. Why are you going on vacation?"

"Oh, it's just a long weekend."

Noah matched Dina's smile. "You and Tim doing good?"

"Any boyfriend that can successfully withstand your well-meaning, but endless scrutiny must be doing pretty good."

Noah shrugged his broad shoulders. "Being a teacher, he should be good with rules, and he seems to know mine pretty good."

Dina lowered her head. "Yes, brother dear, you've schooled him well: respect, unconditional love, and fidelity. He calls it RUF. He claims he's RUFing me up all the time."

Noah laughed with his sister. He had to confess, to himself at least, that he liked Tim Raines. None of Dina's previous boyfriends qualified for that thought.

"You know, I want you to find the same thing." Dina searched the dark brown eyes that looked so much like her own. "Maybe I should inspect your women, but that would be an endless, thankless job."

Noah didn't deny it. He knew women found him

attractive and charismatic, causing him to draw more than his fair share of female attention. He rarely pursued them, but he didn't mind being pursued himself as long as they understood that there were no strings attached. "Believe me, none of them are worth your most casual glance."

"I haven't given up on you. One day, you're going to meet a woman who scales your wall and lands in there." Dina poked him in the chest.

Eve's image popped into his unguarded mind. Before he could analyze her surprise appearance, Dina poked him in the chest again. "This woman's going to see you with more than her eyes. She's going to see you with her soul, and your soul's going to answer."

Their food arrived, and Noah chuckled at his sister's conviction. "Well, while we're waiting for this miracle to happen, why don't we eat breakfast?"

🍅🍅🍅

Domino night fell on Friday again. Noah stared at her boldly, wondering why he bothered. Hell, the woman still wore her dead husband's ring. Why would he want to deal with that headache? Besides, Eve made it clear she wasn't interested, and he had enough other offers not to persist with her. But still he did.

Eve's concentration wavered. Noah's piercing brown eyes caught her glance, daring her to maintain the contact and look deeper. Eve looked at her dominoes and had to check the board twice to remember the spinner. She shook herself mentally and vowed to avoid the challenge in his eyes. It rattled her too much. She focused on his play. Nearing the second night of competing with him, she noticed admirable qualities in her partner. Noah's grasp of the game was absolute. He made swift, accurate decisions and only took well-calculated risks. Their few losses didn't unnerve him; they only made him more purposeful. Playing with Kate had been pleasant, and sometimes enjoyable. Playing with Noah was exhilarating.

They were in the final game of the evening. Noah and Eve had won nine games to Yoshi and Ebony's three. If Noah and Eve won, they would be treated to a free dinner. The fact that they were behind by thirty points, and the others only needed twenty points to win, presented a challenge. The best strategy was for one of them to control the game and be the first to play all the bones in his or her hand or domino. Then, they would get all the points from the bones Yoshi and Ebony had yet to play. The trick was to keep their opponents from scoring, and be the first to domino.

Eve evaluated her hand. It sucked. She had two bones from the same suit. There was no way she could control anything. She looked at Noah. All she saw was desire and that was useless in interpreting his hand. But it did make her heart jump, which made thinking clearly hopeless.

Noah took charge. He seemed to have the bones to dominate. With little help from Eve, he managed to prevent everyone from playing. Eve held her breath. Noah had one more bone and if he could play, they would get their opponents' points. She searched his eyes and caught a glimpse of something that left her clueless. Noah hid the bone with his hand as he moved it to position. Turning it over, he played it with a hard tap on the table. Then he crossed his arms and sat back with a Cheshire cat grin.

Eve yelped and pumped her fist in the air. Ebony stared, amazed at Eve's reaction.

"Damn," muttered Yoshi, throwing the scoring tablet on top of the bones.

Noah looked at Eve's beautiful face, still glowing with excitement, and something inside him softened a little. She finally met his stare. "Where are we making reservations, Eve?"

"It was your excellent play that got us here, Noah, so you decide."

"Okay, the Mexican Kitchen." Eve smiled at his

choice. Mexican Kitchen was known for making the best fajitas in the city.

Eve nodded and said, "Excellent choice."

A week later, Eve sat in her car, watching patrons enter and leave the Mexican Kitchen through the hazy light of the street lamp. It was Saturday. Domino night had been cancelled for the week because they were going to dinner. Leave it to Don Juan to remember that her favorite food was chicken fajitas. Eve arrived early and had seen Ebony, Yoshi, and Noah all enter the restaurant. She knew they were waiting for her, and still, she was hesitant. These feelings were ridiculous. This wasn't a romantic date, and even if it were, her husband had been gone for four years now. There was absolutely no reason to feel guilty. She twirled her wedding ring.

Eve closed her eyes and pictured her husband's face. A long, tan face with soft brown eyes and sandy-colored hair. Nothing like Noah's square, dark brown face with his strong jaw, and wide-set magnetic eyes. He reminded her in stature, with all his muscles and reputation, of the football and basketball players she avoided in college. Eve had attended the University of Washington on a track scholarship. She was so busy, that most of the men she associated with were athletes. Respecting women didn't appear to be high on their list of priorities. That's why she felt so fortunate when she met Todd. Todd was her calculus tutor. With his quiet, mild-spoken demeanor, he was completely different than the athletes, and he was completely different than Noah as well.

Frustrated, she slapped her leg. She was supposed to be remembering Todd, not a womanizing firefighter who was looking for a challenge. But while she was thinking of him, she refused to be a statistic or a notch on a belt. She wouldn't allow herself to be one of the many striving for a crumb of affection. No, not as long as her mind was stronger than her body.

Her mental pep talk did little to convince her to leave the car. She flipped down the mirror, and picked at her short hair, played with her make up. "Just go and get it over with," she scolded herself. "He hasn't asked you out since the first domino night. Maybe he's given up, and you're being silly, hiding in the car!" With that, Eve left her safe haven and entered the restaurant.

The hostess led her to the table where the others were already seated. Suspiciously, the only available seat was directly across from Noah. No problem, she assured herself, she would keep eye contact to a minimum. Eve's logic failed the test. She felt the warmth of his gaze regardless of her acknowledgement. She knew his eyes watched her, and this knowing gave her an uncomfortable pleasure. Her senses were on overdrive, and a warm flush pulsed through her body.

Yoshi asked his usual question, "How many brothers did you send to the guillotine today?"

"None. It's Saturday. But I'm going to send you, if you keep asking me that question with your no working self!" Everyone chuckled, and Eve relaxed a tad.

She sat down and Noah handed her his menu. "Thank you." Their hands touched briefly. She glanced at the menu. "I know what I want. Chicken fajitas. There it is," she pointed.

Noah leaned forward, tilted her menu, and looked. This forced her eyes to briefly meet his. "Yes, that says chicken fajitas." He knew he was being forward, but he couldn't resist barging through any opening provided. He'd take any legitimate excuse he could get to gain her attention. "I think I'll join you, Eve, and have fajitas too."

Eve ignored him.

Noah persisted, "So, Eve, how was your Saturday?"

She looked in his direction. "It's been a pretty good day. It started early because I had to take

Sean to an eight o'clock basketball practice."

"That's your son?"

Eve nodded.

"How old is he?"

With such direct questions, Eve felt funny and childish avoiding his eyes. She looked right at him.

"He's fourteen and already taller than me."

"And I'm sure he's a handsome boy because he has such a beautiful mother."

Eve was proud of herself because she didn't get flustered. She maintained eye contact and said, "Actually, he's the spitting image of his father, and yes, he's extremely handsome."

Noah nodded and gave her a quirky smile that said touché, but I'm not that easy to get rid of.

The waiter arrived, and they all placed their orders. They were still handing their menus to the waiter when Noah commented, "You know, I end up at the courthouse at least once a month, and I've never seen you around. How long have you been a prosecutor?"

Eve sipped her water and gave Ebony a wide-eyed look. She wanted Ebony to join the conversation to take some of the pressure off. Ebony's big grin told her she got the message, and the way she sat back, with crossed arms, told her she wasn't going to say a thing.

"Jeez, I've been a prosecutor for twelve years

now."

Noah leaned forward, putting his forearms on the table, and Eve leaned back still holding the water glass as a barrier between them. "No! You're too young to have worked that long!" Eve laughed, despite herself; Yoshi and Ebony joined her.

"Noah, my son is fourteen. I'm well past thirty." Good, Eve thought to herself, now that he knows maybe he'll leave me alone.

"That's right, Noah, Eve's old enough to be your mother," Ebony volunteered. Eve glared mockingly at Ebony, her eyebrows forming a crease across her forehead. She wanted Ebony to speak, but not malign her age.

"You could be his Aunt E-bone because you're about the same age."

"No, I'm younger than you, remember?"

"Two years, Ebony, two years. The older you get the more a difference like that doesn't matter."

"How old are you, Eve?"

Both women turned to Noah, and Yoshi said, "Noah, don't you know you're never supposed to ask a woman her age? That's right up there with how much do you weigh?"

Noah playfully put his hands up. "Okay, okay, I'll ask another question. Eve, why did you become a prosecutor?"

"There are many reasons, but a couple of the

main ones are that the hours are manageable, so I can spend time with my family; also, it's the type of career where I can give back to the community, and last it satisfies my nosiness."

"Huh?" Noah wasn't following her logic.

"I'm curious. People always say if you possess an inquisitive nature, be a reporter. I say be a prosecutor or a defense attorney because you're always reading police reports about other people's lives."

"Hey, Eve, you're a snoop just like me," Ebony said. "I love it when the shop's alive with gossip." She hunched her shoulders and did a little jiggle that made everyone laugh.

Eve was tired of answering twenty questions. As soon as the chuckling ended, she asked Noah a question before he could ask her another one. "Noah, why did you become a fireman?"

Noah had the choice of being brief, or really answering the question. He chose the latter.

"My pop was a fireman, and I became hooked on fire fighting when he bought me my first wooden fire truck when I was a boy. I learned early that his job was very important, and everybody in the neighborhood respected him. When I was a kid, my pop seemed larger than life. I supposed everybody thinks that way about his or her dad, but I had confirmation. My pop would take me to the fire station, and I could see the admiration in other firefighter's eyes and attitude. I knew my pop was one of the best firefighters in Seattle, and my little chest puffed with pride as I walked through the station with him."

Eve gazed at the body part in question. She had a hard time imaging his chest being anything but burly and brawny.

"I remember the other firefighters punching me in my shoulder, saying, 'you're a chip off the old block, and we have a bunk ready for you next to your dad's.' I grew up wanting to be just like Pop."

Noah shrugged. "Now that I am a firefighter, I love it. It's exciting. You're going into a situation that everyone else is trying to get out of. It really does make you feel brave." Yoshi barked a laugh and nodded his head. Noah continued, "Although, I think it's more fortitude than bravery, more guts than intelligence. There is something about facing a fierce, destructive enemy that could harm you, and using your skills to hopefully defeat it. It's teamwork at it's best, and it satisfies my competitive nature. Also, there's nothing like the camaraderie I have with my fellow firefighters."

"Here, here," Yoshi said, and lifted his water glass. Noah lifted his, and the glasses clinked as they touched.

Noah took a sip before continuing. "Danger isn't what makes us close. Grief is what does it: a child fatality or losing a firefighter. The unspeakable stuff. What you can't tell your family about in detail. You don't have to tell another firefighter unless you want to. You just look in the person's eyes after the horrific event, and you know they're feeling what you're feeling. That kind of thing makes for tight bonds. I'm talking about a shared understanding."

"I'm impressed, Noah. I didn't know you could be so eloquent. I couldn't have said it better." Again, Yoshi raised his glass to toast with Noah.

"You said 'was' in reference to your dad. Is he retired?" Eve asked.

Noah fought the sorrow that swept through him. Eve saw something flicker in his eyes, and then it was gone before she could decipher it.

"He passed a few years ago."

"I'm sorry." Eve said the words automatically.

"Don't be. The last five years of his life, he suffered greatly with Alzheimer's. In the end, it was a stroke that finally killed him." Noah's eyes shifted upward as he delved deeper into the past. "When he first found out he had Alzheimer's, he tried to kill himself. The man was too independent to willingly let himself become a burden. My mom wouldn't let him out of her sight. She knew he was too concerned about the effect it would have on her, so he wouldn't do anything too crazy in her presence. After a time, he was too disoriented to attempt suicide, so at least we didn't have that to worry about."

Noah's focus came back to the people at the table. "I never understood how people could say their loved ones found peace or relief with death, but after living with my father the last year of his life, I understand completely. I think the father I knew growing up was locked up in a confused brain, and that death released him to enjoy the benefits of heaven." They were all silent as they contemplated Noah's words.

Eve spoke first. "That's a beautiful way to think about it. Your father must have been a wonderful person."

Noah dipped his head in acknowledgement. "Thank you. He was."

There was an awkward pause that was quickly filled when the food arrived moments later. Noah and Eve's fajitas sizzled as the waiter, accompanied by a chef, placed the hot platters on the table. Among oohs and ahs, all four of them scooted back as they watched the chicken pop and hiss. The waiter set tortillas in front of Noah and Eve, along with a big plate of guacamole, sour cream, cheese, and salsa. Eve licked her lips in anticipation of rolling the chicken, cheese, and salsa into the tortilla. It had been at least a month since she'd last had fajitas, and she was really looking forward to the first bite. She remembered Noah and looked up.

His question let her know that he'd seen her tongue cross her lips. "The food or me?"

"Definitely the food."

"Oh shucks." He grabbed a tortilla and began wrapping a fajita.

Ebony and Yoshi were engrossed in the delivery of their meals and missed the exchange. Yoshi had a big burrito plate, which included rice and black beans. Ebony had a shredded-beef enchilada. Soon everyone was eating. The fajitas were a mess, and Yoshi and Ebony had a good time making fun of them as they ate. Noah was happy to see that Eve wasn't shy about eating. She dug in and ate with as much enthusiasm as he did.

At the end of dinner, everyone said good-bye, and Eve and Ebony hugged. Eve headed to her car, and Noah pointed to her, indicating to Yoshi and Ebony that he'd escort her. Eve noticed Noah following her. "Oh, I parked right out front. You don't need to walk me to my car."

Despite her protest, Noah walked beside her. When they reached her Volkswagen Beetle, he extended his hand, "Thanks for being my domino partner and not giving in to second thoughts. We make a good team."

His hand enveloped Eve's. She let hers linger in the strength longer than convention dictated. As she slipped her hand out of his grasp, her fingers brushed over calluses. The roughness reminded her that he was a man who worked with his hands. She denied the fact that it excited her. She also decided to ignore the second thoughts comment. "We would be better if I wasn't guessing. I'm not good at reading you yet."

"Well, we could remedy that. I know I embarrassed you the first night. I never should have asked you out in public, so I'm asking you in private."

Eve unlocked and opened the door before answering. She needed time to settle her nerves. With the car door between them, she said, "I accept your apology, but I believe we should just remain domino partners."

"Is it your husband or my reputation?"

The question pissed her off. "I don't date babies, and this may be hard for you to believe, but I'm not attracted to you."

"Come on, Eve, at least be honest. Your eyes, your hands, your slight anxiety tell me you're attracted, and if you haven't noticed," he pointed to himself and puffed up his chest, "I'm hardly a baby."

Oh, she'd noticed all right. That knowledge and anger made her stiffen and grip the edge of the door. She leaned forward. "It's almost worth one date to get rid of you. I've heard that all that's going to happen will happen on that date. No morning after, no calls, no letters, no commitment beyond one night of sex."

"Maybe it'll be different with you. What you've heard describes women who pursue me. I'm definitely the one pursuing you, so I'd hang around for the morning after. At least for breakfast. Can you cook?" He thought she was going to hit him. He could see it in her eyes. He loved the fire and wanted to see more of it.

She sat down hard, and he grabbed the car door before she could slam it. "Listen, all I'm saying is let's get to know each other better, and we might find we're looking for the same things in life."

"What makes you think I want to be a test subject for you? I'm sure Ebony's told you that I'm a widow. I know what it means to be part of a wonderful, long-term relationship. My relationship skills are fine. You'll have to go explore yours with someone else." She slammed the door, and he watched solemnly as she drove off. She couldn't resist looking in the rearview mirror at the lonely figure watching her drive away with his hands in his pockets.

CHAPTER 3

*E*ve, you have a lot of Johns this morning because the police ran a prostitution sting last night. The decoy must have been very pretty and convincing 'cause she sure caught a lot of flies."

Eve chuckled. "Yes, I saw that when I prepped the files this morning." Eve was sitting in her office, chatting with Lila who was standing by the door. Lila worked in the Case Preparation Unit, and she'd organized all of the documents that went into the files for the jail court.

It was the Monday following the dinner, and Eve had to work the jail calendar, which was in the jail. The court's location made Eve hate doing the calendar, even though it was easy. As the jail prosecutor, all Eve had to do to prepare was read a police report, decide what and if charges should be filed, and appear in court. In court, if she were filing charges, she would inform the defendant, and argue with the defense attorney about bail.

"Eve." The pain in Lila's voice made her look up. "Have you ever had a person you know end up in one of those reports?" Lila pointed to the files.

"Yes." Eve had been born and raised in the same city where she prosecuted. It was inevitable that she ran across someone she knew.

"Well, my cousin's husband was one of the guys picked up for soliciting last night."

"Oh." Eve sat back in her chair.

Lila rubbed her face. "I'm so embarrassed for him and her."

I would be too. Eve didn't voice her thoughts.

"Has such a thing ever happened to you, Eve?"

Eve looked at Lila's red eyes and flushed cheeks. She kept twisting a long lock of brown hair around her finger. Eve felt sorry for her. "No, Lila, I haven't been in your exact situation, but let me tell you about Ronald Mattocks."

Lila closed the door and sat in the chair across from Eve's desk.

"Ronny used to date my friend about six years ago. My friend and I had lost touch, so you can imagine my surprise when I saw her name in a

Edwina Martin-Arnold

police report!"

"So, she was a victim? How horrible."

"Yes." Thinking about what Ebony had been through still made Eve see red. "The jerk called her up and warned her not to go to the beauty shop where she worked. She went to work, and the fool came to her job, chased her around, slapped her, and pushed her down before one of the male customers stopped him. When my friend fell, she hit her head on the metal piece of a chair and was knocked unconscious; she suffered a mild concussion. The aid unit had to be called." Eve didn't mention how she had to stifle a gasp when she looked at the pictures of Ebony's multicolored bruise. Eve had seen things ten times as gruesome as the bump on Ebony's head, but this was an old friend she was looking at. She remembered that the wall she usually kept firmly in place slipped a little, and tears actually came to her eyes.

Lila was incredulous. "He embarrassed her and jeopardized her job like that!"

"Yes. Working here, Lila, you know the whole thing is about control. He wanted to bring her to heal, like a dog with its master." Eve continued the story, "Boy, was I apprehensive when I called the number listed in the police report. It wasn't exactly the best circumstances for a reunion."

Lila bobbed her head in sympathy.

"When my friend answered, I used my child-hood nickname for her. Always exuberant, she screamed into the phone." Eve smiled. "The years dropped away, and it was like we were teenagers again. Thirty minutes of silliness went by in a sec-ond. Both of us were anxious to see each other again, so we made arrangements to meet for dinner that night. I decided to wait until dinner to bring up the case."

"Wise move," Lila commented.

"At dinner, I told my friend how I got the number, and her enthusiasm dropped considerably. In a subdued voice, she told me about Ronny. She said that they'd been dating for about four months when Ronny first went into a tirade because things hadn't gone his way. About two weeks before the beauty shop incident, he hit her in a fit of anger."

"Of course, he apologized later and swore he'd never do it again, right?" Lila interrupted.

"Right. After some soul searching, my friend decided she didn't want to take a chance on 'again.' She ended the relationship. Ronny showed up at the shop and stopped her in church to plead his case, but, as my friend put it, she wasn't hearing it. Then, she started getting hang-up calls at all hours of the night, and last, Ronny's warning not to come to work."

"Eve, it must have been hard for you to see a

close friend go through this."

"It was. But I was so happy she'd avoided the vicious cycle."

Eve knew Lila understood what she meant. The violent act would occur, and then the honeymoon period would happen where the abuser would swear that he'd never hit the victim again. He'd be so charming and sincere that the victim would believe him. Then, the tension would start building again until it resulted in another violent act, and the circle would repeat itself. The same couples came across Eve's desk over and over. She knew the problem was bigger than she was. She saw herself as a stopgap; a relief from the vicious cycle, and maybe, the intervention of the court system might actually break the cycle in some cases.

"My friend assured me she wanted no part of any cycle with Ronny, and she was more than willing to prosecute. Despite numerous witnesses, stubborn Ronny still made us go through the embarrassment of a trial. You know what, Lila? Ronny's case certainly wasn't my biggest or most important trial, yet I wanted to convict him so bad that's all I thought about. I rehearsed my opening statement in the shower, I thought about my direct examination as I ate breakfast, and I tried to antici-pate every defense objection during my commute to work. My heart soared and sang when the jury foreman stood and said guilty."

"I bet it did! I'm glad you got the bum."

"Oh, yes. And, as my friend put it, the Lord truly does work in mysterious ways. She got a husband out of the whole mess."

"Really!"

"Uh huh. It was one of the firemen assigned to the aid unit that responded to the call at the beauty shop." Noah's face filled Eve's mind. She pushed him away. "My friend's husband claimed he fell in love with his damsel in distress when he saw her lying unconscious on the floor. I suspected it was the killer dress she wore when she testified. I don't blame him though. My friend's gorgeous. She's about the same height as me, but the similarities end there. She's voluptuous."

Lila giggled. "Eve, you look great."

Eve laughed too. "I know I look all right, but I've never been accused of being well endowed!"

Lila's chair screeched against the wood floor because she was laughing so hard.

When Lila was calm, Eve continued. "My friend's husband is no slouch himself. He has a unique look because he's Japanese and black, but he has dark brown skin. The skin tone, combined with his almond-shaped eyes, give him an exotic look. Anyway, he and my friend were married a year later, and I was the matron of honor."

"That's a wonderful story. Well, not the Ronny part. Oh, you know what I mean."

"Yes, Lila. I know. You should see the two of them together. Just like in the movies; they're still walking off into the sunset." Looking at her stack of files and then glancing at the clock, Eve said, "Lila, I don't have the perfect answer for your situation. All I can advise is that you stay out of it. If your cousin finds out and wants to talk to you about it, she will. I would just assure her that you don't talk about what happens at work. The issue is between your cousin and her husband, not anyone else. If it becomes a problem, they have to resolve it. Now, I have to get to court."

Lila rose to leave. "Thanks, Eve. I really appreciate you taking the time to help me."

As Eve walked toward the metal detectors at the jail, she consoled herself with the thought that she'd already suffered through one week. Prosecutors usually did two-week rotations in the jail; thus, she only had one more to go. She couldn't wait to be done. The problem was that the court was in the jail, and it depressed her. A friend once asked her how she could send people to jail when she hated the actuality so much? Eve answered philosophically and truthfully. Jail was a necessary evil. In a civilized society, wrongdoers had to be punished to avoid vigilante justice and anarchy. As Eve told Noah, she thought of it as her contribution to maintaining the community. An important element because she wouldn't be happy in a career unless she felt like she was giving back. But still, the downside of being in a jail and looking at people in chains remained.

Eve went through security, walked down the short hall, and entered the courtroom. Automatically, she glanced through the bulletproof glass wall to see how many visitors had showed up. Two women who looked worried sat in the bench seats. Eve knew they were probably mothers, wives, or girlfriends.

The minute Eve placed her files down, the judge came out and sat at a high desk. He looked down at the lawyers, standing by their assigned metal tables, which Eve knew were Army castoffs. Eve had a table to herself, while the numerous defense attorneys had to share the other one. Two court clerks sat between the judge and lawyers. Right now they looked relaxed, but soon they would be working feverishly updating the computer, and trying to keep track of the endless paperwork being passed around.

"Good morning," the judge said to everyone. Without waiting for a response, he looked at Eve. She was responsible for running the calendar. "Madame Prosecutor, since everyone is here, I thought we could start a little early. Do you mind?"

"Of course not, Your Honor." She hoped everyone was ready to rock and roll. The overanxious judge had entered before she had a chance to check with the clerks and other attorneys. She called the first case. The five gun-toting marshals that protected the courtroom went into action. Two stood as watchdogs, and the other three shuffled the prisoners in and out in groups no larger than three. The marshals got the prisoners from a holding cell right beside the courtroom. The female inmates came in the morning, and the male inmates usually came in the afternoon. The two were separated to maintain control. Sometimes, the prisoners got impatient; they would scream obscenities and bang on the holding cell door, making Eve feel like she was about to be part of a riot. The feeling only increased when the prisoner developed an attitude in court. Someone was always struggling with the marshals. Gun butts, Mace containers, or handcuffs would hit the walls and furniture causing numerous dents and scratches that no one bothered to fix.

The day was running smoothly until Jerome Keller's name was called. He came out smelling so foul that Eve almost gagged. She covered it with a small cough. One of the clerks gave Eve a sympathetic smile, and then pulled out a scented hanky that she held to her nose.

One had to smell pretty awful to be noticed over the normal jail smell. The place was an odorous brick wall. Eve had been warned, but the smell still physically stopped her the first time she worked the jail court. Its source was elusive. Oh, some of it was easy to detect. Eve recognized urine and funk. She suspected that poor hygiene was a tactic used by some to make themselves an unattractive target.

Assault or rape was less likely if the attacker was afraid of getting a disease, or couldn't stand the smell or appearance. But there was something else that made the smell sharper, more disgusting. Eve finally decided that this something was fear. Fear of the other prisoners, or fear of the unknown. Eve didn't know, but this fear mingled with the other smells and created a stench more odious, more fetid. Daily bleaching deadened the smell, but it was never completely gone. It was a part of the building, ground into the floor, and rubbed into the walls. The courtroom was saturated with it, and it clung and hung there even when it was empty.

Eve had no idea what the motivation or cause was for Keller's smell. His jail-issued overalls looked clean enough, however, his long, red hair looked matted, and he appeared to be very thin and pale. Keller was a frequent visitor to the jail court because he was constantly committing petty crimes to support a drug habit.

"Hey, judge," Keller shouted, "this persecutor hates me! I want a different one."

Eve hid her smile. Keller was known for hating the prosecutor and loving his defense attorney. Whether the person representing him was male or female, she or he could expect to get adoring phone calls for at least six months after his case was resolved.

"Mr. Keller, I'm sure the prosecutor has no feelings for you one way or the other. Do you understand that you're being charged with a crime?"

Ignoring the judge's question, Keller looked over at Eve suspiciously. "No, judge, she's convicted me many times. She's just a prostitute for the state, and I know she hates me!"

The clerk snickered behind the handkerchief. Eve didn't suppress her grin this time. Having a sense of humor was essential to being a successful prosecutor.

The judge immediately came to her defense. "Mr. Keller, I must insist that you address Madame Prosecutor appropriately, or I will have to send you back to the holding cell. Would you like to wait until tomorrow for your case to be heard?"

"No, no, judge. Don't send me back. They hate me in there too."

After this exchange, Keller was cooperative.

However, as he was leaving the courtroom, he leaned toward Eve and whispered, "You're still just a state whore." Eve shook her head at him.

The rest of the week in the jail court passed agonizingly slow. She was so happy by the time Friday rolled around that she didn't care that it was raining. Winter in Seattle always meant rain; you got used to it. Besides, all the rain made you really appreciate the appearance of a rare sunny day. As she left the jail court on Friday, she felt exhilarated walking in the cool, damp air. She quickly walked the two blocks to her office, not bothering with an umbrella in the light drizzle. She didn't have to worry about her hair since she'd cut it short and besides, the water seemed to cleanse the last of the jail stench away.

On Monday, she'd return to the trial unit. Eve loved trials. The adrenaline rushed through her just like it did for a college track meet. Eve's event had been the mile. Running had always been important to her, and she still engaged in it avidly. She smiled while she walked; her happiness increasing when she remembered that Sean had a basketball game that night. She always looked forward to seeing him in action. Because of the game, domino night had been cancelled. Eve's smiled wavered. She couldn't decide if she was happy or sad about that.

❀❀❀

Eve watched her son, pride booming through her heart. Sean dribbled the ball upcourt, and right after he passed the half court line, he dished a pass to the player in the wing position. The wing zinged the ball back to Sean, who stood about five-feet away from the top of the key as he ran the offense. Sean quickly passed the ball to the wing on the other side. Shedding his defender off the pick set by the center, Sean got the ball back and sunk a three-pointer.

Eve and her mother both jumped up yelling. Eve gave her mom a shoulder nudge. "I taught him that. The perfect shooting form--elbow straight in front of his face, and the way the ball rolls off his fingers to create that beautiful spin." Eve demonstrated the form that made her a formidable opponent in high school. Her mom grabbed her raised shooting arm and urged her to sit.

Smiling indulgently. "I know, dear. You were a great player and you've passed those skills on to Sean." Laughing, Eve sat and hugged her mom's wide girth. "You know, being here makes me forget myself sometimes. It brings back the glory days, and makes me want to get out there and play!"

"I know, dear." Her mom squeezed her knee. "But you must contain yourself. You know how easily Sean gets embarrassed."

The two women commanded attention. Eve's mother, Beulah Johnson, had dark brown skin surrounded by a full head of beautiful white hair. She wore it in an Afro. Gracious and elegant, she favored colorful Afrocentric clothing that looked dramatic against her skin. A former English teacher, her wide dark brown eyes were smiling now, but they were known to pin unruly students to their seats.

Eve had come straight from work. She wore a black wool pantsuit with a white silk blouse. Though not as elegant as her mother, she possessed a natural grace and composure that drew a second look. Her face glowed as she watched her son.

Sean's team was playing man-to-man defense. Her son avoided a pick and managed to deflect the pass to his man. Sean's teammate scooped up the loose ball, and he and Sean streaked to the other end of the court. At the last minute, his teammate flipped a no-look pass, and Sean scored an easy two.

Her mom squeezed her knee. Eve put her arm around her ample shoulders, and kissed her age-softened cheek, instead of jumping up and cheering loudly. "Just like me, Mom. He can light 'em up from the outside and inside."

"Yes, you were good in your day," her mom answered. Years of cigarettes had made her naturally deep voice even deeper. She'd finally quit smoking, but the baritone voice remained.

Holding hands, both women turned their attention back to Sean. By the fourth quarter, he had twenty points and ten assists. He was in a zone. No one could stop him from the outside. He landed three pointer after three pointer. Sean's team, Garfield Junior High, was up by a point with a minute left in the game. The other team scored two points and was up by one. Sean headed up the court with thirty seconds to go. He started the offense. A teammate set a high pick. Sean used it to shed his defender and dribbled around the right side. Another defender left his man to pick up Sean. Sean zinged the pass in to his open teammate, but he was covered before he could get off a shot. The player sent the ball back out to Sean. With five seconds left, Sean faked one way and went up with the shot. The defender slapped at the ball, missed, and caught Sean in the chest while he was in midair. Balance gone, body twisted, he landed badly on his ankle. Her son's anguished yell drowned out the swish of net, and the sound of the buzzer. Garfield had won by one point.

Her mother didn't restrain her mad dash to Sean. Instead, she followed her lithe daughter at a heavier pace. Eve reached her son before the coach. His eyes were squeezed shut, and he curled into the fetal position with both hands holding his right ankle. The coach and Eve managed to soothe him enough to examine the ankle. The coach thought it was broken, and Sean was in so much pain, they decided to call 911. The fire station was near the school, and the tortured wail of the fire truck soon pierced the air.

Eve was incredulous and extremely irritated with herself. Her heart pounded with worry for Sean, and still the distinctive siren made her think of Noah. She couldn't quite erase him from her mind.

"Murphy's law," she whispered to herself. It was surreal, watching Noah stride across the gym floor. It was Friday night. Yoshi was off, and he and Noah worked the same shift, so why was Noah there? Back straight, he moved with natural grace and confidence. Time slowed as she watched him. She saw surprise in his eyes when he recognized her. Then a big grin spread across his face.

"Is this your son?"

She nodded. Sean lay on his back with one of his hands enclosed firmly in two of hers.

"Okay, son, I'll be as gentle as I can, but it's going to sting a bit when I take off your shoe." Eve was surprised Noah possessed a humane side. She knew he was a womanizer and could pour on the charm, but his compassion seemed sincere.

Sean's fingers bit into her hand and tears

leaked from his eyes, yet he didn't make a sound. She resisted the urge to cradle his head and tell him to let it out. She knew it would only embarrass him. Instead, she held his hand tighter as his nails pierced her flesh. Eve suppressed a gag at the sight of Sean's bare ankle. It was grotesque, swollen, and beginning to darken. Eve shut her eyes and took deep, even breaths.

"I'm sorry, it looks like it may be broken, son. We need to get you to the hospital." Noah spoke to her son as he and the others prepared him for transport. "I heard from your coach that you were the hero tonight."

Sean grunted.

"Yeah, the shot we all practiced on the playground, and you hit it." Noah's words made Sean smile, despite the pain. "You know, you're going to be it next week, maybe for two weeks. All the honeys are going to be offering to carry your books once they see the star on crutches."

Noah looked at her and winked. Her heart softened a little. This side of Noah was completely unexpected. She wouldn't have believed it existed if she weren't witnessing it. His praise and gentle teasing were having the desired effect. Sean didn't say much, still he laughed and visibly relaxed. This eased Eve's tension, and she found herself chuckling at Noah's comments.

Two of his colleagues lifted Sean onto a stretcher. After he was in the ambulance, Noah turned to Eve. He placed a hand on her shoulder, "He's going to be fine." Her shoulder tingled.

"Do you two know each other?" A stately woman in a bright, multicolored outfit asked.

"Yes, Mom. This is Noah Russell. He's my new domino partner." She knew she should move, but the massaging fingers had her paralyzed.

"Oh, how fortunate," her mother said, beaming. "Can you pull some strings, so we both can ride in the ambulance?"

Eve was relieved when Noah removed his hand. "No, there's a space problem. I'm pushing it by allowing Eve to ride with us." Eve handed the keys to her mother and kissed her on the cheek.

Noah called the hospital and let Emergency know they were coming. With Eve's permission, he gave Sean a painkiller. She couldn't believe that even under these circumstances, she felt Noah's pull. She tried to ignore it.

Now that they were away from Sean's friends, she indulged herself and rubbed his forehead. He allowed her touch, and, with closed eyes, actually turned toward her lap. You're still my little boy, she thought as tears threatened. She knew his life wasn't in jeopardy, but seeing him injured and lying on a cot, looking so much like his father, brought back memories of that night and how she agonized over the fate of her missing husband.

Noah's warm breath made her jump. He whispered in her ear, "Why are you crying? In six weeks or so, he'll be good as new."

She didn't know she was crying. Thank God Sean's eyes were still closed. She looked at Noah. I'm an oxymoron, she scolded herself. How can I weep for the loss of my husband, and at the same time crave this man?

Leaning close, he whispered in her ear once more, "We're over the worst part. Don't fall apart now." She nodded and allowed Noah to wipe away her tears. He took her hand and held it lightly. She let him hold it the rest of the way.

Noah wanted to stay with them. His part was done, and the crew wanted to leave.

"Hey, just get the lady's number. We need to get back."

"Okay, okay, just give me a minute."

Noah left the crew in the hospital lobby. He went to sit by the two women, holding hands, watching the doctor put a cast on Sean. He had no way of knowing both were focused on the past, thinking of another time in a hospital when the stakes were much higher than a broken ankle.

"How are you doing? Any questions about the x-ray or what the doctor said?"

Eve answered, "No, we understand what the words broken bone and severely sprained mean. We don't need your assistance any longer." Noah and her mother looked at her. Eve didn't care if they thought her tone was harsh. She was pissed. Angry her son was hurt, angry she was a widow, and angry that even now her heart was doing flip-flops for a man to whom she didn't want to be attracted. She knew the root of the problem was guilt. She hadn't thought about Todd this much in months. Everytime her body acknowledged Noah, Todd popped into her head and guilt quickly followed. She was tired of feeling guilty; anger was much better.

Beulah looked from one to the other. "Maybe we should step outside and let the doctor finish." When they were outside the door, she said, "I'm going to get some coffee. Would either of you like a cup?"

"No," they answered in unison. Beulah slipped away.

"Why are you here? Don't you have tonight off?"

"Yes. Someone was sick, and I was called in."

"Why are you still here? Isn't your job done?" she demanded rudely.

Noah kept his voice soft and even. "I could say my job." He shrugged his shoulders, "but I'm here out of concern for you."

She wasn't impressed. She leaned forward and looked him in the eyes. In her best courtroom voice, she attacked. "I hope you are not using an unfortunate situation and a defenseless boy to get in my good graces."

Noah stiffened and leaned back. The once-warm eyes were now glacial ice. The look was reminiscent of Eve's mother. Both could make you shiver. Noah's tone matched his eyes. "You must be a good lawyer. No one has attacked my honor and insulted me so thoroughly as you have." His jaw moved as he clenched his teeth. "I will overlook it now and hope in the future you can be more open."

"Open?"

"Yes, open. Stop judging me based on rumors. Judge me for myself."

She lowered her voice as her anger rose. She was almost hissing. "Can you deny you've slept with hordes of women?"

"I'm no Wilt Chamberlin."

"I bet you're a close second."

"Why does it matter? What happened before is in the past and out of our control now. I can honestly say the only woman I'm interested in is you, and until we resolve this thing between us, I can guarantee you that I won't be with anyone else." Besides the one time with Sheila the night after he met Eve, which was about three weeks ago, he'd been celibate.

"The past is an excellent indicator of the future."

"I know you don't mean that, Eve. Are you really saying that people don't change?" He continued without giving her a chance to answer. "Besides that, you don't really know my past. All you know is a bunch of gossip. What do you call gossip in court? Hearsay, right?"

Eve nodded.

"Hearsay isn't allowed in court, is it, Eve? It's not allowed because it's not reliable."

Eve leaned away from him, arms crossing her chest, and her whole body tensing with fury. "Noah, this isn't a criminal court where someone's freedom is at stake. Lots of hearsay is admissible in a civil trial where all you will probably lose is money. In our case, what's at stake is even less important than money, so I can listen to all the hearsay, gossip, rumors, scuttlebutt that I want."

"Look at me," he demanded. Angry eyes clashed. "Confess, Eve. You don't know who I am because you've already convicted me. You decided my character based on faulty evidence!"

They stared at each other. "You are absolutely right," Eve said. Then, she lied through her teeth, pronouncing each word separately and distinctly. "I do not know who you are, nor do I care to know."

Without a backward glance, she walked back into the room where Sean was being treated. A pattern Noah was getting used to: watching her leave.

Beulah waited until they were home and Sean, with his new cast, was in a drug-induced sleep. The late news provided background noise. Beulah sat in a purple, gold, red, and brown robe that looked more like a dashiki. Eve wore her silk pajamas, a royal blue short set. Beulah patted the couch where she sat and said, "What's going on?'

Eve took her mother's invitation and sat down. "Nothing."

Beulah played with Eve's short hair, picking at the curls and then smoothing them out. Eve slouched into her mom's touch, and put her stocking feet on the coffee table. They relaxed into a comfortable silence. After a while, her mother asked again, "So, are you going to tell me what's going on between you and Mr. December?"

"Mr. December?" Eve looked up at her mother.

"Yes. I bought the fire department calendar at Starbucks. Not to look at the hunks, but to support charity, you know? I was going to give it to my friend, Jean; she enjoys that type of thing. Then I looked at it, and somehow forgot to give it to Jean."

Beulah tugged hard on a curl when Eve doubled over in laughter. Eve rubbed her head and managed to say, "Go get it."

Her mom got up. "I didn't tell you, or put it up because I knew you'd laugh, and Sean would tease me unmercifully."

Eve quickly flipped to December after her mom handed her the calendar. Her breath caught. "Impressive isn't he," her mom commented. She didn't answer. Noah was standing in a snow-covered pasture holding an ax, with chopped wood all around him. He wore tan fireman pants and red suspenders. His marvelous torso was bare. Well-developed pectorals, four racks of abdominal muscles, and bulging biceps had Eve mentally drooling. She put the calendar on the coffee table, and leaned back on the couch. Her mom gave her time to recover. "Okay, for the third time, what's going on with you and your domino partner?"

Eve didn't bother opening her closed eyes, "I told you, Mom, nothing."

Beulah sat down shoulder to shoulder with Eve. "So, you're usually extremely rude to someone who has been most helpful and sincere for nothing?"

She chuckled, "Was I that bad?"

"Yes, you were mean, so now explain why."

Eve gave in, "He keeps bugging me to go out."

"Oh, not that!" Her mother threw up her hands.

"He should be shot! Doesn't he know asking you out is a capital offense?!"

Eve sat up and turned to face her mother. "It's

73

more than that, Mom. He's a Don Juan, a womanizer. I don't need more drama in my life. I've had
enough already."

"I can appreciate that. The past few years
haven't been easy, and I admire the way you've
picked up the pieces and met your obligations.

However, four years of celibacy is more than a
show of respect."

"Wait. How do you know I haven't had sex?"

"I can count the dates you've had on one hand.
Besides, a mother knows these things."

"Are you saying I should sleep with him?" Eve
and her mother had always had a close and open
relationship, but this was too much.

"Well, not on the first date, but I am telling you
it's time to take your wedding ring off, and explore
what other men have to offer." Beulah laughed at
Eve's shocked expression. "Look, I saw how you
reacted to him. Your eyes popped out of your head
and rolled around on the floor when he walked into
the gym. That, combined with your uncalled-for
rudeness, means he affects you. Forgive me, but
I'm happy about that. I've been concerned that you
buried your romantic feelings when you buried
Todd. This man brings those emotions to the surface. He's broken through your indifference."

Ignoring Eve's annoyed expression, she continued. "I'm talking from experience, Eve. I know your

father left us and remarried before he died in that plane, but the result is the same. My bitterness did the same thing your grief is doing. I know I didn't share my bitterness with you. I always told you your father was a good man, we just grew apart, and that's why I didn't mind when he moved in with another woman. Essentially, that's true. We let silly spats build up into big stupid arguments and we stopped communicating. After a while, I couldn't remember what the idiotic fights were about. I just knew I couldn't be the first to give in. Your father wouldn't give in either. Stalemate. Our asinine pride killed our marriage."

"But, Mom..."

"No, don't interrupt," Beulah held up her hand and flashed Eve a freezing glare. "I don't want to say anymore on that subject. What I want to say relates more to you, and I should have said it a year ago. I shut the door to that part of myself, rejected all offers, and focused on you and my students. Now, don't get me wrong, I'm not whining or terribly unhappy with my present state in life. I have a wonderful daughter and grandchild, and that's a lot more than some people have. I'm just saying, leave your options open. You're young with lots of years ahead of you. I'm telling you that some of those nights can be cold, and I'm not talking about the temperature. Take some risks before you sentence yourself to Siberia."

Beulah's frankness left Eve speechless. Her mother patted her knee. "I know I've shocked you, dear. It's been a long day, and we're both tired. Just think about what I've said, all right? By the way, you can have the calendar." Beulah tossed it on her lap, kissed her cheek, and went to bed.

Eve sat on the couch, her arms wide, legs stretched out, and Noah staring at her. She remembered when she was eight, she got into a fight with Sally Patterson over the only free swing at the playground. Well, it wasn't really a fight because Sally sucker-punched her in the stomach. She swung happily while Eve writhed in the dirt. Eve had that same feeling now, like her mother slipped in a gut punch. When she got her breath back, she got up and went to bed where she slipped the calendar between the mattresses.

🍎🍎🍎

Sweat dripped in his eyes, his muscles bulged as he strained to get the weight up. With a loud grunt, Noah shoved and barely got the weight back on the bar. One of his coworkers glanced into the fire department weight room. "Lots of clanking going on in here. You okay? You need a spotter?"

"Yeah and no," Noah answered; too tired to get

up from the bench. Shrugging, his coworker left.

"Damn, damn, damn," a whispered litany. He knew he should use a spotter while bench-pressing three hundred pounds, but he wanted isolation. Time to deal with the stuff clanging around inside his head. He went to the weight room as soon as he could when he got back to the station after leaving the hospital. As he lay there, staring at the ceiling, he told the empty room, "The woman is rude and obviously not interested." He wondered why he was drawn to her. When she said she wasn't interested, he wanted to grab her, run his fingers through the short curls, and thoroughly explore her mouth. He wondered if she would be interested then. He wondered if she'd take that damn ring off.

Running a hand across his wet forehead, he admitted Eve probably would have smacked the mess out of him. He tried to convince himself she wasn't worth the headache. She probably still loved her husband, she had a kid, she was a lawyer, and if they got married and divorced, she'd clean him out. Not that he was Donald Trump, but being a single man with no responsibilities other than his own needs, he'd managed to put a bit away. Divorce! Why was he thinking divorce when they weren't even married? Hell, she wouldn't even grant him a date. Why was he so attracted? He knew it was more than her looks because he'd had more than his share of beautiful women over the years. He'd also had a fair number of rebuffs, and it certainly didn't make him want to approach the woman again, so it wasn't some weird rejection thing.

Maybe it was her intellect, which showed clearly through their verbal sparring. Or maybe it was her strength and commitment. She survived a tragedy and was there for her child. He knew if they were together, she was the type of woman who would be a partner, not a noose around his neck, strangling him if he ever tripped. She would be a retaining wall in mudslides, his eye in the worst of storms. Damn, I'm getting corny. He sat up and tried to motivate himself to go take a shower. I sound like one of my sister's silly romance novels.

CHAPTER 4

*E*ight days later and domino night rolled around again. Its ominous presence hung over Eve's head all day long. Like a spoiled child, she kept whispering, "I don't want to go, I don't want to go, I don't want to go."

"Today is Saturday, didn't Ebony call to remind you about domino night?" Beulah asked. "Shouldn't you be getting ready?" Sean, Beulah, and Eve were relaxing in the living room.

"Hey, Mom," Sean said, using his standard address. She used to quip, hay is for horses, but after a while she didn't bother. She philosophized that you pick your battles with children, and this was an okay one for her to lose, but it still pricked her nerves to be addressed in such a way. "Can you

drop me by Nick's house on the way? He has a
new CD I want to check out." Sean lay on the
couch with pillows underneath his cast to elevate
his leg. Eve sat at the end of the couch and gently
rubbed his big toe, which stuck out of the end of the
cast.

"Sean, you just broke your ankle a week ago.
Stay home and rest. Let the thing heal!"

"Mom, I'm bored. All I'm doing is sitting and ele-
vating my leg. I can do that stuff at Nick's. At least
at Nick's, I can listen to the jams and talk to someone."

"Excuse me. Your grandmother and I are people!" She pinched his toe playfully.

"Stop!" She left his toe alone. "You know what
I mean, Mom. Stop teasing me." He gave her a
sappy look: chin down, hands stretched out and
crossed before him, "Pleeeease."

"Seaaaan," she put the same whine in her
voice. "I know he speaks your language, and you
have things in common, but..." She was about to
say that he needed to rest, and besides, she was
going to skip domino night and not go anywhere.
That was before her gaze caught Beulah's. She
read the challenge in her mother's eyes. Either face
Noah, or stay and face me. Noah won hands down.
"I hope it's not one of those gangster rap CDs."

"Oh, Mom, they're just talking about reality. You

know, how they live."

They'd had this conversation before. "Just because it's how they live doesn't make it right. They're not making the problem go away by glorifying it."

"Mom, you take it way too seriously. I'm not going to call women out of their name, or shoot up the world just because they say it in a song." Sean began hobbling out of the room, using the furniture and the wall as handholds, before she could reply. "I'll be ready in five minutes."

She started to follow. "Let the boy go," Beulah advised. "He's a good kid with lousy taste in music. Reminds me of you. Remember when you and your friends used to refer to each other as niggah. Lord, that drove me crazy. It's such an ugly, degrading term, and here you youngsters were using it to describe yourselves. And the way you used to draw the word out niiigggggaaaah, pleeeease! I can still hear you and Ebony saying it. Yuck!" Beulah shuddered and shook her head to emphasize how repulsive it was.

Eve did indeed remember, and found herself smiling, then her brows creased into a frown. She would have drawn a line in the sand then if she knew calling each other niggah back in the seventies and early eighties would lead to being referred to as a bitch, ho, or worse in the nineties. "As I recall, you used to justify it by saying that if you used the term among yourselves, then it wouldn't hurt when white people called you that. You said you were taking control of the word and diffusing it of its power."

Eve nodded.

"Well, Eve, I know it's difficult to listen to that bad music, but Sean's world is too big for us to censor it completely. He's going to hear it whether you forbid it or not. And look at the bright side: You don't use that hideous term anymore. You grew out of it. Chances are Sean will too. But for now, as long as he only plays it in his room, on a low volume, and he's not disrespectful, I really don't think you have much to worry about. He's not on drugs, he loves basketball too much for that; he gets excellent grades; and he's well-mannered most of the time. He will be fine. Knock on wood." She tapped on the windowsill near her easy chair. "You sure turned out okay." The two smiled at each other.

Conceding to her mother's wisdom, Eve contented herself by yelling, "Sean, bring your crutches."

"Ah, Mom, those things make me look like a cripple. I get along fine without them!"

"Boy, you just broke your ankle. Bring your crutches!" Eve got up and headed toward her bedroom. She threw over her shoulder, "You are a cripple, at least for five more weeks." Her son wailed as only a teenager could.

On the way, she plotted her strategy as her son rapped with the radio. Okay, maybe she'd been a little coarse and abrupt, so she would apologize quickly and get it over with. Get the awkwardness out of the way early.

"Hey, Mom, you'll like this one. It's about Rosa Parks. 'Ah ha, what's that fuss everybody move to the back of the bus,' " Sean sang as he bopped around in his seat.

"How so?"

"I don't know, but they say her name."

Eve laughed and shook her head. Then she found herself bobbing her head to the catchy beat.

At Nick's house, despite Sean's look and vow that he could handle it, she helped him into the house, and told Nick's mother that he was suppose dto stay off his ankle, and elevate it to a level above his heart. After seeing him settled, she left to go to Ebony's.

Déjà vu. Here she was sitting in a car scared— no, hesitant was a better word, about getting out. "This is stupid." She gripped the steering wheel. "I face hostile defense attorneys, angry defendants, and intimidating judges every day," she muttered. In comparison, Noah was a piece of cake. A delicious-looking chocolate cake, and she could probably handle more than a slice. Whoa, where did that come from? Giving herself a mental slap, she told herself that the dessert and Noah were too lavish and rich for her. She needed to steer clear of both to avoid indigestion and heartache. Nodding her head firmly, she got out of the car.

Eve let out the breath she'd been holding when Ebony told her Noah wasn't there yet. When Noah arrived, they began playing immediately. She admired the fact that he was a gentleman. He was his usual polite, gracious, entertaining self. No uncomfortable pauses or embarrassing silences. He treated her as he always did, which meant she was still caught and held occasionally in the warmth of his eyes.

At the end of the evening, Eve and Noah found themselves down by a game. Full of pride, Yoshi pushed out his chest as far as he could. He put his hands on his hips and swaggered behind them to the door. He teased them all the way, claiming the prior series had been a fluke. Eve suggested tonight was the oddity, and Noah readily agreed. Ebony scolded her husband by telling him if he bragged too much, he'd jinx them. Standing beside Yoshi in the doorway, with her arms around his waist, Ebony reminded them they wouldn't be able to play for a while. Ebony was going to California to spend time with her sister who had just had a baby, and then she and Yoshi were going on vacation.

"It must be nice having your own shop," Eve teased.

"You know this is my first vacation since opening a year and a half ago. I'm kinda nervous about leaving."

"Don't be." Yoshi hugged her hard. "You have a great manager, and everything's going to be fine."

Noah walked Eve to her car. Halfway there, Eve turned to him. "I want to apologize for the other night. I'm glad my behavior didn't stop you from coming tonight."

"No, it takes more than a nasty attitude to scare me away."

Eve smiled a real smile at him and Noah's breath caught a little. "I promise to be more objective, and I'll try not to assume things."

Noah didn't address whether he'd ask her out again. They reached her car. "Look, Eve, I'll be honest with you. I haven't been a choirboy. That reputation didn't appear out of thin air. But it's been grossly exaggerated and blown out of proportion. It has a life of its own and grows despite the real me. It's impossible to live up to and it's equally impossible to live it down. So, I try to ignore it. I'm hoping one day I'll meet the woman who can see past it to the real me."

Eve was speechless. She was scared of the

real him. She was more comfortable with the reputation because she could keep avoiding the man the reputation described. Finally, she found her voice, "I hope you meet her one day."

"Maybe I have. Now that we've got that cleared up, how about dinner and a movie?"

She had to laugh. "You are so persistent. No, Noah."

"I just thought I'd try. On a serious note, the fire department is very involved with the Middle School Career Day. I've been asked to help find speakers, and it would be a real treat for the kids to hear from a prosecutor. It's two weeks, on a Friday. We could have lunch afterward. What's your address? I'll send you an information packet."

Shaking her head, Eve said, "You don't give up do you? You know your strategy is very obvious?"

"As you can tell, I'm desperate. Put me out of my misery and say yes."

"Send me the packet at work. I'll let you know." Eve handed him a business card and got in her car and left.

🦋🦋🦋

On Tuesday, he did one better and hand-delivered the packet. He had to testify, and would be at the courthouse already, so he had the perfect excuse. He took the stand in a case where a man was charged with burning down his house so his wife wouldn't be awarded it in the divorce proceedings. Noah's team was the first crew to arrive. His testimony was routine and unchallenged. The State just needed him to establish that a fire definitely took place. He was on and off the stand in fifteen minutes.

After he was excused, he went in search of Eve. The receptionist at the prosecutor's office looked him up and down as he approached. Her husky voice purred when she asked, "May I help you?"

"Yes, I'm looking for Eve Garrett."

"Is this about a trial or personal?"

Noah smiled knowingly, and thought, at least she's being tactful. "Neither. It's about a community event she may participate in."

"Oh." The woman checked the sign-in sheet. "She's in trial in court six. By the way, my name's Regina Vincent. I'm here every morning part-time."

Noah shook the lovely brown hand with long, lacquered fingernails. "I'll keep that in mind. Thanks for the information."

Noah found courtroom six and slipped into the back. The judge glanced at Noah and finished reading the jury instructions. "Ladies and gentlemen of the jury, you have been instructed in the law of this case. Now you will hear from each attorney before you will retire to the jury room to deliberate. Madame prosecutor." He nodded to Eve.

Eve and the defense attorney sat at separate tables below the judge's elevated platform. The attorneys' backs faced Noah and the five or so others in the audience. The jury sat against the wall to Noah's right on the side of the attorneys.

As Eve rose, so did Noah's heartbeat. She wore a dark blue power suit with classic lines. The skirt ended at her knees and allowed Noah to see her shapely legs for the first time. He shifted in his seat.

"Ladies and gentlemen of the jury," she began in a strong, confident voice, "Mr. Graff had a bad day. Super Bowl Sunday, and everything was going wrong. His friend didn't show, so he had to watch the game alone; his beer was warm; the TV had fuzzy reception; and to top it off, his team lost the Super Bowl, and he was out a hundred bucks. So, what did he do?" She raised her hand and paused. "He vented the way he usually does. He took it out on his wife, Sue Graff.

"Now, the first thing defense counsel is going to rant and rave about when it's his turn to address you is that you can't convict because Sue didn't testify. But is that really true? Sue didn't take the stand, but we still heard from her. We heard her voice on the 911 tape pleading with the operator for help." Eve pushed play on the recorder that rested on the bench in front of the jury. A piercing wail filled the courtroom. Some of the jurors leaned back in their seats. Next, they suffered through a woman sobbing for help because her husband was beating her. In the background, there was the sound of a man cursing loudly. Then abruptly, the line went dead.

Eve shut off the recorder. "Yes, we have certainly heard from Sue; not only from the tape, but also from the officer's testimony. Remember Officer Clark described how Sue ran out of the house to meet him. She was crying and saying that her husband attacked her. Remember the officer said Sue was hysterical when near the defendant. She shook uncontrollably and couldn't get out her words. Obviously, poor Sue is terrified of that man." Eve pointed to the defendant. "Couldn't that be an explanation for why she isn't here? Doesn't that seem more logical than she isn't here because it didn't happen?"

Again, she paused for effect. Then she strode to her desk and picked something up. "But we have more than Sue's words, don't we? We know what she looked like." As Eve showed the jury the enlarged photos, Noah could see glimpses of a woman's head and torso. The torso was criss-crossed with several purple, yellowish bruises.

"This is what the defendant did to Sue on Super Bowl night because he was unhappy about his beer." Still holding the photos, Eve continued, "When you viciously attack someone and cause these types of injuries, you're committing a crime. That crime is called assault. Because of this," Eve shook the pictures, "you should find the defendant guilty." Eve spread the three photos out in front of the jury and returned to her seat.

Noah was impressed. Her appearance captivated, but her words drew the audience in, especially him. He was doing more than looking at her; he listened. The way she stood, spoke, and carried herself demanded attention. She didn't scream or use antics to capture them. She had a quiet authority that made him, the jury, and even the judge lean forward and take notice. Beauty and brains. A powerful combination.

The defense attorney wasn't up to the task. He did what Eve warned the jury he would do. He harped about Sue's physical absence. The jurors fidgeted in their seats, and the judge didn't look at the lawyer once. Everyone seemed relieved when he sat down. Eve gave a very brief rebuttal. A veteran of many trials, Noah was delighted with her strategy. She knew the jurors were tired, hungry, and already siding with her, so she kept it short and sweet.

The jury was excused for lunch and then deliberations. Noah slipped outside of the court and waited for Eve in the foyer. God, she's beautiful, he thought as she came through the door. Her short curly hair framed a heart-shaped face, giving her look a touch of innocence. But her cinnamon skin tone and eyes were spicy. Her eyes weren't as almond shaped as Yoshi's, but they had a slight slant to them that Noah thought was incredibly sexy. Compared to his six-two, she was short. He guessed she was about five-four, a short fireball.

Eyes widening were the only sign of surprise when she saw him. She hoped he failed to realize that she thought he looked great in the dress blues of the fire department. His pants and shirt were creased to perfection, and underneath his arm, he carried a hat. Eve was tempted to ask him to put it on. She had a soft spot for muscular men in uniform.

Taking a mental deep breath, Eve resorted to sarcasm to control herself, "What? Are you stalking me now?"

Noah laughed, "No, just good service. I'm delivering the career-day packet." He handed it to her, and fell into step with her as she walked away.

"Thanks." She glanced at him as if to say go away.

Noah ignored the look. "I saw your closing. The

jury's crazy if it doesn't convict."

"Thanks. This is the third time Graff's been charged with domestic violence. Hopefully we can get him this time." Eve pushed the elevator button to go to her office. It was in the same building as the courthouse.

"He got off the other times?"

"Yes. Usually Sue shows up and messes up the case. Graff tells her he's sorry, gives her some flowers, and promises not to hit her again. Then, Sue comes in and tells the jury how clumsy she is. How she really slipped on the rug and the doorknob caused all the injuries. She's very believable." Eve stepped on the elevator. Noah followed.

"This really isn't necessary. I have the packet." Eve held it up.

"Well, if you'd slow up a minute, I could ask you to lunch."

"I brought my lunch." Eve stepped off the elevator and headed to her office.

"Hi, Regina." She waved to the receptionist. "Any messages?"

Regina handed her a stack of pink slips. "Yeah, one's right behind you." Regina's seductive tone annoyed Eve. She frowned at Noah and went down the hall.

Noah smiled back at Regina and followed Eve to her office. Once inside, he closed the door.

"So, what's for lunch?"

Eve made an exasperated noise. "Now you want my food! Open the door before people start to gossip."

"Okay, after I talk to you for a minute." Noah joined Eve at the window. "What a beautiful view."

"I know. It's the only thing that makes this cubbyhole bearable." Eve's senses were electrified as they quietly stood at her window, enjoying the blue waters of Puget Sound. She felt Noah's warmth, and her nose quivered as she tried to identify the pleasant, slightly spicy scent that drifted from him. Eve guessed that it was his natural essence mixed with some after-shave--an alluring combination. He distracted her so much that she had to close her eyes and nose for a moment. When she opened them, she forced herself to concentrate on the water. It was a rare sunny day in Seattle, and Eve admired how the sunlight hit the water, sending off a blinding glare. Kind of like what Noah standing behind her was doing to her system. The intensity of it dazzled her senses, making it hard for her to think clearly. Eve tried to empty her mind and focus only on the water. After a time she spoke. "I get so worked up during trial, that I like to come here and look at the water. It helps bring me down."

"I would have never guessed looking at you during the trial. You appear calm, authoritative, so in control."

Standing so close to him was testing her control. If she turned slightly, her breast would brush his arm. The knowledge made her nipple harden.

"Let's go walk by the water." Before she could protest, Noah grabbed her lunch and put on his hat. "Come on, we'll be back in a half hour." Eve looked at his glowing face, the hat, and the uniform. She couldn't resist. She followed him. He led the way to the waterfront. Downtown Seattle rested on the shores of Puget Sound. Eve's office was five minutes from the water. They strolled along the waterfront until they came upon an empty bench that faced the water. Noah's large hand gracefully swept across his body and toward the bench. Laughing at his antics, Eve sat down. Noah sat also and handed her the lunch. She pulled out a turkey sandwich, and handed Noah half.

Both of their heads turned as a police officer rode by on a magnificent brown horse. Mounted officers were common in downtown Seattle, but that didn't stop Noah and Eve from admiring the big bay. Recognizing Noah's uniform, the officer nodded to him. Firefighters and police officers shared a bond born out of both groups' willingness to risk their lives for the safety of the community. Eve waved to the officer and he stopped in front of them.

"Hi, Eve. I didn't notice you sitting there." The

officer leaned on the pommel. "How's it going? We haven't had a case together in a while."

"It's going good, Officer Peltzer." Eve turned to Noah. "Noah, this is Officer Peltzer; Peltzer, this is Noah Russell." As the two men said hello, Eve resisted the urge to stroke the horse's velvety nose. She knew the officers didn't like people to touch their mounts.

"What a beautiful animal," Noah commented.

Officer Peltzer leaned over and rubbed the animal's strong neck. "Yes, she is. We've been together now for two years, and she's a great partner." The horse snickered and raised her head as if she to say yes. "See, she agrees. Well, you two enjoy your lunch." With a wave, the officer was on his way.

Noah and Eve watched the horse and rider amble away. Noah's thoughts traveled back to his father as he watched the animal's powerful muscles. "My dad loved horses."

The touch of sadness in his voice made Eve turn to him. Noah had a distant look as he continued to gaze at the retreating horse.

Eve enjoyed his profile as he spoke: long, thick neck; strong jaw; full lips, straight, majestic nose. She had to snap herself out of it to listen to him. "He and I would go to the race track, and he'd place a bet or two, but his real reason for being there was to admire the horses. One time he said, 'Son, one of these days I'm going to buy me a horse.' Being a smart-mouth teenager I said, 'Pop, stop talking about it and do it.' He laughed saying, 'I don't want one if it's not on my property, and I can't see your mom moving to the suburbs with me so I could have a horse.' I said, 'Forget Mom! What about me? I don't want to live in the sticks!' " Noah chuckled and twisted to Eve, "Looking at that beautiful horse, I can see why Pop wanted one so bad."

Noah looked at Eve again and felt a little embarrassed that he'd shared such a personal memory. "Sorry about reminiscing. You probably don't want to hear about all of that." Noah pointed in the direction of the horse. "It just reminded me of my pops, and I found myself talking."

He smiled warmly, and Eve's heart accelerated. She was touched by his words and excited by his appearance. "No, Noah. I do want to hear it." Then Eve surprised herself and began talking about her father. "My dad died when I was thirteen, a plane crash. My parents had been divorced for a year when it happened, and I didn't see him much, but it still hurt like hell. It's not easy to lose a parent."

"I'm sorry, Eve." Noah wanted to put his arm around her. Eve sensed that was what he wanted to do, and a large part of her wanted that comfort. She inched away from him to keep herself from leaning into his touch. Noah noticed the move and pretended that it didn't bother him.

"Anyway," Eve continued, "I feel like what I went through was a blessing compared to your experience. My father's death was quick; one phone call, and he was gone. I was spared what you went through, watching your father decline." Before Eve's mind stopped her, the force of the moment had her gently rubbing the back of Noah's hand as it rested on the bench between them. Her mind caught her, and she stopped.

Noah grabbed her hand and held it before she could pull away. He nodded and once again, he found himself revealing what no one outside of his nuclear family knew. "I remember when they first put my father in diapers. I lost it." Noah ran his free hand over his hair and stared out at the waters of Puget Sound. "My big, strong Pop who could scale a ladder faster than any other, who could carry a ninety-pound hose like it was nothing, who could put out any fire, in diapers. My hero reduced to soiling his own pants. I couldn't take it. I yelled at my mom and sister, 'How could you? Pop can still go to the bathroom, and if he can't, I can take him!' I stormed around the house, and managed to break a lamp or two before my mom grabbed me. Mom tried to explain why. You know, she said stuff like, 'Your dad's weak, it's too difficult for him to make it to the toilet, and this is for the best,' I stood there, with my arms welded to my sides because my mother was holding me so tight. I glared up at the ceiling, and knew I had to get away or I'd hurt somebody. My mom let me go, and I raced out of the house. My sister tried to stop me, and I pushed her so hard, she fell."

Noah glanced at Eve. Her eyes were full of compassion, and he interlocked their fingers as he continued to hold her hand. They both ignored the quiver in his voice when he turned back to the water and spoke again. "I hadn't hit my sister since I was eight. I still feel guilty about that. I hopped in my dad's pickup and took off. I didn't make it far. I pulled over to the side of the road and cried for two hours. My sister found me and we cried together. I had been pretty strong throughout his illness, but seeing him in diapers broke me. I realized I wouldn't have Pop much longer. I knew he was sick, but I wasn't ready for him to die. It was a reality check, or more like reality slamming me in the face. Pop died six months later."

Eve squeezed his hand, and Noah looked at her. "Thanks for listening to me. My sister claims I keep things too bottled up. It's easy to talk to you."

The connection between them was so strong that Eve felt breathless. She spoke without thinking. "You can talk to me anytime."

Noah felt weird and a little numb after sharing so much of his personal feelings. He didn't really question why he did it. He knew it was instinctive; it felt so natural with her today that he relaxed, and things just came out. Eve was an enigma with the power to bring him out of himself. If he didn't watch it, he might get lost in the puzzle. Noah tried to defuse his feelings with amusement, "Oh, really. How about Saturday night? I'd love to talk to you all night long."

Eve laughed. "I have to watch you, Noah; you're tricky."

"I guess that means no."

"You're right, but you can go get us a couple of hot dogs from that vendor," Eve pointed to a nearby stand. "You ate all my lunch."

Noah got up to get the food, using the time to compose himself. He bought the hot dogs and handed one to Eve. She looked at him sideways and said, "Why do you bother?"

Noah knew exactly what she was talking about. Originally, his only intent was to deliver the package and bug her about a date. He hadn't planned on talking about his dad, or making any grand statements or proclamations, and he certainly didn't see himself giving her an ultimatum or an out. However, that's exactly what he found himself doing. "Despite your impressions of me, my real success with

Edwina Martin-Arnold

women hasn't been great." Noah ignored her blank stare. "I'm telling you this because I want you to give us getting to know each other a chance." Noah looked out at the water. "In high school and college, women wanted the image of Noah Russell. The stud football player. I looked good on their arm, and I would make a rich husband. I was young, and I didn't care or really understand why they were attracted. I flourished in all the attention. Then, I met Natasha. The first woman I thought I cared about. I made a commitment, and I knew she had to be the happiest woman in the world to be with the fantastic Noah Russell."

Noah laughed and ate the last bite of his hot dog. "Well, when the Denver Broncos let me go, so did my little gold digger. That was a difficult time for me. It made me assess what I wanted in a relationship and how others saw me. I swore off women for a while, but that didn't last long." Noah paused for a moment, and then, turned and looked at her. "There were others who wanted to take Natasha's place, but all those women seemed more interested in the package than the man. My parents had a great love for forty years. They both would have tears in their eyes if they separated for more than a day. I may not have experienced it, but I know what true love looks like. That's what I want."

"I'm not looking for love." Eve spoke the words,

despite the turmoil in her body.

He stared into her. His eyes were magnetic. Eve's turmoil turned into heat. It traveled through her body, making her fingers and toes sizzle, then, it settled in a pool just below her abdomen.

"I know. I'm not asking for marriage or even commitment. I want you to know I'm not the playboy everyone thinks I am. I want more than that. I want the opportunity to date you, to get to know you better."

Eve tried sarcasm. "That's all you want?"

Noah smiled seductively, "You're a beautiful woman. Of course, I want you, but getting to know you is more important. If we like each other, that can come later."

"Noah, I'm a lot older than you."

Noah shifted on the bench so he was facing her and put an ankle across his thigh. "Eve, how old do you think I am?"

She turned her and studied him. "You're not a day over twenty-six."

"Nope, I'm twenty-nine."

"You're still too young. Noah, I'm thirty-six almost thirty-seven."

He looked her up and down and shook his head in disbelief.

"I know, it's amazing what taking care of your body can do."

"All I know is that it works."

The pool in her stomach began a slow boil.

"Hey, Eve. What did you say to Ebony the night we had dinner? Oh yeah, the older you get the more a difference like ours doesn't matter." He paused. "Eve, look at me." Reluctantly she did. "Your age isn't important to me. You are an extremely beautiful woman on the outside, and from what I've seen when you're not picking on me, on the inside as well."

His words and tone drew her focus to his sensuous, teasing lips. Her heart beat like one of Sean's rap songs. She closed her eyes, denying the instant it would take to mentally give herself to this man.

"Eve?" Her eyes opened and faced his honesty. As they stared at each other, she also saw and felt something else. Something she couldn't describe or explain, but it scared her. "I'm not used to this role, and frankly, it isn't fun. It's a little degrading and horrible for my ego. Say the words, Eve, and I'll leave you alone." Noah was silent. He didn't move or make a sound.

Eve knew he was being completely open and sincere. All she had to do was say the words, and he wouldn't bother her again. Once more, she closed her eyes to break whatever hold he had over her, and to give herself strength to tell him to go away. Still, she couldn't do it.

"Why don't I go to career day and we can take it from there."

"That sounds great." Noah spoke the words quietly. He sensed she was skittish, and ready to bolt like a wary doe. An awkward silence followed. The hush of two people who were surprised about how far they've managed to come. Noah wanted to continue to move forward, but he was so relieved about where they were, he was unsure of what steps to take.

Eve was hesitant and scared. Running from her decision, she looked at her watch, "I have to go. No, don't get up. I'll see myself back. See you at career day." Noah didn't say a word. He settled back on the bench and released a huge sigh.

Regina called to her when she returned to the office. "So, you're dating the lover of the fire department?"

Eve's heart stopped. "No, he was just dropping off some information I need."

Regina's drawn out "uhhhh huuuuuhhhh" followed her down the hall.

Eve made it to her office and collapsed into her chair, forehead on her desk. She uttered, "Does this man's reputation have no end?" She chastised herself for not taking the opportunity to get rid of him. She couldn't stand the thought of being one of his statistics, and she vowed that she wouldn't as long as her mind was stronger than her lust. Todd's death and being a single mom proved to her she had mental toughness. But she was in uncharted territory. Never had she felt such a strong attraction to someone. She and Todd took a pleasant journey, growing into their love for each other. She compared it to taking a walk through a flower-filled meadow on a sunny day. Her attraction to Noah was like waiting until there was a big storm, and then taking a wild river ride without a paddle. Her body and emotions took off before her head knew she was taking a trip.

To make matters worse, the connection wasn't all physical. After he explained to her what he was looking for in a relationship, and she looked into his eyes, Eve felt a link that had nothing to do with lust. And as she sat analyzing it, looking deep within herself, she tried to blame it on empathy. The heart-wrenching story about his father had really gotten to her. But she knew she was lying to herself. Eve had been a prosecutor for a long time now. She heard or read about gut-wrenching stories almost every day at work. She'd even managed to become friends with quite a few of the victims that came through her door. So, she was well aware of what compassion felt like. What passed between her and Noah was much more than sympathy.

Eve grabbed a tissue and rubbed her sweaty palms. She looked at her hands, recognizing that the moisture wasn't the result of pity. She was scared; nervous that what Ebony called the knowing was to blame. It seemed to Eve that Ebony and Yoshi had gotten together overnight. When Eve asked Ebony how she knew she was in love, she said, "It's the knowing, Eve. We looked deep into each other's eyes, and it was like our spirits were connecting. Our souls knew we were right for each other." Eve had trouble with the concept, and believed the melodramatic Ebony had been listening to too many love songs. But as she'd stared into Noah's eyes, she wasn't sure Ebony had been exaggerating. There was something going on between them that she'd never felt before; it was something she couldn't describe or put a name to. Questions pounded in her head. Was Noah her soul mate? Could the other half of her dwell underneath a playboy persona? The very thought was inconceivable, laughable, if she wasn't so terrified that there might be a grain of truth to it.

It gave her some comfort and hope that she believed him when he explained himself and his crazy reputation. However, she wasn't quite sure what she was hoping for. Confusion and indecision pounded through her head. Decisive by nature, she was unaccustomed and very uncomfortable with what she was feeling.

Her phone rang. She answered. "Eve, this is court six. Your verdict's in." Setting aside the issue, Eve went to hear her verdict. She didn't realize how tight she was until she heard the judge say guilty. She released a slow breath. Eve managed to keep thoughts of Noah away by focusing on the sentencing, and later, by focusing on her family and nighttime rituals. But as soon as she lay in her bed, Noah forced his way into her head.

Restless, Eve rose and made her way to the kitchen. She heated milk in the microwave, and then nestled into the couch. "Oh, God," Eve muttered. This is exactly what she did for months after Todd died. Tears spilled down her cheeks as she reflected that if Todd hadn't died, she wouldn't be in this predicament. Frustration burned through her. She put the cup on the coffee table and drew her knees up to her chest. The soft sound of a robe brushing against slippers preceded Beulah's gentle hand on her head. Without words, her mother sat beside her.

"Todd?" Beulah handed her a tissue.

Eve sniffed and wiped her nose. "Yes, but not the way you think. I'm so mad at him, Mom." Eve punched the seat cushion beside her. "Why did he have to work late? Why didn't we wait 'til morning? Why wouldn't he let me drive? Why didn't I insist on driving? I'm furious. Then I start to feel guilty because I'm angry." Eve cried harder. "It wasn't supposed to be like this, Mom. We had so many plans, so many dreams, all flushed down the toilet because Todd was too arrogant to let me drive, and I let him be that way."

Through her tears, Eve saw her mother's confused look. She'd never shared the details of that night with anyone. Eve got up and began pacing in front of the couch. She spoke as she walked. "I know Todd and I appeared to be the perfect couple, but there was one big thorn in our rosebush."

Beulah's nod encouraged her to continue. Eve took a deep, fortifying breath, and let her mother into her pain. "Todd was a workaholic. His job at the computer company meant the world to him. Even when he was at home, he spent lots of time on the computer. Sometimes I would watch him. He'd be so absorbed; he wouldn't even know I was there unless I touched him. His feet would move in rhythm with his hands on the keyboard. I swear, Mom, it was like I was seeing him dancing with the other woman." Eve stopped her pacing and was silent. She wrapped her arms around her body.

Beulah spoke. "Eve." She glanced at her mother. "I know Todd was addicted to his job. You never complained to me, but I have two very perceptive eyes." She continued in a soft voice, "It's more than that, isn't it?"

Eve looked down and nodded her head.

"Tell me, baby."

Eve began pacing again. She focused on the floor as her lips moved. "Todd had an epiphany that night." Beulah sat up, but she didn't say a word. Eve noticed her movement, and knew her mother was probably thinking, what. "I still remember it like it was yesterday. We started out late. Todd's promise to leave work at three melted into seven. By the time we got Sean to your house and hit the road, it was after nine at night. Irritated, I suggested that we wait until the next day, or that I drive. Todd said no. Despite the bags under his eyes, he insisted he wasn't tired. I guess I was so happy he suggested the trip, that I let him have his way." Eve paused, gazing at the ceiling for a moment.

"Eve, hindsight is twenty-twenty. You didn't know what would happen."

Moving her head up and down, she started walking once more. "I know, but that knowledge doesn't ease my guilt. Anyway, we'd been driving for about an hour when Todd grabbed my hand and said, 'I do understand, Eve.' " Eve put her hand to her chest. "My heart began to pound because I hoped he was talking about what I thought he was talking about. He told me a coworker had a son on Sean's basketball team. The guy came to work, raving about how great Sean was in a game. Todd was embarrassed because he didn't even realize that Sean had a game. He said the guy's innocent comment hit him like a ton of bricks and made him truly reflect on all I'd said to him over the years."

Eve stopped moving and stared into her mother's concerned eyes. "He finally got the point, Mom. He understood that he needed to spend more time with Sean and me. After twelve years, the man finally got it! We needed him more than we needed Microsoft stock!"

Eve returned to pacing. "You know how poor Todd was growing up. Love was abundant, but money was tight. He always said, My parents worked themselves into an early grave, and they had no financial success to show for it.' Well, he admitted it, Mom. He confessed that somewhere along the way, he got confused and equated money and providing with love. He told me he wanted to work less, and if he couldn't do that at Microsoft, he would leave. Can you believe it, Mom?" Eve didn't look her way or wait for an answer. "And then, poof, he's gone. One of the happiest moments of my life. I go to sleep with a smile on my face, and all of a sudden, I'm fighting with a river for my life."

Eve turned to Beulah, tears streaming down her face. "Even the good memories hurt, Mom. How could his light be extinguished when he was just starting to see it? I feel like I was standing on the edge of Utopia, and it was cruelly snatched away from me. It makes me burn with anger."

Beulah stood and wrapped Eve in her arms. Eve's sobs shook both their bodies as Beulah guided them to the couch where she eased her daughter down. She didn't say much; she just maneuvered her arms around Eve, and let her clear out the wound infecting her heart. After a time, the crying stopped. Then, Beulah spoke. "Is it possible your attraction to Noah brought this on?"

"Yeah. I hate to admit it, but yes. I was so hurt and angry when Todd first died, but I thought I had dealt with it. The last couple of years, the pain eased, and I found myself fuming less. Yet, every time I'm with Noah, Todd and all these unwanted emotions force their way into my head. Then I find myself seething." Eve smiled weakly at her mother. "How'd you know, Mom? You don't miss a beat."

"Sitting in the living room in the wee hours of the morning is a good clue. Although, you can strike it up to mother's intuition." Beulah squeezed her.

"As usual, you're right." Eve rubbed her tired eyes as she expressed herself. "Noah gets to me, Mom. I have to acknowledge it. He's blasted through all my shields, and I'm drawn to him. It scares the heck out of me."

Beulah removed her arms from Eve, turned

toward her, and lifted her chin so they met eye to eye. "I'm going to give you some excellent advice, and I suggest you take it. First, let go of the anger and guilt; they're holding you back and holding you down. It's a shame that the accident happened right after Todd came to his senses, but it was God's decision. It wasn't your decision or Todd's decision. It was fate. Do you hear me, Eve?" She grabbed her shoulders and leaned closer, "It was fate! It doesn't make any sense to be angry about the decisions that God makes for us. We have to trust in His will, and let go of emotions like anger and guilt. What did you tell Sean? That it's like acid erasing your common sense?" She squeezed her shoulders before letting go.

"Yes, how did you know I told him that? Gosh, that was so long ago. Right after Todd died. I was sitting in the living room, just like tonight, crying when he touched me on my shoulder. I looked up, and Sean was crying. I tried to tell him that it would get better, and he should focus on the good times, and he said, 'What good times? Dad was never here for a good time.' "

Beulah gasped.

"I know, Mom. Shock stopped my heart, and I needed time to let it start up again. When it started, the beat was so rapid, I needed more time to reduce it to a level were I could talk. Then, your grandson informed me that he was almost eleven, so I shouldn't treat him like a kid. He told me that sometimes when he got up late to go to the bathroom or something, that he could hear us. He said I was right when I told Todd he was a slave to the almighty dollar."

"Oh, goodness," Beulah moaned.

"My sentiments exactly. That's when I grabbed the boy by the shoulders, just like how you grabbed me, and I said that bitterness and anger are so destructive. I told him how all those bad thoughts mix around in a person's head, contaminating it, and jumbling up their common sense."

"That explains it then," Beulah said. "I got mad at him for something he did. I don't remember what, and he said, 'let go of your anger. It's wiping out your good sense!' " Both women laughed. "I asked what he was talking about, and he told me that's what you said when he was complaining about his father. He informed me that it worked for him, so I should chill out and stop being mad before I couldn't think clearly."

"That boy." Eve shook her head.

Beulah became serious again and touched Eve's shoulder. "You've talked about it. You've vented. You've had a good cry. Now it's time to move on, give yourself permission to feel again." She took a deep breath and resettled her girth.

"Now my second point: let me begin by saying that I've met a lot of people in my long, illustrious life, and I'm a damn good judge of character. I saw this Noah with Sean, and saw how he reacted when you were a bitch." Eve's head snapped to her mother. "I know that's strong language, but it accurately describes your behavior."

Eve was shocked. "Mom, did you eavesdrop?"

"Not intentionally. The coffee machine wasn't far away. You both were talking loud, so I heard most of the conversation. But let's get back to my point. I think he's good in here." She tapped her chest. "He seems strong enough to be dependable, emotionally and physically. Yes, he is quite a sight physically!" Shock didn't stop Eve from laughing. "Do what the man says. Try to be open. And maybe, Eve, it's time to take off Todd's ring."

Eve looked down at her ring. It was a carat, a large solitary diamond that sat at the base of her finger. It used to annoy her because it got caught on everything--pockets, coats, blouses, desk drawers, even Sean. She felt terrible when she nicked him a couple of times when he was a baby. She thought it was ostentatious, and she rarely wore it. But after Todd's death, she clung to it. Her finger was bare when he died, adding red pepper to the emotions boiling over in her stomach. So, she wore it all the time.

"Eve, I know you didn't much care for that ring before the accident. I've never asked you why you wear it, and I'm not asking now, unless you want to tell me, but it might be time to end the penance. You've done nothing wrong. It's okay to let go."

Both women were silent. Eve wasn't ready to face the ring issue, so she avoided it. After a time, she spoke, "What about kids, Mom? Noah's bound to want some."

Beulah shrugged her big shoulders. "You and Todd were always talking about having another child. There's no problem there."

Eve knew her mother spoke the truth. She loved children and wanted more of her own. After Todd's death, she stopped all of those thoughts and labeled them as impossible. Her flesh began to pimple at the thought of having children with Noah. Not because of the actual having, but because of the process. Erotic images flashed through her mind. Hard, muscled legs covered with hair entwining with hers; her hands and arms wrapped around broad, strong shoulders. She saw the side of a torso, filling out into part of a buttock, and her hand grasping the moving cheek. Eve realized she was seeing Noah as if she lay beneath him, and they were in the act of joining. Gathering herself, she whispered, "I guess I'm not too old at thirty-six."

"Shoot, I'm not too old these days with all these

new medical advances!" Beulah pointed to the blank television. "Yesterday, on the news, I saw a couple in their sixties having a baby. If those old fogies can do it, you can too. And you're in excellent shape, unlike myself." Beulah affectionately rubbed her big stomach.

"Mom, you look great." Eve hugged her. Once more, the two women sat in silence. Eve's musing went beyond the actual baby making, and she fantasized about having another child to cuddle and watch grow. She loved the thought, and knew that Noah would be an excellent father. A soft snore drew Eve back to reality. She looked down and saw that Beulah's eyes were closed. Eve gently shook her mother awake and helped her back to bed.

Beulah laughed when Eve tucked her in. "See, you do need another baby. Are you getting me confused with Sean?"

"No, I know you're my wonderful mother." Eve gave her mom another big hug and kissed her on the head. "Thanks, Mom. I've never shared the details about that night. I feel better now that I've told you."

"Eve, it's like a bandages. Sometimes keeping it on only makes the wound worse when what the sore needs is air to speed the healing. I'm not saying tell the world your problems, but don't keep so much bottled up. As long as I'm on this earth, you can talk to me."

Eve had tears in her eyes when she whispered, "I love you, Mom."

CHAPTER 5

Ten days later on Friday, Eve and Sean stood at the back of the crowded auditorium. "Okay, Mom, are you sure you're prepared? You can't mess up and embarrass me up there!"

"Sean, believe it or not, I'm used to public speaking. I'm prepared, and I'm not going to shame you. But now you know how I feel when you and your friends get loud when we go somewhere."

"That's different. We're just having a good time." Eve cocked her head to the side and looked at him with a half smile. "Okay, okay, maybe you have a point; but still, you're used to that trial stuff, not this speech stuff. A lot of my friends and teachers are out there so you have to be on."

Eve held back the laughter, and with all seriousness she said, "Okay, baby, I'll be on." She went to hug him and crossed her arms instead. Mother hugs were absolutely forbidden in public. She was surprised he didn't complain when she called him "baby."

"Don't worry, Sean. Your mom will be super." A warm flush rushed through her. Eve turned to the voice coming from behind her. Noah was taking off his heavy, fire repellent jacket with the reflector strips to reveal a crisp uniform. Eve felt like Pavlov's dog. She lightly wiped her mouth just in case she was drooling. Noah looked fantastic in his uniform. It suited his tall, impressive frame to perfection. The light blue shirt, sporting different insignia, hugged his shoulders, and the starched pants outlined his long legs. The shirt was short-sleeved, revealing formidable arms and strong hands that a construction worker would be proud of.

"Hey, you're the fireman." Sean pointed to the cast. Noah nodded his confirmation. "You're right. The cast is a real chick magnet."

Noah and Eve burst out laughing.

"What?" Sean looked from one to the other.

"We have to sit now, Sean. I promise not to embarrass you."

Each of the seven people on the panel would have five minutes to speak, and then questions would be allowed for twenty minutes.

It was hard for Eve to concentrate on the people who spoke before her. She sat shoulder to shoulder with Noah, and her senses were very aware. You'd never know it, though, because she put on her best lawyer persona to protect herself and rose to the occasion.

She felt Noah move. He stretched his arm out and began lightly tapping his long fingers. From the elbow down, Noah's arm was visible. The tapping made his forearm move. Watching the sleek muscles glide beneath the skin had her drooling again. Inhaling sharply, she shifted her focus to his fingers. Erotic fantasies slipped past Eve's defenses. She imagined them tapping their way up the back of her calf, over her thigh, across her stomach, between her breasts, along her neck, to her mouth where she would capture those roving digits with her lips.

Noah cleared his throat. Eve's eyes shifted to his for about three seconds. He gave her that knowing smile, like he was reading her mind. Damn him, she thought. He's doing this on purpose. Annoyance didn't stop a tingle from electrifying her nerves. How can I be irritated and aroused at the same time? Noah continued the secret smile as he rose to the podium.

"How many of you here are going to be professional athletes?" Several kids raised their hands. "At your age, that's what I thought too. And I prepared for it. Lord, did I prepare." Eve listened as Noah described his rigorous eating and exercise program. "Football taught me teamwork and how to set and achieve goals, so I'll never regret the dedication I gave to it. And I was good. I was rated the top high school running back in the state for three years in a row. In college, I was all conference three years in a row, and you know what?" The crowd and Eve were captivated. "I didn't make it."

"I was the starting running back for USC in my junior year when my dad became seriously ill. There was no choice for me. I went home to be with my family. I didn't stay there long, but when I came back, I was so out of it, Coach benched me. I'd never been second string before. By the time my senior year rolled around, we had my dad's situation stabilized." Noah knew he was exaggerating, but he didn't think the kids needed to know that his father was getting worse, and his sister had quit her job with an airline in Chicago to come home. Dina insisted that she'd hated Chicago and was planning to come home anyway. She told Noah to take his butt back to school, so she could watch her baby brother score touchdowns on TV. He never got that chance.

"My head and heart were back with football; however, my backup had done a phenomenal job during my physical and mental absence. He got the nod, and I got splinters."

The students groaned.

"Still, I was drafted into the National Football League. I guess because I'd played so well before I had to go home. I was released with the first wave of cuts."

The students groaned again. Noah didn't bore them with the fact that the Broncos had so many running backs, he'd have to have been Eddie George to make the team.

"I knew I could bounce around the league, trying to make other teams. Steve Largent was released by the Houston Oilers and ended up making the Hall of Fame with the Seattle Seahawks. However, I felt like it was a divine message from above that it was time to go be with my family. I don't regret any of my decisions that I made during that time because family will always be more important to me than a game. Yet, not making the NFL did result in one of my toughest challenges. That's when I thanked the Lord for my parents. They drilled in me the value of an education. So, when football didn't work, I still had my degree. I used it to get hired and advance at the fire department. So no matter what your dreams are for the future, an education can only help. Once you have education, knowledge in your head, and a degree in your hand, that's something no one can take away from you. I know it sounds corny, but it's true a mind is a terrible thing to waste." He sat down to a standing ovation.

Eve whispered, "You're a hard act to follow." She got up and took her place at the podium.

When the room quieted, she said, "I want everyone here to stand up and get on top of their chairs. Yes, you heard me right. If you can, get on top of your chairs and if you can't," she hoped Sean was listening, "imagine standing on top of the chair." With lots of noise and laughter, the students followed her instructions. When everyone who could was standing on a chair, Eve said, "Now dance a little bit. Not real hard, we don't need anyone to get hurt. Just groove a little." Eve rocked from side to side. Noah leaned forward, staring intently at the gently swaying hips.

Sean, with his broken ankle, stood beside his chair, squirming. "Oh man, what is she doing?" he said under his breath.

"Now you know how I feel. Many young people have asked me how it feels to be a lawyer. It feels like I'm dancing on top of the world. Okay, have a seat now." Eve waited for the room to quiet again. "I'd always dreamed of being an attorney but I was scared. I didn't see any Johnny Cochrans when I was growing up." The students chuckled. "The biggest career challenge I faced was finding the courage to get started. A wonderful man helped me."

Noah listened in growing despair as Eve described how his competition, her deceased husband, made her dream a reality. "I hated my job at Boeing. Sitting at a desk all day buying parts for airplanes was incredibly boring for me. I cried every Sunday night. My husband got tired of the routine and asked me, 'What do you want to do?' Between whines, I said 'Be a lawyer.' He said, 'Do it then.' I was afraid. I didn't think I was smart enough. My husband went out and got all the information. He signed me up for a class to prepare me for the Law School Admission Test. He even went to class with me. The admission test took four hours. My husband waited outside and gave me a sandwich during the fifteen minute break." Students sighed at his thoughtfulness. Eve smiled inwardly. It was a happy memory of Todd. One of the few times when she became more important than his work. "I did well on the test. This would have been impossible without his love and support. When I saw the results, it gave me the self-confidence to do for myself. So believe in yourselves. Support one another's dreams, instead of laughing at them. Anything is possible if you have confidence, and you work hard. I'm living proof of that."

She sat down to thunderous applause and whistles. Beaming with pride, Sean cheered the loudest. Noah flashed her a smile that vanished when she looked elsewhere. Damn, he thought, I'm up against one hell of a memory.

At the end of the event, things were wrapping up, and the students were leaving. Sean hobbled over to her and gave her a brief, quick hug. "That was a great speech, Mom."

Eve was stunned. Did my son really just hug me in public? Before she could react, he was limping away to leave with his class. For a second time, Noah sneaked in behind her. "I agree. You are great, so great that I'd like to take you to lunch. I'm meeting my sister. You can think of her as a chaperone if it makes you feel better. I'd really like you to meet her."

"All right." Eve told herself she'd agreed so swiftly because she was still in shock over Sean's behavior. Besides, she didn't have to go to work because she'd taken the entire day off. She waited while Noah went to change. Eve remained in a white silk blouse and brown slacks. She was tempted to ask him to keep the uniform on because he looked so good in it. He returned in jeans and a black T-shirt, and to Eve's dismay, he looked even better. Minus the cigarette, he reminded her of the hunks that used to be featured in the cigarette ads. When she was young, she and Ebony used to drool over the Winston model. He was tall, dark, and handsome in his jeans and cowboy hat. Here I am with a real-life Winston model, Eve thought. What in the world am I going to do? They had decided to leave Eve's car and ride together in Noah's black Jeep Cherokee. Eve watched the play of his arm muscles as he steered the Jeep. "Where are you taking me?"

To heaven if you'd let me. Out loud Noah said, "The Space Needle restaurant."

"That's pretty fancy, isn't it?"

"I'm lunching with two special women." Noah glanced at her and saw she was becoming uncomfortable. "Hey, what happened in that case?"

"Guilty." Eve pumped her fist.

"That's great." Noah grabbed her hand from the seat and squeezed it quickly before he set it back down. He held it just long enough to jolt her. Eve wondered, no she knew, he was doing it on purpose to unsettle her. She wanted to pinch his arm, right at the peak of the big bicep that bulged as he drove. They couldn't reach the Space Needle soon enough for Eve. The sexual tension was so thick and hot she felt like she was melting. They walked to the Needle, and the cold air helped to cool and settle Eve's overwrought emotions. As they neared the building, Eve reflected on how she always thought it was strange looking. Its base was a needle that mushroomed into a sixties version of a flying saucer. The restaurant sat in the saucer, which slowly revolved, allowing the patrons a wonderful three-hundred-sixty degree view of Seattle. It took an hour for it to go around once. Riding the elevator, which was mounted on the outside of the building also provided a magnificent view of the city. Even though Eve had been born and raised in Washington State, she could count on one hand the number of times she'd been in the Space Needle. The two of them entered the restaurant, and Noah found Dina already sitting at a window table. Brother and sister embraced warmly.

"Hey, handsome, how were the kids?"

"Great." Noah pulled out the chair for Eve. "Eve stole the show. She got a standing ovation. Eve, this is my sister Dina; Dina, this is Eve."

The two shook hands. "Pleased to meet you," Eve said. "Your brother is being too kind. He was a big hit, and he also received a standing ovation. He gave the kids a wonderful message about education."

"Yes, my brother's very impressive when he wants to be." Dina reached over and rubbed her brother's broad shoulder.

The three of them sat in a triangle around the circular table. Dina stole glances at Eve who sat to her left. Eve seemed familiar for some reason. Dina looked in her eyes when her brother introduced them, and there wasn't a glimmer of recognition from her. Dina racked her brain and came up empty. Oh well, I meet lots of people on the airplane, she rationalized. Maybe Eve was a passenger, and for some reason her face stuck in Dina's brain.

Eve quickly relaxed. She liked Dina instantly. Her conversation was open, animated, and expressive. Eve enjoyed seeing another side of Noah through his sister. She heard about a Noah who made life hell for Dina's dates. Most of the boys had heard of Noah because of football and were already intimidated. Noah showed them no mercy. If he were in a good mood, he would just shut the door in the boy's face, and not tell Dina he was there. If he were feeling surly, he would let the boy in and practice his golf swing while he asked him about his plans for the evening.

"Because of my brother, I learned to get ready quick and meet my date at the door!"

Eve also learned about a compassionate person who had climbed the tallest tree to rescue his mother's precious cat. Ignoring the increasingly thin branches, he reached the cat, got scratched, and got stuck himself.

"One of my better moments," Noah quipped with a hint of a sexy smile. Dina couldn't get the words out, so Noah, in an emotionless voice, told her how

fun it was to be rescued from a tree by the fire
department at sixteen years old. He explained how
it was especially exciting because he knew the people who responded to the call, and they teased him
unmercifully. Noah chuckled at the humbling memory, and real amusement passed between the three
of them.

Like a video camera, he recorded Eve's every
move. The way the silk shirt clung to her back as
she bent over in mirth. The sparkling gold hoop
earrings that danced erotically as her head bobbed.
The laughter quieted to a chuckle. Eve felt good.
She hadn't laughed so much in ages. She felt a
comfort with Dina, and she had to admit Noah, too,
that usually took months to develop. Still grinning,
she excused herself to go to the bathroom.

Dina watched Noah watch Eve. "I see you like
more than the food here." Noah's roving eyes came
back to Dina's teasing gaze.

"I know. It shows?"

"Every time you look at her. I've never seen you
so smitten before."

"Smitten? I like that. I'm smitten. You've never
seen it because I have never felt like this before."

Dina clapped her hands and exclaimed, "Noah!
You're in love. I'm so happy for you. I know I've
only known her a little while, but I can tell she's a
grand person, not that shallow shell you thought

was a human before. I've been waiting for this for a long time. I'm so happy you can feel this way after that creature."

Crossing his arms, Noah confided, "I'm consumed with her. I go to sleep with her. I wake up with her. Her presence fills me. Her smile floors me."

"My God, she's turned you into a poet. This is unbelievable. So, you're sleeping with her. Have you told her how you feel?"

"No, I haven't told her, and I haven't kissed her, much less slept with her."

Absolute disbelief covered Dina's face. "You haven't been to bed with her, and she consumes you! This is priceless." She giggled. "You do nothing in moderation, do you? When I told you to open your heart, I didn't mean use a shotgun!"

Noah turned serious and quiet. "I think that's the trouble I'm in for. She only wants to be domino partners."

"Oh, that's not how she looks at you, brother. She sneaks glances at you when she thinks no one else is looking. She's not used to your nosy sister who takes in everything."

"Yeah, I'm not sure I'm used to her either."

"Stop, Noah. It's only because I care. But back to what I was talking about. Make your moves." Dina ducked and shifted like a running back.

Noah laughed. "I'm telling you, Dina, I've made them. In fact, I'm damn tired of making them. She's killing my ego."

"Good. I like her more already if she's getting rid of that monster."

Dina had more to say on the subject, but she swallowed her comments when Noah motioned with his eyes that Eve was returning. The rest of the lunch continued in much the same vein. Eve laughed as the siblings lightly teased each other and her. The love between them was evident and refreshing for Eve to see. Eve was surprised how much time had passed when Dina announced she had to leave.

Noah drove Eve back to her car. It wouldn't start. After the accident, Eve couldn't get in a car. It took all of her willpower to ride the bus to work. Sean gave her the courage to try. He was used to being driven to his many events. Therapy and Sean's encouragement allowed her to first sit in a car, and then, eventually drive. The accident occurred in a Lexus. Eve bought a car that was completely different. A reconditioned 1972 Volkswagen Beetle. The type she drove for four years, during her undergraduate days. Her candy-apple-red Bug reminded her of those days. But presently, she wasn't real pleased with her car. She slapped the dashboard and tried the ignition again.

Nothing. Not even a click. She watched Noah get out of his Cherokee and tap on her window. She tried one more time before she rolled down the window.

"Mind if I try?"

Frustrated, she handed him the keys and got out of the car. He turned the ignition once, got out, and went to the back of the car to look at the engine. He leaned on the bumper as he looked. Eve pretended not to notice how his muscles strained against his T-shirt. Noah leaned further in, and his shirt came out of his jeans. She caught a flash of tone brown skin that reminded her of the calendar. Eve salivated. She walked to the front of the car and tried to calm herself. She was leaning against the hood, taking deep breaths when she heard him shout, "Damn!"

Eve rushed back to find him sucking on a finger. "Let me see." Eve grabbed his forearm. She thought her heart would come out of her chest when she held his warm hand and looked at the wet, blunt-tipped finger. She studied the small cut longer than necessary for the visual effect, and to give herself time to recover. Finally, she stopped staring at his finger and said, "I have bandages at my house." Was that hoarse voice hers? She realized she was still holding his hand and let it go.

He knew the cut didn't justify a bandage, but

he'd use any excuse, whether provided by him or her, to spend more time with her.

"Can you drive?"

He swallowed the urge to chuckle, "Yes, I think I can handle it." The ten-minute ride to her house was accomplished in silence. Noah drove with one hand just in case she decided he really wasn't hurt. She lived in Madison Valley. An upscale area that was popular because it was close to Lake Washington and fifteen minutes away from downtown Seattle.

She lived in a two-story, large Victorian-style house, which was very much like the other houses in the neighborhood. All of the homes had similar architecture and the lawns were equally plush and green. He parked in the driveway, and Eve led him through the black iron gate and up the three steps to the front door.

Noah entered her home to find that it was very comfortable. Everything was done in earthtones: browns, greens, and dark blues. The front door led you into a large room that took up most of the first floor. The couch and matching loveseat were inviting with their heavy structure and big cushions. Noah enjoyed the artwork on the walls. He especially liked the Jacob Lawrence piece, featuring a black family walking in the rain. But the picture above the fireplace mantel dominated the room. So this is Mr. Wonderful, he thought to himself. He acknowledged that it was a beautiful family portrait.

Sean looked as if he was about nine, and Eve's hair was long and flowing. She looked gorgeous whether her hair was long or short. He wondered when she cut it. Her husband stood behind her and Sean with his hands resting on Eve's shoulders. Now he knew where Sean got his coloring. His father was a handsome light brown man, and Sean looked just like him except for his hair, which was darker than his father's. The man stood ramrod straight, and his look and bearing shouted that he was extremely proud of his family. Noah didn't blame him; he'd be equally proud to be in his position.

Noah was so absorbed with the picture he failed to notice that Eve had gone right to the kitchen. She yelled, "I'm in here, Noah." He followed the voice and found himself in a place where a master chef would be at home: Pots hung from the ceiling. Recessed lighting beamed down upon an island stove. A microwave was tucked under a counter. She was standing by the sink, looking so magnificent that Noah's heart momentarily paused. He decided that he preferred her hair short. Long hair hid her lovely forehead, downplayed her noble cheeks, and took away from her mesmerizing eyes. "Put your finger under the water." He did as he was told, and Eve disappeared into a small powder room off the kitchen. She returned with a bandage.

"You have a beautiful home."

"Thank you." Without looking at him, she dried his finger with a paper towel.

"How many bedrooms?"

"There's three bedrooms and a couple of bathrooms upstairs." Eve focused on opening the bandage. "It has antiseptic in it."

"Oh," he murmured, loving the attention.

They were standing very close as she wrapped his cut. Eve was aware that if she moved slightly to the right, she would be nuzzling his strong neck. She felt his breath in her hair. She stopped breathing in the middle of an exhale as she contemplated her choices. Beulah left a note on the kitchen table saying she'd be back around five, and Sean would be home around 3:30. It was 1:30, plenty of time to relieve the ache robbing Eve of her strength. It was hard. Damn near impossible to stop her hand from gliding up his arrogant neck, and allowing herself to melt into his embrace. It had been so long since she'd felt the heat of a man's body intimately; damn, was she craving it. And if she were being completely honest, she'd have to admit that not just any male would do. She wanted Noah with all her heart and being.

Once again, Noah sensed her internal turmoil.

He stood absolutely still. She would know the decision had been hers. Without eye contact, she entertwined her fingers with his and rubbed her forehead against the soft skin of his neck. She ignored her wedding ring as it moved while their fingers rubbed against each other. She felt his neck muscles glide as he swallowed. Her nose was inflamed. He smelled fresh and clean. Eve felt drunk and swayed a little. He dipped his head and brushed his lips across her short curls.

I'm in trouble, she thought to herself. This is the Don Juan for real, not the reputation or the image, but the genuine, attractive, charismatic, erotic, seductive man in all of his glorious flesh. She breathed deeply, intoxicated by his scent. Noah claimed the rumors were overrated and blown out of proportion, but standing there, immersed in the vibrations, convinced Eve that the rumors were underrated, not even close to how captivating and sweet his spell was. She remembered her mother's old saying, "If it's too good, it must be bad for you." Noah had to be rotten.

"Let's go back to my place where we can take the next few hours letting this heat develop into a full-fledged fire. After we've burned up, we can practice reviving each other." She felt the words on her scalp, sinking into her brain, making her more dizzy.

In high school, Eve and her girlfriends would hop in the car and speed down a steep hill by her house. All of them would scream at the dip as their stomachs dropped. That's exactly how her stomach felt now. The sensation kept repeating itself, vibrating her pelvis, making her legs weak.

Her defense mechanism kicked in automatically. Without thought, she spat out, "Is this the part where I melt into your arms and say 'Have your way with me?'"

"I don't know, is it?" He lifted his lips from her soft, springy curls.

Mentally slapping herself, Eve stepped out of the embrace and let go of his hand. "No, it isn't." She risked looking into his eyes, and glared at him defiantly.

His hypnotic eyes were unreadable. Eve felt their pull and turned away. "Thanks for lunch and the ride."

"You're welcome." Noah waited, giving her the chance to change her mind. "Do you need help getting your car?"

"No, I'll just call and have it towed to the repair place up the street. They always fix the Bug."

Noah waited a second longer, then left without another word.

Eve immediately called the repair shop to have the car towed, and then she began cleaning the house. She had to keep herself busy, or she'd batter herself with thoughts of what she should have done. Within the hour, the shop called and told her the car would be ready that afternoon. The starter was bad and needed to be replaced. Eve looked outside the window and debated on running or calling a cab. It was an overcast day, but so far, it hadn't rained. She decided to risk it and changed into running shoes and sweats to jog the three or so miles to the repair shop.

She needed a good run to calm her nerves. Running had always been important to her, and it became a salve after Todd's death. She cut her hair soon after he died to facilitate running. It was difficult for Eve to explain how she felt when she ran. At first, it was hell. Air felt and tasted like Drano, and her limbs and brain refused to believe they were part of the same body. Eve considered this part of the ritual to be a character builder. She'd concentrate on three breaths by nose and one by mouth because some coach told her this would keep her from hyperventilating. Maybe, but Eve did it because it took her mind off her burning chest and her aching thighs. After about five minutes, she'd hit nirvana and remember why the torture was worth it. She'd groove into her sweet spot where she felt like she could run for days. This was the place where she could think and things seemed cleared, answers came easier.

To get to the shop, she had to go up a large hill on Madison Street. As she puffed her way up the long hill, she passed the Philadelphia Fevre Steak & Hoagie Shop. If she didn't have to get her car, Eve would have stopped in to eat. Cheese steaks were a close second to fajitas, and Philadelphia Fevre was the only place in Seattle that made them close to the real thing. Todd was from Philly, and he always bragged about the sandwiches. Before they were married, Eve had a track meet in Philly and Todd came along so he could show her his old haunts. She had her first cheese steak and was hooked. She and Todd almost danced a jig when Philadelphia Fevre opened, and the sandwiches tasted like the genuine article. Eve ran by it quickly or else she would have succumbed to the temptation to stop and have a bite.

Once she passed it, she slowed to a leisurely pace to kill time. Running wasn't producing answers today. Her feet pounding pavement wasn't taking away the tingle she still felt for Noah. To avoid thinking about him, she concentrated on dodging potholes, the people she passed, the houses, the cars. Maybe it was time to buy a new one. By the time she reached the shop, the Bug was ready. She settled the bill and drove home where Sean was hopping around her mother in the kitchen, asking her when the fried chicken would be done.

"Go away, Sean. It'll be done when it's done." She pretended to swat him with the spatula.

"I can't wait, Grandma. Your chicken's so delicious." She shooed him away when he tried to kiss her.

Eve entered the fray, fussing at Sean to use his crutches. The rest of the evening she was able to keep thoughts of Noah at bay by interacting with her family. However, bedtime was difficult. Sleep didn't come. Indecision tortured her all night. Her decision to be intimate with Todd had been nothing like this. He'd been Eve's first lover, and in the beginning, there was all the pleasure of exploring something new. Their lovemaking settled into a comfortable pattern that was enjoyable, but far from spine tingling. Eve strongly suspected that being intimate with Noah would not only wake up her spine, but also blow her mind. All the man had to do was walk in the room, and her nether regions started doing unmentionable things. He excited her too much, made her too eager, and left her too agitated.

As she toyed with her wedding ring, twirling it around her finger, Eve was surprised that thoughts of loving another man didn't bring gut-wrenching guilt. After wondering if she should be upset about that, she began to feel self-righteous. Dammit, she

was so tired of guilt and depression. She was confused about Noah, but he did make her feel alive
again. Maybe too alive, she thought as she
stopped herself from rubbing her belly. Turning on
her stomach, she resisted the urge to move against
the sheets. This is ridiculous, she scolded herself.
Thank God it was Friday, and she didn't have to go
into the office tomorrow. She wondered if Noah had
to work. She slammed her fist into the pillow. He
wouldn't get out of her head. She gave up and
pulled the fireman's calendar from between her
mattresses. She quickly flipped to December, and
he filled her brain and took over her body. Of its
own accord, she told herself, her hand drifted below
her belly, and she lost herself in fantasy, but in the
aftermath, she still couldn't sleep, and she was just
as frustrated.

CHAPTER 6

Noah opened the front door to his condo in West Seattle on Saturday, and almost dropped his coffee. Some sloshed over the rim and hit his big toe. "Damn!"

"Not the reaction I expected," Eve said, standing on the landing outside his door.

Noah let her in. "Not you, the coffee." He made a comical picture as he held the cup with one hand, and wiped his toe with the other. He put his foot and the coffee down. Then, he looked at her. His expression went from shock to disbelief to guarded. She didn't take her eyes off him as she removed her coat. She boldly looked him up and down, drinking in his brown muscles, which gleamed against the white tank top and boxers he wore. She loved how his immense shoulders tapered into lean hips and long heavily muscled legs. She traveled back up and asked, "Do you live alone?"

A sleepy Ebony said he lived alone when she got the number and address from her during an early-morning phone call. She and Yoshi had returned in the wee hours of the morning, and she was so groggy, she didn't even ask Eve why she wanted the information. Next, Eve called Noah, and hung up when he answered the phone.

"Yeah. How do you know where I live? Why are you here?"

Eve didn't answer immediately. Instead, she began taking off the clothes that she'd chosen wisely that morning. She got out of bed with a very determined attitude after a restless night. She took a hot, long, lingering shower, each pelt exciting her body, confirming that she was doing the right thing for her sanity. Afterward, she rubbed vanilla-scented oil into her skin. She loved the slightly spicy aroma, and she hoped Noah would too. Next, she surveyed her closet. She didn't want to wear anything that would be difficult or awkward to remove.

So, she donned a tan, silk shell shirt over loose-fitting brown slacks made of light wool. Eve began unbuttoning those very same slacks. "I'm giving you what you want." Her hands stopped on the second button of her pants. "You still want in my panties, don't you?"

Noah was dumbfounded. Not something he was used to. She was on the last button when he said, "I wouldn't have put it that way, but yes, I desire you."

Their eyes locked. Eve's communicated her determination. He understood the message even if the reasons eluded him. The air grew thick with anticipation of what was to come. Eve's fingers grasped the end of her shirt; she pulled it up and off in one smooth motion. Unhooking the front clasp of her black lace bra, Eve took his hand and said, "Where's the bed? Let's hurry up and get this over with."

Laughing, Noah showed her. "Don't get too romantic; you might ruin the mood."

She pushed him on the bed and shrugged off her bra. Noah leaned on his elbows and watched. She hooked a thumb in her underwear, and with a hip twist, pushed them down with her slacks.

"My God," Noah uttered. Eve tossed the pants, not caring where they landed. "I knew you were in shape, but this is heavenly."

She thought she might be a little embarrassed, but she found she enjoyed being the vamp. His reaction made her brazen. She slowly walked to him. "I ran track in college. Coach made me lift weights, and I discovered I liked it. I don't lift as much anymore, just enough to stay toned. And, of course, running helps."

"Well, whatever you're doing, keep it up."

Eve laughed.

Noah was no stranger to the female body. He had seen more than his fair share, and still, he was moved. His hungry eyes took in broad shoulders; small, firm breasts; and a tight, trim torso with well-defined abdominal muscles, and long, chiseled legs. His tongue touched his lips. He was fixated on her legs and what lay between them as she progressed. She stopped at the edge of the bed. He sat up, wrapping his arms around her.

Reveling in the feel of his large, rough hands on her skin and his lips on her belly, Eve tilted her head back. She was dizzy with desire. She couldn't remember ever being this aroused. Lovemaking with Todd had been mildly exciting and satisfying but, as she expected, this was something else: it was exhilarating, eye-popping, spine tingling, and just plain wild.

She suffered small tremors as he planted whispery soft kisses up her stomach. Panting, she willed him to take a breast in his mouth. Lips, open and hot, brushed across each nipple, causing a moan from deep in Eve's belly.

Toying with a peak, he asked, "Why now, Eve? Are you sure you're doing the right thing?"

"Who the hell knows if I'm doing the right thing."

Desire added a harsh edge to the whispered words. "I just know I can't take it anymore. You've been driving me crazy for weeks."

He moved to the other nipple, still not taking it completely in his mouth. "You've only known me a few weeks."

"Precisely. Now stop playing with me and get on with it!"

He leaned back, so he lay on the bed, and Eve was above him. Yes, yes, yes was her only coherent thought, as he grabbed the hanging fruit and sucked gently at first, and then with increasing intensity. Sensations tore through her body. Reasoning was impossible. All she could do was feel. Why had she avoided this intense pleasure for so long? All of her rules designed to protect her from emotional danger seemed insignificant when compared with such rapture.

The rippling began in her stomach and below. She almost lost her balance when he cupped her. The shock of those big, long fingers moving lightly outside her lips had her swooning. When Noah's fingers reached her wetness, he couldn't contain a small smile of satisfaction. He gently reversed their positions, so Eve lay on the bed, and he was above, then he began kissing her mouth deeply. She imprisoned his neck with her arms. Hot skin against hot skin. Oh yeah, he's done this before, Eve thought. He's managed to kiss me senseless, and undress himself at the same time. Both her hands caressed his large chest. She pulled at the sparse curly hair between his firm pecks. One hand ventured down the hard stomach. She loved how his skin trembled as her fingers passed. He squirmed against her, and Eve felt the heaviness against her leg. He was blessed. She confirmed this with her hand, causing him to groan deeply, and then, hiss while he enjoyed her lips.

Fear made her hesitant. She hadn't expected there to be so much of him, and it had been so long for her. "There's been no one since my husband," she blurted out, feeling anxious.

"Shush, it'll be fine." He brushed a kiss over her lips.

Strong hands touched her gently as he tenderly moved down her body. Eve closed her eyes, savoring each stroke, each new sensation. Her breath caught when he reached the place where her legs met. Anticipation made her taut. He kissed the top of her thighs to soothe her, then he slowly parted her legs, and gently stroked her open. How fingers so big could be so tender continued to be a mystery to Eve. It was no mystery what was about to happen next, and she knew that even if a fire started in the bed right beside her, she wouldn't have moved. Noah found what he was looking for and blew on the exposed jewel. Eve's hips jumped involuntarily. She settled, leaned on her elbows, and looked at him. Her eyes begged him to do it. Noah ended her torture and thoroughly enjoyed her. Again, Eve's only coherent thought was yes. However, this time she repeated it loudly until it blended into one long moan.

The rhythm of her hips, the sound of her moan, the grimace on her face told Noah she was almost there. She tried to pull back, and he held her firmly, quickening the pace. She gave in and suddenly thrust her hips forward while she cried out and began shuddering, allowing pleasure she had buried for years to burst forth. Noah thought it best not to rush although the restraint was killing him. He slowed his movements until, after a time, she grabbed his head to still him. "Damn, you're good." She squeezed her thighs.

Noah would have chuckled if he weren't so anxious. He kissed his way up her body as she recovered. His lips never left her flesh as he reached into a nightstand by the bed, and proceeded to protect them with short, choppy movements. Eve was amazed at his speed and skill when she realized he was already wearing a rubber. Things had progressed so quickly, she forgot to get hers out of her purse. No need to now. She realized, there is some benefit to sleeping with a womanizer.

He leaned over her, preparing to enter and said,

"You thought that was good, wait until you feel this."

Eve laughed as he slowly entered her body. "Oh, yeah, you have to remember that my impression is colored by four years of abstinence. I'd think anyone is good at this point."

Noah buried himself, and was too overcome with feeling to immediately answer. When he could breathe again, he said, "Four years, huh? That means we'll have to do this again and again, so you'll really be able to judge." Any reply Eve was going to make was forgotten when he showered her face with kisses. Discomfort came and went quickly when he began moving inside her. She grabbed his head and kissed him deeply. The taste and smell of her coming from him renewed the tingles. Groaning, he lost his breath and began breathing loudly through his nose. He let her set the tempo of their lovemaking. Eve's body surprised her. She had never been blessed with multiple orgasms, but she had a strong feeling that could change. In her need, she gripped his buttocks and urged him to move faster.

"Oh, baby," he hissed against her neck. Clutching her hips, he quickened the pace. Eve locked her arms around his shoulders and matched him stroke for stroke. Their harsh, fast panting filled the room. Stimulated beyond reason, Eve broke the rhythm first and came. Her pleasure was just as mind-boggling the second time around. Hearing her moan was too much for Noah to bear. One, two, three more thrusts, and Noah joined her with a loud, lingering bellow.

Noah shifted most of his weight to the bed, and, with limbs tangled, they held each other as their breathing slowly returned to normal. Noah reflected that neither of them had spoken of love or their feelings for each other. As he nuzzled her neck and gently rubbed her stomach, he realized he wanted more than sex. It was scary. His last attempt at something more devastated him, left him full of holes, and sucked him dry. His thoughts made him stiffen.

"What's wrong?" Eve croaked into his hair.

Noah loved the way her voice sounded, very sexy and husky. He wondered if it always sounded that way after lovemaking. "Nothing." He nibbled at her neck and relaxed his body. He took a deep whiff. Umm, he loved how she smelled. He wondered what it was; it was kind of a hot scent, spicy. It went with this fiery woman who was such an interesting enigma to him.

Eve purred like a well-fed cat. She felt exhausted; that good exhaustion that comes with mind-blowing lovemaking. Looking inside herself, she also realized that she felt content and happy with Noah's arms around her waist, his leg trapped between the two of hers. She rubbed her thigh against the tantalizing hairiness. It felt right, like this was how it was meant to be. She wrapped her arms around his head and pressed her nose in the short curls. He rewarded her by licking her neck. Without thinking she said, "Umm, there's some truth to the rumors. You are a fireman with quite a hose, and you certainly know how to use it." He chuckled, and his hose stirred against her. Then, Noah rose and looked at her. Their eyes caught, and Eve felt such a strong connection, it set the core of her on fire. Not with lust, but with feeling. A feeling so intense, Eve knew it must be Ebony's knowing. Fear settled in, encasing her like a force field. Noah put his head down and nestled into her upper chest. His actions only escalated Eve's dread. She was so frightened because of whom she was with: Mr. Love 'Em and Leave 'Em. What she just got was the most she could expect out of a relationship with Noah, and the humiliating thing was, that she knew that before she came over.

This morning she told herself, sleep with him once and get him out of your system. How naive of her. She now knew that sleeping with him had put him in her system forever. He was fantastic! The experience was fantastic, and if she didn't watch herself, she would be in love. In love with a man who would never return her feelings. She felt stupid, and to top it off, she was beginning to feel claustrophobic. Noah's arms felt like restraints, instead of heaven, and all she wanted to do was bolt. To hide her panic, she slowly stretched and began untangling herself.

"Hey, where are you going?" he asked as she pulled away. She didn't answer and he sat motionless, like the eye of a storm, while he watched her whirl around, searching for clothes, holding the sheet she clutched to her front. Despite his confusion, his body continued to react to the sight of her.

She didn't realize her tush excited him just as much as the front. He pushed himself up and leaned back against the headboard. "Do you mind telling me what this is all about, and why you're leaving?"

She retrieved her bra from the curved end of the sleigh bed, and her panties and slacks from the lampshade. Showing him her back, she pulled the garments on. She grabbed her shirt and faced him after she had pulled it on. "Satisfying an urge. Getting rid of an annoying itch."

He chuckled and grabbed her hand as she reached across him to get her socks. He kissed her fingers and stared at her face in an effort to force eye contact. Their eyes caught. "Were you pleased? Do you need to be scratched again?"

"It's not polite to kiss and tell." Eve eased her hand from his and balanced on one foot while she pulled on her sock.

"Not even to your lover?"

She stopped putting on her shoe, and looked at him sharply. "We're not lovers."

"Then what the hell are we?" Frustration made him raise his arms and lean away from the headboard.

She looked at him. Way too sexy for her own good. He settled against the headboard, completely comfortable with his nakedness, and looked exasperated. She continued putting on her shoes. She didn't answer because she didn't know how. Her sharp wit was failing her. Telling him the truth would leave her too vulnerable. She couldn't admit she was drawn to him because he was gorgeous, but even more than that, she feared she was falling in love with him for the things she couldn't see: His sense of humor, his kindness, and his love for his family, his strength. She decided to change the subject. "I'd appreciate it if you kept this to yourself."

"What?!!!" He threw up his hands.

She stood before him fully clothed, arms crossed in front of her. "Don't tell anyone we slept together."

He sat up. "Well gee, you bolted before we actually had a chance to sleep together!"

He had a point, she had to admit. She resisted the urge to laugh, knowing that would drive him crazy. "Touché. Look I'm a prosecutor, a mother; and you have a reputation known throughout the legal community. I won't be a notch in a belt, a known conquest. It would be embarrassing to me, my mother, and my son."

He stared at her. She sighed painfully, "Look, when you get tired of our liaison, I want to deal with that in private."

"So, you've finally answered my earlier question. That's what this is to you, huh? A liaison, a secret tryst. Tell me, did you park your car around the block?" Eve's look became defiant. Damn, he didn't want to argue with her. He wanted to reach her, make her understand that maybe they were looking for the same thing. "Listen, Eve, forget I said that. I'm not out to hurt you. Why do you just assume that? Why don't you ask me what I want?"

"Okay, what do you want?"

"I want more than secret sex. It may sound crazy, but I want to court you, to get to know you, to see if we can have what my parents had, a wonderful long-term relationship." He got up and stood before her. Without touching her, he said, "I would never intentionally hurt you or embarrass you. I respect you too much for that."

Eve stared at his chest, unwilling to meet his eyes. "Hurt is just as painful when it's unintentional."

"Speaking of hurt." He put a finger under her chin and lifted until their eyes met. "Let me ask you something." His eyes bore into hers, connecting with Eve, and making her quiver. She briefly closed her eyes, trying to break the bond growing in her, trying to stop the knowing. Noah waited until her lids lifted. "This may be a shock to you, but I do have feelings too. What particular emotion do you think I feel about the fact that you're willing to have sex with me, but not be seen with me? Do you think I feel anger, sadness, humiliation, shame, or all of the above?"

His words moved her. She touched his hand, drew it into both of hers, and rubbed it gently. He felt warm metal and looked. Brain cells burst as he realized she came to him wearing her wedding ring. "I'm asking for time. Time to build the trust in private." Shock left Noah speechless. When it became apparent he wasn't going to answer, she stood on her tiptoes and softly kissed his lips.

She was almost to the front door when her name from his lips stopped her. She turned and looked at him in all his naked glory, and had second thoughts about leaving. "Remember when you told me you didn't want to be a test subject so I could explore my relationship skills?" He didn't wait for an answer. "Isn't it ironic that that's exactly what you want me to be, your secret experiment." He turned and walked back into the bedroom.

Eve had faced some of the toughest defense attorneys the city of Seattle had to offer, and she had always held her ground. She reminded herself of that as she fought the impulse to run back, beg Noah to forgive her, and forget her stupid request. She needed to sever this hold he seemed to have over her. She wanted to deny the knowing that she told herself she didn't believe in. Yet at the same time, she thought that maybe that was the reason behind the incredible urge she had to go back and curl up in his strong arms. However, she had too much going for her and her family to risk it on a playboy. She stood still, with closed eyes, and reminded herself that she wasn't being stupid. Noah was just like the jocks she avoided in college. Hell, he was an ex-football star. Women were like underwear to men like him, and had to be changed once a day, sometimes twice. Her pride, her son, her job all were reasons not to risk it. This became her litany, and she repeated it over and over as she forced herself to walk out the door. Noah squeezed his eyes shut, and refused to shed a tear when he heard the door close.

🍎🍎🍎

At home, Beulah was reading the Saturday newspaper, and Sean was already out and about. Eve knew her mother assumed she'd been at work. As she passed her mother, sitting on the living room couch, Beulah looked up and told her, "Ebony called." Eve wasn't ready for that conversation. She took a hot shower, and did go to work to avoid thinking about the truth of Noah's words.

Ebony caught up with her later that day. She got right to the point as soon as Eve picked up the phone. "Why was I searching for Noah's address after only one hour of sleep? And did you ask me if he lived alone, or am I going crazy?" Eve took the cordless phone into her bedroom, and told her the sordid tale minus a few intimate details.

Ebony was incredulous. "You, Ms. Conservative, went over there for a booty call!?!"

"Leave it to you, Ebony, to reduce this to teenage gutter terms."

"I can't help it. I hear it all day in the shop; besides, it accurately describes your behavior."

Eve lay on her bed and gazed at the white ceiling. "No, it doesn't. I want more than one time."

Ebony interrupted her. "So, he lived up to the hype?"

"Ebony! I feel like I'm talking to Sean. All I'm going to say is that some of the rumors are true. Now where were we before I was rudely interrupted? Oh, yeah, I want to see him; it's just that I want privacy. The whole world doesn't need to know if it doesn't work out."

"Eve, I can see where you're coming from, but look at it from his point of view. He thinks you're ashamed of him. What real man would want a woman who feels that way?"

"That's not how I feel." Eve tossed a pillow at the ceiling, "I just want time for our trust to grow."

"Shame or distrust, both are bad for the start of a relationship. Don't be so concerned about what others think because you can't control their minds or tongues. You're good at reading people, and that's why juries love you. Trust your gut, girl, and stop asking Noah to lower his pride and self-esteem." Eve didn't answer. Ebony knew she was sulking on the other end of the phone. "I guess we're not playing dominoes any time soon."

"No, the games are on indefinite hold."

"You know, Yoshi is going to think you and Noah planned this because we're winning?" Ebony's comment had the desired effect, and Eve chuckled. "Yeah, tell him I schemed to have all this unwanted drama in my life just to thwart him."

Thwarted, frustrated, baffled. None of these

terms adequately described what it was like being at a Sonic game with Noah ten rows down and with a date. Horrible, sickening, loathsome, those words were more precise. It was Friday night, usually domino night, and almost a week after the event. Eve counted the rows again, yup, ten exactly. Sean saw him first. He yelled excitedly, "Hey, Mom, there's the fireman!" Then, he looked at her in that weird way kids do when they're trying to figure something out. Head cocked to the side, he said, "You like him, don't you?"

Her heart dropped and rolled around between her feet. She picked it up and put it back in her chest and stalled. "Why do you ask, son?"

"I don't know. Just a vibe I had. You know, Mom, Dad's been gone a while now. I know me and Gramma are pretty terrific, but it's okay if ya wanna date this guy."

Eve wasn't ready for such wisdom, coming from Sean. Where had her little boy gone? "Well, thanks. This is interesting, coming from bat boy." Her tone and head nod were sarcastic. Both of them remembered her first date a few years ago. Sean hovered around the door, unnoticed in the excitement. He answered the door with a bat after the first ring. He chased the poor man around the front yard swinging with all his might. Eve frantically ran behind him while her mother shouted admonishments from the doorway. Eve struggled to catch him before he pulverized the man. Not an easy feat in high heels, but she somehow managed to do it. Dragging him back into the house wasn't accomplished easily either. Her mother had to leave the safety of the porch, and enter the fray to help her. The man retreated to his car until Sean was in the house and the door was closed. Eve was so ashamed, she cancelled the date. The poor man didn't call her for another one.

"Ah, Mom, that was a long time ago, and Gramma's been working on me." Eve stared. He sounded so mature in a hip-hop sort of way. "Gramma keeps telling me not to be selfish, and she keeps asking me if I would like to grow old alone, and she tells me that Dad would want you to find someone else. Besides, it would be nice to have a guy to talk guy stuff with."

"What guy stuff?" Her heart began to patter, and her thoughts raced. She knew he didn't mess with drugs. She constantly watched him for signs and there were none. But sex was another matter. Besides locking him up, there was no way she could monitor that. Fourteen is too young for sex! "Guy stuff, you and Gramma wouldn't understand." She understood sex. Eve looked at her son and was filled with self-doubt, wondering if she should get him a Big Brother. "Don't get worried, Mom. I'm fine. I'm too smart to mess with drugs."

"What about sex? You're awfully girl crazy."

"Mom!" Sean looked around to make sure no one was paying attention. "I've had sex education. I'm not talking about that stuff. It would just be nice to have a real man to talk to sometimes. So, I guess I don't mind you dating the fireman, but I'm not sure about the marriage thing yet."

"Sean, I can assure you I'm not getting married anytime soon."

"Ah, Mom, in few years I'll be a senior, and I'm outta here. I don't want you to be lonely."

She hugged him with one arm. "Oops, sorry. I forgot we're in public." She withdrew. "I appreciate the thought." Eve was truly touched.

The crowd jumped to its feet and booed a call. She and Sean rose to see what was happening. The referee called a foul on Sonic guard Gary Payton, and they jeered with everyone else as Kobe Bryant went to the foul line.

The invisible string tugged at Eve's eyes again, drawing her attention to the back of Noah's head. Every time he moved, her head jerked to him. He and the woman spoke animatedly, and she constantly touched Noah's arm. From her profile, Eve knew it wasn't his sister. Whoever she was, she was beautiful and Eve wanted to scratch her eyes out. She chastised herself for the jealousy burning a hole in her chest. The two of them had said nothing about commitment, and how could she complain when she didn't want to be seen in public with him. Noah rose and walked up the aisle. "Hey," Sean yelled, waving his arms. He saw them and waved back. His eyes were blank, completely unreadable when they fell on her face briefly.

Noah was gone for half-time and the whole third quarter. Curiosity was eating Eve alive. She resisted the urge to turn and look behind her at the exit again. She didn't want Sean to get suspicious. His date seemed unconcerned as she watched the game intently, never glancing up the stairs. The date may not care, Eve fumed, but she wanted to know where the heck he was. Probably getting some woman's number, she thought cattily. "Sean, you want anything from the concession stand?"

"No, thanks, Mom. I'm straight." He shoveled more peanuts in his mouth and took a big gulp of Coke.

Eve got up and negotiated her way upstairs to the facilities. Key Arena was a big circle. The court was at the center, and the seats spiraled out into increasingly larger rings. Eve decided she would walk her level of the circle once. She hadn't gone twenty feet when she saw him. He was sitting on a stool beside the information booth with a girl, who looked to be about four years old, sitting on his lap.

He didn't see or feel Eve's gaze because he was so absorbed with the child. Eve became a fly on the wall as she stood about five feet away, and watched Noah dry the little girl's tears.

"Do you know this is the church?" He interlocked his fingers and pointed them down. "This is the steeple." He put his two index fingers in the shape of a steeple. "Open the door." He opened his thumbs, "and there are the people." The child squealed with laughter and grabbed Noah's wiggling fingers, trying to copy him. He patiently showed her how.

Someone bumped Eve from behind and kept going without a word. The rude woman reached Noah and grabbed the girl, hugging her furiously. The girl cried, "Mama, Mama!" Noah stood back from the stool, smiling.

Eve's heart melted, and then froze when Noah saw her. He stopped smiling and looked at her with such desire a reaction started immediately between her legs. Her eyes followed his hands as he put them in his pockets, and by the time she got back to his eyes, his look had become cold and questioning. Eve never considered herself a coward; at least that's what she told herself as she walked over to him. "Rescuing damsels in distress?"

He shrugged, "Only when they need it like you did the other morning." Eve blushed. "How about now? Are you in distress?"

Eve was silent because she hadn't completely recovered from his first verbal jab. She acknowledged she was losing the war of words.

"This is a public, crowded place, and we're standing awfully close together. I know that causes you distress, so I'll rescue you and go back to my seat."

"Wait!" Eve blurted. He stopped and looked at her. Indecision was killing her, and she had no idea what she wanted to say. She just knew she didn't want to part this way. "Can we talk, or do you need to get back to your date?"

Noah sighed heavily and shook his head. "You don't deserve an explanation, but I'll give you one because for some strange reason, your opinion is still important to me. I went to college with one of the Lakers, and we're still friends. The woman I'm sitting with is his pregnant wife." Eve felt lower than the grime on the Key Arena bathroom floor at the end of a game. "While you digest that, I'm going to watch the rest of the game." He turned and left.

She didn't attempt to stop him this time. She slinked back to her seat and put on a happy face for Sean. When the crowd stood, she stood. When others cheered, so did she, but the last quarter was lost on Eve. She didn't even know who won the game.

CHAPTER 7

The next evening, Beulah stood in her bedroom doorway and watched. "You ought to be out like your son, cast and all, and out on a date. That's what Saturday nights are for, instead of in here torturing that treadmill. How fast are you going?"

Sweat poured in her eyes, making it difficult to see the control panel. Eve wiped her eyes with a forearm and squinted. "8.2." Her breathing was so labored, she barely got the words out, "Only two minutes to go." She cranked the speed up to 9.5 miles per hour, and forced her aching muscles to respond by pumping her arms harder and raising her knees higher. Her mother shook her head and left the doorway.

Eve almost collapsed when she heard the beep, signifying the end of her hour run. She grasped the side bar and slowed her legs with the machine. She knew her heart rate would be astronomical, so she didn't check it. She set the speed at 2.5 and walked until she could breathe normally. Stepping down, she kicked off her running shoes and socks. She grabbed a towel from the bathroom attached to her bedroom, and went downstairs to the kitchen to get a water bottle from the refrigerator. Taking a long drink, she slowly made her way to the living room couch her mother was sitting on. Beulah stayed focused on the sitcom as she patted Eve's sweaty knee after Eve sat beside her. Wiping her wet hand on the towel around Eve's neck, she said, "You need a shower, but before you go, what are you running from?"

Eve looked at the TV while she answered. "Let's see, I'm running from flab attacking my hips and thighs, cholesterol building up in my blood." Her mother's voice and look cut her off. "Don't get cute with me. You look like you were running from the devil himself on that treadmill. Is Mr. December that bad?"

Sighing, Eve said, "Why ask if you know the answer?"

"Stop stalling and playing lawyer with me and answer the question. Is it Todd or the fireman?"

"You know, Mom, you'll have to learn his name if we get together. It's Noah." Again, her mother gave her the look. "Okay, okay I'll stop stalling." But the silence grew as Eve contemplated how much she wanted to tell. She sipped the water, and rubbed the ice-cold bottle across her forehead.

Beulah broke the silence, "Eve, either tell me or go take a shower. You stink!" They both laughed and the tension was erased. Eve looked into her mother's concerned eyes. "It's not Todd, is it?"

Eve shook her head and released the flood-gates. She told her about the guilt she was still struggling to overcome. She explained, not in detail, how she accepted her attraction to Noah and made him a conditional offer. She described Noah's anger and silence, which she took as rejection. Beulah listened in stillness until Eve ran out of words. Eve looked at her, "Why are you so quiet? Don't you have anything to say?"

"Actually, no, you've done a pretty good analysis on your own. As a matter of fact, I think you're very lucky."

"What?"

Beulah chuckled. "You are. How many women get the chance to have two good men in their lifetime? Don't waste your good fortune. You don't know how many good ones will happen along." Patting her knee, Beulah said, "I'm tired, and I know

165

you'll figure this out. Grab a glass of wine and go soak in the bathtub. That always helps me decide what to do. Good night."

They both got up, and Eve kissed her mother on the cheek. Then she turned on the hot water for her bath, and while it was filling up, she went to the kitchen and poured a large glass of red wine. Smiling to herself, Eve murmured, "Momma always does give good advice." After drinking half the glass, Eve fell asleep in the tub. Her sleep was so sound, she didn't even hear Sean come in. Eve left the water feeling mellow and with skin a raisin would be proud of; however, she was no closer to answering her problem.

🍎🍎🍎

Noah was sick and tired of Eve. Two weeks of reliving his intimate morning with her was driving him crazy. Here it was Saturday, and thoughts of Eve spoiled any plan he had of going out. He just didn't want to bother with all the games and trite- ness that were intertwined with the single's scene.

Again, he thought of the family picture hanging in Eve's living room. He mentally replaced her hus- band with himself. Then, an image of them in his bed flashed into his mind. His hand drifted to the phone right next to him. He found himself picking it up to call her and agree to any conditions that she wanted as long as they made love. He came to his senses and slammed the phone down. Dammit, he had a couple of days off; he didn't have to report to the station until Monday, and he refused to spend another day, much less an off day, fantasizing about her. He picked the phone back up and dialed his mother's number. "Hi, Mom."

"Hi, baby." This is a nice surprise. You're usually out or at work this late on a Saturday night."

"Yeah. I'm off and I miss you. How about I pick up some movies and come by."

Noah pulled into the driveway about an hour later. He grew up in a modest three-bedroom house in a working-class area of West Seattle. Sitting in the car for a moment, he looked at the single-story, dark blue house. He rarely got nostalgic, but this was one of those times. Pangs vibrated through him when he looked up at the basketball hoop attached to the roof. The net was gone, and the faded backboard had holes near the bottom. It was becoming an eyesore, and he should probably take it down, but it represented so many memories for him. If this piece of concrete could talk, it would tell of many battles fought between him and his father.

When he was young, his father used to let him win, and he was so deceptive, it took Noah a while to catch on. The tables were turned as the years went on, and Noah gradually began letting his father win just so they'd have something to argue about.

Noticing the rim was bare except for one string that was struggling to hang on, he remembered the day his father put it up. He was so excited to have his own hoop in his very own yard. He and his friends watched his father mount the hoop and shouted directions as only seven-year-olds can. "A little to the left, no to the right, that's straight, no it isn't, it's leaning a little." He thought his father would blow a gasket when little Bobby Newman took a shot before the hoop was ready. His poor father looked hot, tired, and exasperated after two hours on the roof, but he still played an inaugural game with them. They were all too young to realize it wasn't regulation height, and Noah was so happy, he probably wouldn't have cared if he had known.

The memories brought feelings of love and pride.

Pride reminded him of Eve and how much she had damaged his ego. Maybe he was so upset because as he watched her dressing frantically, to leave him, all he could think about was Natasha. After leaving Denver when he was released from the Broncos, he detoured to USC to ask Natasha to marry him. She'd stayed with him through the bad times, and she deserved to be his wife. Natasha didn't say much while he vented about his father or about being benched, but she was always there with a soothing backrub, and the peace that her body offered. He arrived at their shared apartment to find her packing. He remembered how she screamed at him. "I wasted two and a half years on you! We could have had a nice life together, but what do you do? You fall apart just because your dad got sick. You run home, like a baby, and mess up your timing. Even after that fiasco, I sacrifice and keep you together, and I thought it was working when you got drafted. Then you screw that up and get cut. How dare you get cut!"

Noah's mind had reeled. He had the opportunity to cheat on her every day of the two and half years they'd been together. He didn't because he'd made a commitment. Back then, he couldn't believe she was just about the football! He remembered struggling against emotions raging through him so quickly that he had to sit down on the bed. He fought the onslaught, and was repulsed by the fact that he might cry. Feeling angry, and a lot of cursing and yelling were what he should have been doing. Not sitting on a bed, with a lump in his throat, surrounded by a horrible feeling of hopelessness. He didn't move until she was gone.

When he got back to Seattle, Dina was the only

person he told. There was nothing like Dina's biting humor to bring perspective to a situation. "Good, that woman was nothing but a lapdog, fawning after you, waiting for you to say fetch. You need someone who's going to spice things up with her own ideas and opinions!"

Noah laughed, remembering her comments. Yes, sitting on his bed watching Eve dress to leave him, reminded him of sitting and watching Natasha pack, but the similarities ended there. He quickly got over Natasha. She'd put a gaping hole in his ego, and he used the experience to avoid women who were only after the window dressing. He didn't really miss Natasha. Not so with Eve. It had been two weeks, half a month, and she still lived in his mind, popping up at every unguarded moment. His heart jumped out of his chest when he saw her at the game a week ago. Anger and disgust pushed his heart back to its proper place and made him a little rough. "Here I go again," he whispered to himself. "Stop thinking about it." He got out of the car. He used his key and let himself in the front door. His mom greeted him in the hallway. "Hi, honey." She kissed his cheek and gave him a big hug.

"Mmmmm." They both made the comforting noise; a tradition somewhat unique to his family that started when his mother first hugged his sister after receiving her from the doctor at birth. They all made the noise when they embraced.

"What movies did you get?"

"It's a Babyface night. I got *Hav Plenty* and *Soul Food*."

His mother looked at the videotapes, reading the covers. "Who's Babyface?"

"He's a singer, with his own record company, and he and his wife have started producing movies."

"Oh, I've heard *Soul Food* is good. I've been wanting to see it." He followed his mom into the kitchen. "The pizza is here. I got pepperoni and that gross stuff you like, Canadian bacon and pineapple. I just don't see how you can like sweet stuff on your pizza."

Noah grabbed a slice and took a huge bite. His mother handed him a plate. "I like it because it's delicious and nutritious." He flashed a silly smile and put three more pieces on his plate.

His mom laughed at him. "Well, you have a large to yourself."

Noah put the movie in and stretched out on the big couch; his mom settled on the loveseat. As the previews played, Noah asked, "How have you been?"

"Fine. I have some bad days when all I seem to do is think about Dad, but it's happening less frequently. I keep busy with church activities, and I'm volunteering at the Women's Clinic."

"Good." Noah was truly happy his mom was keeping busy.

"So, how have you been?"

"Oh, I'm doing all right." It was weird, but he didn't feel like confiding in his mother. When he was growing up, his father was the one he always went to. He knew his mother would be understanding, supportive, and would give excellent advice, yet he was hesitant.

His mother looked at him with her mouth slightly open and her brow creased. Noah could tell she wanted to question his answer that he was doing all right. She didn't. Instead, she closed her mouth and turned to the movie. A little while later, his mom did speak. "Noah, you know you can always come here to relax or whatever?"

"I know, Mom. Thanks for telling me though. It's nice to be reminded that I'm not a burden."

"You're never a burden, son."

The rest of the evening was peaceful and uneventful. They enjoyed the movie and each other's company. After the second tape ended, Noah stayed a while, and they talked about nothing in particular. Noah left happy that he had spent time with his mother, but still he was haunted by Eve. She hovered around in his subconscious, refusing to be completely vanquished. It was really beginning to piss him off.

Soon after he left, his mother called Dina. "You need to talk to your brother. Something is wrong."

"What?" a sleepy Dina asked. She had an early flight and it was after midnight.

"Your brother. He spent a free Saturday night with me, watching movies."

Dina made an undignified noise. "That is strange. He's usually out clubbing." She rolled over, turned on the lamp on her nightstand, and looked at the clock. Her fiancé, Tim, covered his face with a pillow. "Jeez, Mom, I have to be up in three hours. I have a trip for four days. I'll see him when I get back, and I'll ask him what's wrong. Okay? I have to get some sleep."

"Okay, honey. Sorry I woke you up. Get some sleep and have a safe trip."

Dina flopped back into Tim's arms and was asleep within ten seconds.

🍎🍎🍎

Noah yawned and looked at the clock--almost six in the morning. After working Monday, he'd been off until Friday, which was yesterday. It was Saturday morning, and close to the end of his twenty-four-hour shift. It was time to get up and get ready to go home. Stretching, he sat up and looked over at Yoshi sleeping in the next bunk. Smiling, he let the alarm clock ring and watched a startled Yoshi wake up.

"You're sick, man," Yoshi mumbled as Noah left to take a shower.

"Get up and go home to your lovely wife," he said over his shoulder.

Yoshi sat up and rubbed his eyes. "Today is Saturday, isn't it? I'm looking forward to some days off." Noah dreaded it. It was harder to elude thoughts of Eve when he was off.

As he showered and dressed, Noah couldn't help wondering if Eve had told Ebony. He assumed Ebony and Yoshi shared everything with each other because they seemed to have that type of relationship. Neither of them had said a word about Eve or domino night, and Noah wasn't about to bring up the subject.

The new crew had arrived, and breakfast was on the table. Noah and Yoshi grabbed a plate and helped themselves to scrambled eggs, sausage, and toast. "What're you going to do tonight?" Yoshi asked.

Noah shrugged his shoulders, "I don't know. I haven't really thought about it." He knew he would have to do something, or else his thoughts would pound him into calling Eve.

"You want to go to Sydney's?"

"No, I don't want to be a third wheel to you and Ebony."

Yoshi took a sip of orange juice. "I wouldn't let you." Noah laughed. "I meant just you and me." Noah looked at him funny. "Ebony know about this?"

"Look, even though I didn't necessarily want to hear it, Ebony told me a little about you and Eve. You know how my baby likes to gossip."

Noah chuckled. "I know."

"She didn't tell me much, just that you two got together, and it didn't work out."

Noah nodded. "That about sums it up."

"I'm not butting in your business, but I hate to see you so quiet, so reserved. It's much more fun to tease you when you fight back." He playfully shoved Noah's shoulder. I want to cheer you up, so let's go kick it!"

Noah laughed. "Okay, I'll see you around ten-thirty or eleven.

Noah got to the club a little before eleven. It was still early, so he had no trouble finding a parking spot. He approached the door to Sydney's, which was a no frills, tiny place tucked into the corner of Second and Vine in downtown Seattle. About the only decoration in the place was a large disco ball left over from the seventies that twirled from the ceiling in the middle of the dance floor. Noah paid the cover charge and entered the dark, smoky room. He surveyed the empty dance floor and the assortment of vinyl tables with mismatched wooden chairs. He didn't see Yoshi, so he headed for the bar.

Regina saw him the moment he stepped in. As he paid, she clearly saw his face illuminated by the light at the cover booth. Her girlfriend, Tisha, tapped her on the shoulder. "Girl, look at the brother that just walked in. See him? He has on the olive-colored slacks and the white shirt."

The top two buttons of Noah's shirt were loose, drawing Regina's eyes to the beautiful brown skin. "Um hum, I see him." Regina noticed her head wasn't the only one turning as he made his way to the bar. "Excuse me." She left a wide-eyed, stunned Tisha and headed in Noah's direction.

Noah bought a beer and leaned against the counter, studying the crowd, waiting for Yoshi. The large room was about a quarter full and already it was hazy. Usually smoke didn't bother him. He knew that inhaling the fumes went hand in hand with clubbing, but tonight it irritated him. He wondered how he tolerated it before. A waving hand caught his eye. He looked at the woman and mentally shuddered as she took a long drag from her cigarette. Once the smoke cleared, he recognized the receptionist from Eve's office. So, that's where the raspy voice comes from, he thought cynically. He watched her saunter over to him. She maneuvered gracefully between tables and patrons in her tight red dress. She stood right in front of him, and without a word, reached around him to grab an ashtray on the counter. Her arm leisurely moved against his waist, and she managed to brush a breast against his chest. She ground out her cigarette, and reached back around to return the ashtray. Noah didn't move as her entire front pressed against him.

Lately, he had been thinking of life as before Eve and after Eve. Before Eve, he was sure his lower region would have at least twitched at Regina's outrageous conduct. Despite the cigarette, she was a pretty woman in a dress that left little to the imagination. But his after Eve body, just wasn't interested. He hadn't been with anyone since Sheila. She and others had called to see if he wanted to get together, but he shunned all offers. Noah straightened and lifted his beer to create space between him and Regina.

Regina ended the silence. "Hi, gorgeous. Remember me from the prosecutor's office?" Noah nodded. "Are you here by yourself?"

Noah chuckled at her boldness and straightforwardness. No room left for doubt with this woman. "Right now I am, but I'm expecting a friend later."

Edwina Martin-Arnold

Regina didn't ask if the friend was male or female because she didn't care. "Well, while you're waiting, would you like to dance?" As she spoke, Regina took the bottle from his hand and put it on an empty table near the dance floor. She began dancing, her fingers motioning for Noah to join her. Noah had a strong urge to ignore her invitation. He wanted to show her his back and just turn around to the bar, order another beer. Yet, he didn't want to hurt her feelings. A fast song was playing, so Noah figured it was relatively safe, and he agreed to dance. Regina moved smoothly around the barren floor. At times, she moved in close, but she stayed within the bounds of respectability. Still, Noah couldn't wait for the song to end.

When the song was finally over, Noah saw Yoshi by the bar. Touching Regina's shoulder, he bent to her and said, "Thanks, my friend's here. I'll see ya later." Noah grabbed his beer and walked to Yoshi. Regina followed him at an easy pace, thinking, You're not getting away that easy, big boy.

"Who's your friend?" he heard her say from behind him. Noah turned and introduced her to Yoshi. "My girlfriend and I have a table. Would you like to join us?"

"Sure," Yoshi said quickly. He ignored Noah's irritated glare as he followed Regina to the table. Muttering, Noah did the same.

Introductions were made, and they all settled in at the table. Tisha looked at Yoshi's fingers and groaned. "Why are the good-looking ones always married? I don't suppose you're separated?"

"No, I don't supposed I am," Yoshi answered good-naturedly. "It'll be five years next month."

"Congratulations. If I promise to be good, will you dance with me?" Laughing, Yoshi agreed, and they went to the dance floor.

Noah looked at Regina. He'd met her type before and knew what to expect. Bulldoze her way to the bedroom, and either she would be done with him or completely obsessed. Noah wasn't interested in either option. He leaned across the table, so she could hear him over the music. "Look, Regina, I'm catching the vibes you're sending, and I'm very flattered. You seem to be a really nice woman." God wouldn't begrudge him one small lie. "But I'm really not looking for a relationship right now." So, he told two-insy whinsy lies. He wanted nothing more than to begin a real relationship with Eve.

Regina trailed a fire-engine-red, blunt-tipped, lacquered fingernail down the back of his hand. Noah couldn't help comparing it to Eve's natural, clean, curved nails. "I'm not looking for a relationship; all I want is a good time, and according to the grapevine, you're lots of fun."

Noah wondered if he'd ever be able to converse

with a woman without his damn reputation popping up. "You shouldn't believe everything you hear." Noah's tone was terse. Regina removed her hand and sat back.

"Oh believe me, I'm a skeptic. I tend to have more faith in my own eyes and gut than other people's mouths. Right now, my gut is telling me you have a thing for the Queen of the Prosecutor's office." Regina held up her hand, "Don't bother denying it; you're body language says it all. I wish you all the luck in the world, melting the Ice Princess. Others have suffered many freezer burns trying." Her hand stopped him again, "Let's just dance, talk, and enjoy the evening. I'll pretend that you're married to my best friend and not available, okay?" She held out her hand.

"Okay." Noah shook it.

Regina lived up to her end of the bargain until the last dance of the night. It was around 1:30 and Yoshi informed everyone he would be leaving soon. Noah began preparing to go when Regina asked him for one last dance. The two joined the others on the crowded dance floor. The music pulsed through Regina's body, making her feel mischievous. She gyrated in close to Noah, and then moved away. She took the chance that he was too much of a gentleman to leave her alone on the floor, and she came as close to touching him without actual contact as humanly possible. At one point, she showed remarkable balance as she moved in and shimmied down to his crotch, and slowly worked her way back up in three-inch, red high heels.

Noah was more irritated than embarrassed. Regina knew he wasn't interested and was pushing him for selfish reasons of her own. He was tempted to turn his back on her and leave the club without another word. Glancing around, he saw Yoshi laughing. While Noah was distracted with Yoshi, Regina turned her back to him and was attempting to do a lap dance standing up. Noah grabbed her hips to still them and whispered in her ear. "Cut it out, or I'm leaving." Anyone observing them would have thought they were lovers.

Regina turned around and laid her arms around his neck. "I just want to be sure you know what you're passing up."

Oh, I know, he thought to himself as he removed her arms.

"Well, you can't blame a girl for trying." Regina behaved herself for the rest of the song.

Outside, Yoshi put his hand to Noah's forehead. Noah pushed him away. "Yoshi, what're you doing?"

"Man, are you sick? The Noah I know wouldn't be leaving the club with me. That girl was all over you."

Noah smiled and didn't answer him. "Go home to your wife, pick on her for a while." He waved as he walked to his car.

CHAPTER 8

Competition was ingrained in Regina. She didn't even think about the need to compete. It was just the way it was. If she took the time to analyze it, she would have reflected that she learned rivalry from the crib. She and her mother participated in a silent war over her father. Like most new parents, hers were enthralled with their new baby. They hugged her, cooed to her, and rubbed her belly while they counted her fingers and toes numerous times. After a while, the newness and wonder settled in for her mother, and she eased into the role of raising her child. However, Regina remained a bright new penny for her father, and he was blinded by the miracle of her. When he looked at Regina, he was awestruck and thankful that the Lord had blessed him with such a child. He treasured Regina because he truly believed that she was the better part of him. If asked, he would have honestly answered that he loved his wife, but she wasn't a part of him; his blood didn't run in her veins as it did in his daughter. Regina was his precious gem, and hearing her laugh or seeing her smile made his heart thump with joy.

Because Regina's father wanted the best for her, he insisted that his wife be a stay-at-home mom. Living on a mechanic's salary left little room for luxuries. So, when a young Regina pestered her father for an expensive Cabbage Patch doll, her mother quickly said no, claiming the doll cost too much and was ugly. Her father didn't say much while she and her mother battled. He just got a weekend job at a car wash, and one Sunday he came home with a bag that he dropped in Regina's lap. "Take good care of her," was all he said. The doll still had a place on Regina's bed.

When his wife's and daughter's wishes collided, he twisted in a wind that usually blew his lovely daughter's way. His wife suffered these indignities with quiet pride and bitterness. Young Regina was far different. She fussed, pouted, screamed, made faces, and threw mammoth tantrums when her father didn't side with her. As she grew, her visible reactions lessened when she learned her father didn't like such displays of emotion. He saw the behavior as his bad side coming out. Regina became less demonstrative and more calculating. Over the years, she learned to put women in two categories: threat or unimportant.

Eve and she were the only black women in the Seattle Law Department, and this alone was enough to place her in the threat category. But Eve's indifference to Regina riled her. It made Regina want to get under Eve's skin like pepper spray and burn the hell out of her composure. The fact that Eve was an attorney, and she was a part-time receptionist had made Regina hesitant to challenge her in the past, but she had recently been accepted to Grambling University in Louisiana. She was about to graduate from a local community college, and she wanted to get out of the boring Northwest. She couldn't wait to be on the campus of an all-black college. So, she didn't care if she ruffled the feathers of the pristine Eve. To the contrary, she was looking forward to it.

Instinctively, Regina knew Noah was the path to shaking up Eve. It was the Monday after Noah's rejection, and Regina's self-esteem didn't like the blow. Also, it didn't help that Eve's demeanor reminded her of her mother's quiet dignity that she could never quite shake. Likewise, it didn't help that they were both in the lunchroom that reminded

Regina of the kitchen where many a battle took place. So, without any real conscious thought, she slipped back into the patterns established early in childhood. Eve became her mother, the lunchroom became the kitchen, and Regina went for the jugular.

Later, Eve would be thankful that very few people were present. She usually bought a sandwich at the deli in front of her building, and quickly ate it there or in her office. But she didn't want to eat alone today because Noah was always with her, just beyond conscious thought. She knew he would burst to the forefront if she didn't occupy herself. So, she found herself in the lunchroom, which consisted of a long table in the library. She got stuck in court, so it was almost 12:30 when she arrived, and only three women were present.

Eve sat down next to Sally Trenton who worked in the Case Preparation unit. Both of them faced Regina who sat directly across the table. Sally gave Regina the perfect opening when she innocently asked, "Did you meet anyone interesting during your adventures this weekend?"

"As a matter of fact, I did. Someone Eve already knows." She leaned across the table and spoke in a conspiratorial tone. "Is it true, Eve? Does he make you feel like a natural woman?"

Eve felt as if the entire universe imploded, had

been shoved in her mouth, and then exploded when it reached her throat. She didn't need a name to know to whom Regina was referring. A weird silence filled the room as the others wondered what in the world was going on. Eve was known as a straight shooter, an aggressive prosecutor who was extremely fair. She didn't hide evidence, and if she had proof someone was innocent, she dismissed the case without hesitation. But everyone knew her private life was just that. They knew the basics: she was a widow with a teenage son, but that was about it. She rarely discussed her life away from the office. Regina was known for being quick with her hands and her mouth. She handled the switchboard and disgruntled citizens with saucy professionalism and ease. Both women were likable and easy to get along with; hence, the present tension had everyone in the lunchroom, including Eve, confused.

"Come on, Eve, you can tell us. Should Dr. Feelgood really be his name?"

Eve took a sip of her Coke, trying to get the cosmos past her throat and to compose herself. Jeanne McNare, another attorney who sat at the end of the long table, came to her rescue and gave her time to collect herself. "Gee, Regina, I didn't know you were such an Aretha Franklin fan?"

"So many of her lyrics seem to fit everyday life.

Don't you think so, Eve?"

Anger eradicated confusion. Who does this bitch think she is, baiting me like this?

"What's wrong, Eve? Does the cat have your tongue?"

Eve shot her a look that sizzled the air between them. Regina looked into the fiercely cold eyes and had second thoughts about challenging her.

Eve wanted to snatch Regina by the hair, and throw her narrow behind across the room. It would feel so good to watch her bounce off the wall and crumble to the floor. Eve knew physical violence wasn't as powerful as ripping one apart with words. She'd learned that from her mother who was known to take a person apart with fifty words or less. She'd watched unruly students, rude shopkeepers, and aggressive solicitors wither under the power of that woman's tongue and voice.

Eve spoke quietly and distinctly. "There is one very important Aretha Franklin song you obviously know nothing about, Regina. It is called 'R.E.S.P.E.C.T.' I'm sure you've heard it, being such a big fan. In it, Aretha sings 'R.E.S.P.E.C.T., tell you what it means to me.' It's obvious the word means nothing to you, Regina, in regards to your-self and to others."

"Whoa!" Regina sat back in her chair as if she were reeling from a blow, "So, the Ice Princess can get hot. The rumors must be true if he has you reacting like this!"

"Oh, but you're mistaken, Regina. You give him too much credit. It's you and your rudeness I'm reacting to."

The other two shifted uncomfortably in their chairs, wondering if this confrontation was going to have a violent end. Eve and Regina seemed to have forgotten they were there.

"Are you sure you're not all hot and bothered about him, Eve? He's quite a specimen." Then Regina took a well-placed shot in the dark. "He certainly was under your spell. In no uncertain terms, he told me your romantic charms had ruined him for other women."

The universe moved to Eve's head and exploded. Anger helped her fuse her brain back together, and she managed to meet Regina's eyes and calmly say, "You are such a lovely girl, Regina. Do you always discuss other women with attractive men? Does this give you some perverse thrill, or are you really a closet lesbian? Bisexual maybe? Or did you have a bad lunch? Tell me, Regina, which is it, heartache or heartburn that is making you so bitchy?"

Eve's words had the desired effect, and Regina was momentarily speechless. Taking advantage, Eve discarded her lunch remains and escaped to her office.

Jeanne chuckled while watching Regina prepare to leave the lunchroom. "I don't know what brought that on, but you're a pup when it comes to verbal sparing with a master like Eve," she commented as Regina left.

Fury, exasperation, rancor all fought for dominance in Eve's mind. She sat at her desk, rocked back in her chair, and threw back her head. Finding Noah and killing him would be nirvana. She could think of nothing better than having her hand sting from slapping the hell out of him. How dare he discuss them when she made it very clear how she felt about privacy! Rubbing her temples, she tried to focus. "Damn, I don't have time for this," she muttered. She was due in court in fifteen minutes, so she had to get her raging emotions under control. Closing her eyes, she started a routine she perfected in her track days. She hadn't had to use it since the early days of Todd's death. She imagined a net that she used to gather all her emotions. Once they were contained, she rolled them up into a ball, opened a small corner of her mind, and shoved the ball inside and firmly shut the door. Her mind quieted as she took slow, deep breaths. Poise finally came. Noah would remain in the ball until she had time to deal with him. She rose, grabbed her briefcase, and headed back to court. Jeanne saw her and caught her by the elevator.

"I haven't had the opportunity to see you in court, but now I know what the defense attorneys are talking about. Your mouth should be a lethal weapon." Eve gave her a slight smile as she pushed the down button. "Look, I know you have court, so I'll be brief. Sally and I spoke, and we just want to let you know that what happened in the lunchroom stays in the lunchroom."

Eve was touched, but she was scared to show it; scared that the ball would expand, the door would be forced open, and she'd get fired for being a raving lunatic at work. The elevator arrived, and she escaped inside after a whispered "thank you" to Jeanne.

Court was agonizingly slow. It was a theft trial with a new defense attorney who was determined to try every trick in the book. Eve was ready to scream if he brought up one more stupid pretrial motion. Even the judge looked annoyed and rolled her eyes when the attorney interrupted her just as she was asking the bailiff to bring in the potential jurors.

"Excuse me, Your Honor, but I do have one more motion that should be addressed before we bring in the jurors."

"What could that possibly be, Mr. Novak? I think you've brought up just about every motion imaginable." The judge's elbow rested on the bench; her hand supported her chin.

"No, Your Honor. I have one more motion that could be determinative of the case."

With a sigh, the judge said, "Go ahead, Mr. Novak."

The young man patted the defendant's shoulder, moved a lock of blond hair off his forehead, and stood with an air of self-importance. "Your Honor, it is the defense's contention that the statements made by my client to the security guard should be suppressed because the guard was acting as a police officer when my client made the statements. Thus, the guard should have mirandized my client before he questioned him. I believe that we will need to take live testimony from the security guard for me to establish that the guard was in fact an officer of the law."

Eve almost groaned the argument was so stupid. According to the Miranda rule, police officers had to inform arrestees of their constitutional rights before they could question them. Eve hid her irritation behind a straight back and a blank face. No way was she going to sit through the hour it would take the defense attorney to question the guard when she knew the chances were slim to none that his motion would be upheld.

Eve stood. "Excuse me, Your Honor. May I briefly address the Court?"

"Yes, Madame Prosecutor."

"Your Honor, I don't believe live testimony is necessary. I anticipate Counsel is going to argue that the store in question was involved in a training program conducted by the police department. I will stipulate or agree that the training took place."

"Thank you, Ms. Garrett. That should save us some time. Counsel do you agree to the stipulation."

The green attorney looked from Eve to the judge. Eve could see his mind ticking through his eyes. He was trying to figure out if she was playing a trick on him. Oh come on, she thought to herself. I'm not being sneaky; I just want to speed this thing up.

The judge spoke. "Counselor, I'm not trying to tell you how to try your case, but I see no harm in accepting the stipulation. It just eliminates the need for the guard to take the stand. Finally, the young attorney acquiesced.

"Good," the judge said. "Now we can move to argument. Tell me, Mr. Novak, do you have any authority to support your proposition?"

"Your Honor, I do not have any direct authority, but please let me explain my reasoning." The judge nodded. "As the Court is well aware, the store in question here, The Bon, is a large clothing retailer in the Northwest. To protect against theft, The Bon has enlisted in the Retail Theft Program. This is a program where police officers come into the store and actually train security guards. The officers tell the guards how to spot, detain, question, and even write reports pertaining to the people detained. Therefore, the police department is in essence deputizing these security guards, and they are acting as officers when they apprehend individuals in the store. If it acts like a duck, it's a duck, Your Honor. If these guards are trained and behave just like police officers, they must be held to the same standards as the police, and thus, they must mirandize citizens before they question them." The attorney sat down.

The judge looked at Eve. "May I address the Court?" she asked.

"Yes, you may, Ms. Garrett."

Eve stood. "Your Honor, Counsel is wrong on several points." Eve raised a finger to elaborate each point. "First, it takes more than the Retail Theft Program to convert a common citizen into a police officer. The program is a seminar where the police department comes into the store and gives a tutorial on how to detect and prevent theft. If this were enough to make one an officer, the police academy would be a terrible waste of time and finances. We could just have recruits attend a short training, and then send them off in our streets."

That drew a small smile from the judge. "Also, if what Defense Counsel argues is true, every time police officers meet with community organizations and give them advice on crime prevention, they would unwittingly be deputizing these ordinary citizens. Clearly, counsel is mistaken when he claims that the security guard was the equivalent of a law-enforcement officer.

"Second, the defendant's statements were voluntary and not made in response to questions. In the police report, the security guard wrote a statement. I would like to refer the Court and opposing counsel to the second paragraph of that statement."

Eve grabbed the report, which was already turned to the pertinent page. "I'm paraphrasing, but basically the guard writes that he saw the defendant lift up his shirt and shove the watch down his pants. When he approached the defendant outside of the store and grabbed his arm, the defendant said, 'Okay, you got me. Will you let me go if I give it back?' The defendant's statements were spontaneous and unsolicited. Even if the Court were somehow persuaded that the guard was an officer, the defendant's confession would still be admissible because Miranda is not required when the officer fails to ask a question."

Eve sat down, hoping that the Court would end the nonsense, and not let the defense attorney have a rebuttal argument. The attorney stood and straightened his suit jacket as he prepared to speak. The judge intervened before he could get a word out. "Mr. Novak, I am well versed on this subject; thus, further argument from you is unnecessary. Please sit down. I'm ready to make my ruling." The attorney sat down. "The statements are admissible. They were completely voluntary and not in response to questioning, so this Court does not really need to address whether or not the guards were officers in disguise. However, I will address the issue because I know it is bound to repeat itself in the future."

Everyone in the courtroom was aware that Mr. Novak was a new attorney except for the defendant. The judge didn't want to embarrass him by pointing this out, so she was trying to provide guidance somewhat discreetly. Eve was once a new attorney herself, and had been the recipient of lots of friendly, and not so friendly, guidance by numerous judges. Usually Eve had more patience with rookies, but the fight with Regina left her with frayed nerves, and very little tolerance. She just wanted to get on with the trial.

Looking directly at Mr. Novak, the judge continued. "It takes significantly more than an instructional program to convert citizens into law enforcement officers. The police academy consists of months of training where the cadets are schooled on a variety of subjects: like how to question a subject, how to apprehend someone, how to write a report, and how to handle a gun. It would be impossible for the same amount of material to be covered in a seminar like the Retail Theft Program. Thus, it is equally impossible that the guard in this case was really an officer."

The judge paused and looked at the clock on the wall. "It is now 4:15. Court is scheduled to end in fifteen minutes, so it is too late to pick a jury today. Consequently, I'm recessing early." Again the judge focused on Mr. Novak. "There will be no more pretrial motions; a jury will be picked first thing tomorrow morning." The judge banged her gavel and left the bench.

"Thank goodness," Eve whispered under her breath.

Walking back to her office, she plotted her strategy. She planned to call around, find Noah, and in the basest terms she could think of, tell him off. She called his condo, no answer. She called the fire station and found out he was off. She banged the phone on her desk in frustration, and then, hurriedly checked to make sure it wasn't broken. She hated to do it, but she called Ebony. Yoshi answered the phone. As casually as she could, she said, "Hi, Yoshi, it's Eve."

"Hey, Eve, how's it going. Ebony's not home yet. She has a late customer at the shop and probably won't be home 'til about nine. You can call her there."

Eve tapped her fingers on her desk and bounced around in the chair, but her voice hid her anxiety. Calmly she said, "Actually Yoshi, you can probably help me more than Ebony. Do you know where Noah might be?"

"Yeah, I know where he is. He's at the Links thing, representing the fire department."

Eve thanked Yoshi, said bye, and hung up quickly, cursing herself. She'd forgotten all about the Links Fashion Show, and she'd promised Beulah, who was a member of the Links, that she would go. Her mother would be upset and disappointed if she missed the annual charity event. Checking her watch, she saw that it was 4:45. The event officially started at 6:00. If she pushed it, she could go home, get dressed, and make it just on time.

Eve practically ran to the Bug parked in the building's garage. She had to drive up Capitol Hill and down the other side to reach Madison Valley were she lived. If there was no traffic, she could make it in fifteen minutes. Traffic could slow the commute up to an hour or an hour and a half. Eve drove like a maniac, dodging in and out of cars with

the skill of a stunt driver. She made it in twenty minutes. Beulah was just getting into her Buick Regal
when she arrived. Being a member of Links,
Beulah had to arrive early and was in a rush to be
on her way. Still, she took the time to twirl for Eve.
"Wow, Mom! You look stunning." Her mother was
wearing a full length, all-white dress that looked
dramatic against her dark skin and white hair.
White was the theme color so all the Links were
wearing it. However, Beulah refused to completely
supress her vibrant side. She wore a necklace
made by the Maasai tribe in Africa that she'd
ordered off the Internet. It was choker style that
covered her throat with a plethora of beads. The
red, blue, yellow, and brown beads all fought for
attention against her mother's neck.

"Thank you, honey." Her mother bowed and
started to get in the car. "You better hurry, or you'll
be late."

Eve ran in the house and went straight to the
shower. Fifteen minutes later, she ran out and
kissed Sean on the head. "Hey, Mom, stop. I'm
watching my favorite *Sanford and Son* rerun."
"Sorry. I'll be back around nine. Be good."

She got to the Westin Hotel at six on the dot.
The Westin was distinctive against the Seattle sky-
line because it had two very large and very uneven
twin towers. Eve had the valet park the car, and she

speed-walked to the escalators. By the time she reached the second floor, the lights were being dimmed to signal the guests that it was time to take their seats. Eve crossed the enormous lobby to the main ballroom. Beulah greeted her just inside the door. She told her the number of their table, and then she rushed to join the other Links for the introductory ceremonies. Eve passed through the tables, straining to see the numbers so she could sit down before the event started. At last, she found her table where she sat down and breathed deeply. There were three others at her table, and they nodded and said hello.

The evening began with lights and music. The Links Fashion Show was an annual event, and each Link was introduced at the beginning of the show. Eve fought the need to search the room for Noah, and focused on cheering for her mother and her friends.

The woman next to her whispered, "This is going to be a great show!"

Eve whispered back. "It always is. Look, there's my mother." She and the woman clapped loudly.

Next the Links president explained that the Links was an organization of black women whose main goal was the betterment of the community. The president went on to give the Links history in

Seattle, and she explained that the bulk of the money from the fashion show would be awarded as scholarships to minority children in the Seattle area. Eve was a fashion show veteran and had heard this speech, in some form or another, many times. She tuned the speaker out as she scanned the dimly lit room for Noah. Her anger was like a pot of stew set on a low fire to simmer. It hummed through her, waiting for her to corner Noah, so it would have the green light to flare up full force. She couldn't find him. It was a large room, but maybe Yoshi was wrong, and he wasn't there. Dinner was served. Eve was convinced that only two meals were served at functions such as this: either salmon or chicken. They were in luck, it was a salmon night.

Eve was about halfway through her meal when the models' runway lights came on, causing her to blink and rear back. Her table was right next to the runway, and the lights startled her. That was nothing compared to the jolt she received when she saw Noah sitting directly across the runway from her. Here she'd searched for him, and he was very close the whole time. He seemed unaware of her, and that only increased Eve's ire. Her eyes bore into Noah's profile, willing him to look her way. He did, when the swimsuit model walked down the runway.

The model caught Noah's eye because at first he thought she was Eve. Her hair was long and her face was different, but she had the body. Long, firm with supple definition and incredible abs. The way she sauntered down the runway tortured Noah with memories of how Eve walked to him that morning he couldn't forget. His lower body twitched with the memory. He trailed the woman as she passed, lost in fantasy that she was Eve. The real Eve's cold, angry glare brought him back to reality. At first, he didn't realize it was her. He thought his daydream had taken a different turn, and conjured up the upset woman, grimacing across the runway. He blinked, and she was still there. He smiled and gave a small wave before he remembered the circumstances. Her only response was to sneer more.

Eve wanted to throw her wineglass at him, watching him ogle the model. He stared at the scantily clad woman like she was a chocolate bar, and he was a diabetic. The simmer became a boil in Eve's stomach, and it was so intense, she pressed a hand to her belly, shut her eyes for a moment. The emotions she'd shoved into a ball and placed behind a door in her mind began banging and thumping her brain, threatening to overwhelm her. She refused to consider that the cause could be jealousy. No, the thought didn't even enter her mind. She knew the cause was her own stupidity. How could she put herself in such an idiotic position of falling for a man who was incapable of thinking or feeling above his waist. And no, she couldn't suffer this humiliation in private because the dog she chose to lie with had a wagging tongue. Eve was so deep in self-flagulation that she didn't notice Beulah slipping in and settling her heavy girth into the seat beside her. Beulah had to touch her shoulder to get her attention.

"Oh, Eve, isn't the turn-out wonderful?" she whispered excitedly. "I think we have twice as many people as we did last year."

Eve made some innocuous sound her mother took as agreement. Beulah was so thrilled, she failed to notice how straight Eve was sitting, her fingers missed how rigid her daughter's shoulder felt, and her eyes didn't see how tight her face and hands were. As her mother babbled on, Eve stared off in space, mentally looking inward, and she focused on calming herself. Surface-level control came with a lower heart rate and unclenched fingers. Pain made her look at her right palm. She stared at the small angry red cut in wonder. She rubbed it, realizing that she'd pressed her fingers so hard that her nail punctured her flesh. "Get a grip, girl," she whispered to herself. She caught the irony of her statement, and looked at her hand again. "Maybe, I'm gripping too much?"

"Did you say something?" Beulah leaned over, bumping her shoulder.

"No, Mom, I didn't say anything important. I'm really enjoying the evening."

Beulah smiled brightly and hugged Eve with one arm. "I know it was probably hard for you to come tonight after working all day. Thank you, I appreciate it." Beulah turned back to the show.

Eve's attitude was a mystery to Noah. The thought that she might be mad about what happened at the Sonic game was ridiculous. So, he wondered, what in the world had her so ticked? He looked at her again. She was sitting ramrod straight with her head and chin held up a tad at a proud angle. With her short hair and bearing, she reminded him of the Nefertiti picture that hung in his sister's living room. All that was missing was the hat. He smiled, thinking of her as his proud African princess. The smile soured when he reminded himself she was far from being his. Hell, she probably would never be his. Noah turned and gave his attention back to the models and the others at his table. He vowed to ignore Eve.

Across the runway, Eve made a similar promise to herself. She'd ignore him until she could corner him. She breathed slow and easy, telling herself all in good time.

Noah was better at keeping his vow than Eve. By some quirk in the seating arrangements, he was surrounded by four females. During a break in the fashion show, he started a conversation with the woman to his right. He knew she was a firefighter with a lot of years on the force because he'd seen her around and heard about her, although they'd never been formerly introduced. He found out her name was Charlene Bennet. "Call me Charlie," she told Noah as they discussed their different career paths.

Charlie was assigned to media relations, working toward the goal of being the spokesperson for the Seattle Fire Department. Noah wished her good luck and was silent about his unvoiced goal of one day being the fire chief. One of the women across the table joined the conversation, telling them she worked in marketing for Nordstrom, and often found herself dealing with the media.

Noah noticed the Nordstrom banners decorating each of the four walls. Pointing to them, he said, "Obviously, Nordy is one of the sponsors for the fashion show."

With a toothy grin, she nodded. "Yes. We've been sponsoring it for the last five years. We provide ninety percent of the clothes, shoes, accessories, etc., and we give a generous donation."

"Wow," Charlie said, "that's a great thing for Nordstrom to do."

Noah and the others nodded and mumured their agreement. The lights flickered and dimmed, and all of them quieted as the second half of the fashion show began.

Against her pledge, Eve found herself peeking at Noah as slyly as possible. She watched and seethed as Noah interacted with the women at his table. In her state, it looked as if he were flirting with all of them. Beulah was so excited about how the evening was progressing, she dominated conversation at their table during the break. Eve was relieved. She listened with half an ear and managed to respond appropriately when she had to.

At last, the evening came to an end around eight o'clock. Before Eve could jump the runway to corner Noah, her mother grabbed her arm insisting there were new members she wanted Eve to meet. Once or twice a year, Beulah would go on a campaign to convince Eve to become a Link. Eve kept telling her mother she would when her life calmed down a little and she could make a full commitment. Eve wasn't brave enough to tell Beulah no way. She was a loner. That's why she loved track. She was part of a team, but her race was completely dependent on her. It was her skill and determination that won or lost. It was the same at the prosecutor's office--if she weren't trying the case with cocounsel, which was a rarity. She was the one standing up representing the State, attempting to get a conviction. Eve had no desire to join a group where she'd inevitably have to deal with politics and in-fighting.

Unbeknownest to Eve, Noah's eyes were glued to her when she arose from her seat. The lights were bright, signifying the end of the evening, but that wasn't what was blowing Noah's mind. Eve's dress—no, her whole appearance—had him feeling like a heart patient. She was wearing a black silk, boatneck dress that appeared conservative. It was long with a knee-length split in the front. The dress was elegant in its simplicity, and only added to Eve's natural grace. His eyes drank in her sculptured arms and the long lines of her neck. But the shocker came when Eve turned and bent a little to speak to her mother. The dress was backless and dipped down to Eve's waist. Noah salivated, watching her back muscles glide beneath her skin as she moved.

Somewhere, deep in Eve's subconscious, was the nugget of truth that she'd worn the dress because she knew Noah was going to be at the function. Although she'd never admit it in her current state of mind, she wanted him to hunger for her.

Looking at all that supple flesh, Noah knew it was impossible to wear a bra with a dress like that. His nostrils flared, and his thumbs rubbed across his fingertips as he remembered the texture of her skin. His tongue passed his lips as he recalled her taste. Noah shut his mouth when he realized how hard he was breathing. Lord, he knew he had to get out of there, or who knew what he'd say--or do--just to caress that body again.

It took Eve twenty minutes to satisfy her mother's need to introduce her to the world. When she escaped, Noah was nowhere to be found. Eve spent ten minutes looking, and then she went to the pay phones. Her progress was hampered by men who weren't deterred by the fact that she still wore Todd's ring. They approached the fanatastic-looking woman who attended unescorted. Eve's frayed nerves made her less than delicate when she told these men she wasn't interested.

Noah lived about fifteen minutes from the Westin Hotel if there was no traffic on the freeway. So, providing he went straight home, he should be there by now. She called his condo, and he answered. Without speaking, she hung up, told her mother good-bye, and rushed to her car.

Eve raced down Interstate 5--at fifteen miles over the speed limit--maneuvering through traffic, driving on automatic pilot. She knew her control over her emotions was tenuous and she was in the middle of an adrenaline rush because she found herself speeding in the High Occupancy Vehicle lane, when there was no need to in the light traffic.

She hated it when people violated the HOV lane; it was a pet peeve she held dear and close to her heart. Cursing, she changed lanes and tried her breathing technique. Slow and deep, she thought to herself. She wiped her sweaty palms on the seat and pressed a hand to her heart, ordering it to stay in her chest. Her mind kept replaying her witch match with Regina, and she found her fingers tightening on the steering wheel.

The weeks since she and Noah had been together were difficult for Eve. The constant second-guessing and indecision had her so wound up and frustrated, it was easy to assume that "ruining him for other women" meant that he told Regina they had slept together. A very small part of her contemplated that she might be wrong or overreacting, but she ignored it. An even smaller part of her felt some pride that she was so good, he didn't want anyone after her. That pride took a nose dive when she remembered how he drooled over the model. She hit the dashboard with her palm and screamed just to relieve some of the tension. How could he be so rude and insensitive when she was sitting across the runway? How dare he embarrass her in such a way! She yelled again. Her enraged brain stopped her from remembering that Noah didn't know she was there yet.

Eve reflected she hadn't been this mad since

Sean cut up all her stockings to make wave caps for his hair. He'd cut the legs off the stockings and wore the waist part on his head while he slept, hoping his hair would have waves by the morning. She'd bought him a wave cap, but he said the stockings were tighter and stayed on his head better during the night. Eve wanted to kill him after he ruined the third, and last pair, of her new stockings. She had to rush to 7-Eleven at seven o'clock in the morning to buy a pair before work. Of course, the cheap nylon ripped before lunchtime. Finding Sean was her main priority when she got home from work that night. However, she burst out laughing when she found him in the bathroom with the stockings on his head, tying the cut legs together. His expression was so serious and the nylons looked so silly on his head. His mortified look made her laugh harder. After she got over the giggles, and Sean stopped being mad, they reached a compromise. He stayed out of her dresser, and she bought him new stockings every three weeks. If he wore them any longer than that, he claimed they were too stretched out and didn't form his waves right. Eve had to admit his hair was cute when it worked. The memory made Eve chuckle, and relaxed her chest a little.

However, by the time she was hammering on Noah's door fifteen minutes later, she was feeling strained again, and she was frowning. She ignored the doorbell, preferring to slam the side of her fist against wood.

Noah was sitting down to a Salisbury steak TV dinner when the pounding started. The little bit of salmon at the show only dented his appetite. "Who the hell is this?" he mumbled as he answered the door. Eve pushed him away with a forearm, and barged into the condo. Noah hid his surprise and desire behind sarcasm. "Jeez, are you here for a repeat performance? If you are, I'm sorry I'm not up to it. I was just about to eat a lovely steak dinner." Eve whirled around and faced him. She's furious, he realized as her eyes sent daggers at him. Damn, I want her. She's ashamed of me and looking at me like I stole her purse, and all I want to do is shut the door, make love to her, right here and right now. He closed the door and leaned against it while crossing his arms.

He had no right looking so relaxed and gorgeous, leaning against the door in black tuxedo pants and an unbuttoned, untucked formal white shirt. Eve fought the memory of how that chest felt pressed against her breasts. Instead, she focused on why she should be angry. Here, she'd been to hell and back since the time they'd slept together, and he looked so, so unaffected. Eve walked up to him and hissed, "You bastard." He cocked his head

to one side and looked at her as if to say "what?"
Eve's pressure-cooked emotions exploded and she
slapped him. The crack was loud, and the pain to
her hand was sharp. Later, she would suppose that
in her heart of hearts she did exactly what she
wanted to do, yet at the time, her actions surprised
her.

Noah's hand flew to his cheek. The slap transferred his puzzlement into anger. In a cold, hard
voice he said, "No, you're mistaken. My parents
were married when I was born. Did you come all
this way to hit me and question my parentage?"

She was standing very close and glaring up at
him. She fired questions, "How could you discuss
me with Regina after I told you how important privacy is to me?"

Noah's anger mixed with irritation. "Eve,
what're you talking about?"

"Did you see Regina this weekend?"

"Yeah. So what?"

"Did you discuss me?"

Noah threw up his hands, "I don't know. I don't
remember every little thing we talked about! Why?
What's this about? Am I supposed to have slept
with her too? Now that you've had me, I'm not
allowed to touch anyone in your office? I'm just
supposed to stay at home and hope you'll ring my
doorbell? Sorry, sister, that's not how I operate!"

Noah stepped around her and sat down to eat his increasingly pathetic-looking dinner.

Eve followed and stood right beside him as he defiantly chewed. "I don't give a flying flip who you sleep with."

He interrupted her. "Flying flip? What kind of phrase is that? I'll repeat, Eve, what the hell is this about?"

"Okay, I'll talk in a language you can understand. I don't give a damn who you screw. Just don't discuss me while you do it!"

Noah chewed his food vigorously. He was incensed and avoided looking at her as he spoke because looking at her meant strangling her. "To be honest, Regina is so entertaining, I don't remember mentioning you at all."

Jealousy ripped through Eve. The force was so strong, she had to take a step back. If Noah looked at her, he would have seen the raw pain and anguish on her face, and he might have softened. But he didn't look, and the longer he sat there, chewing food he couldn't taste, the angrier he became. Who the hell did she think she was barging into his house shouting accusations? First she didn't want him yet she wanted to control him! It was too much. Loving Eve was maddening. Love! Where the hell did that come from! No, no, no, he refused to be in love with her. Anger and disgust made him cruel. In a cold, even voice, he said, "Eve, if I were enjoying the charms of another woman, you can be damn sure your name would be the last thing on my mind and lips." Noah wouldn't be surprised if his nose grew two inches for that lie. No woman could erase her from his mind.

The green-eyed monster hit Eve again, and she almost doubled over. Such envy was new to her. She felt territorial, and wanted to maim him and any woman who went near him. She'd never felt that way about Todd. Of course, loyal Todd never gave her any reason to feel such gut-wrenching jealousy. The short silence between them seemed like an eternity to Noah. In between bites, he glanced at her out of the corner of his eye. He saw a glimpse of the anguish before she could hide it. Instinctively, he went to her. By the time he left his seat, she was the Ice Princess; her frosty expression and rigid posture made him wonder if he'd imagined the suffering he'd witnessed seconds earlier.

"You're jealous, aren't you?" he said, standing in front of her.

The swimsuit model popped into Eve's brain, and she backed up and spat, "No!"

Originally, he rose to comfort, but her attitude galled him. Noah wasn't sure what his intentions were as he advanced until Eve's back hit the wall, and his body and his eyes trapped her. "What're you doing?" she demanded in an accusatorial tone. "What I should have done when you first walked in the door." He bent to her and brushed his lips across hers. He expected another slap. When one didn't come, he continued stroking his lips against hers.

Flluttering she associated with him began in her belly. She ignored it and raised her hands to push him away. Her palms touched the skin just inside his shirt as he increased the pressure of his mouth. Her body overruled her mind, and her fingers betrayed her by beginning a gentle massage on his chest when they should have been rejecting him. Noah moaned and wrapped his arms around her as his tongue touched her lips. Eve allowed him in, and her arms snaked around his neck while she pressed their bodies closer. Their body heat seemed to melt her silk dress as the material glided between them. Her stomach felt his arousal, and she knew that if he wanted, she would allow him to take her there, against the wall. In fact, maybe that's what she wanted. His lips moved to her neck, his hands gripped her hips as he lowered himself, so he could grind against her. Eve's legs were weak. Noah and the wall kept her from falling.

God he wanted her. More than he wanted any-thing in his life. His ache for her made him a little rougher than usual. His lips pressed a little harder, his tongue was swifter, his hands pressed and rubbed firmly against her bare back. It would be so easy and pleasurable to give in to the gnawing hunger and let himself go. But he held back. Memories crashed against his lust, reminding him of the pain he felt when she left his bed the last time. He wanted Eve so bad, he was shaking like a drug addict. One more fix is all I need, his tortured heart told his brain. No! He yelled to himself. I can't, I won't. Not under these circumstances. I refused to be used again.

While Noah continued his internal battle, Eve couldn't take it anymore. She wanted him--now. She took short, ragged breaths, struggling to breathe as her hands inched down to free him. She had undone the clasp and was moving to the zipper when suddenly he stood back and pinned her arms above her head with one large hand. The other stayed on her back. He kissed her senseless, then released her hands long enough to slip the dress from her shoulders. After her breasts were free, he recaptured her wrists above her head with his hand. He nuzzled her breasts, teasing her. Eve nipped and nibbled at his forehead; she rubbed her lips in his hair while silently encouraging him to hurry. She gasped as he released her hands and captured her nipple with his lips. He used his hands to squeeze and press as his lips worked. Dazed with lust, she reached for him again. Noah knew if she caught him, he would be lost, and when he surfaced, he'd be completely disgusted with himself.

Noah eluded her and moved back. Stunned and cold, it took Eve a second to put two and two together. She leaned against the wall with her dress at her waist, watching him back up farther. As he buttoned his pants, it hit her, slammed into her like a baseball bat to the face. He was rejecting her. The contemptuous look in his eyes hid his desire. Her heart withered and became a pit in her chest. Embarrassed, she turned from him and fixed her clothes. Noah closed his eyes. Her exposed flesh was a powerful magnet.

Eve felt like a newborn baby who had been taken from her mother and submerged in ice water. Turning back to face him was hard; she felt faint at the thought, but she had no choice. She couldn't find her way to the door with her eyes closed. With a deep breath, she turned around and was greeted by a smirk. She wanted to scream at the top of her lungs and pound his chest. How did this happen? She came over with murder on her mind and wound up making a fool of herself in his arms. He spoke, drawing her eyes to his lips.

"Like I said, Eve, I'm not up to a repeat performance. You'll have to get someone else to pro-

vide the stud service for you. I want a real relationship, not this secret-lover crap you're after." Noah
looked at her hand. "Also, it really is in poor taste
to try and sleep with me when you are still wearing
another's wedding ring." Eve's eyes dropped to her
ring finger. Noah moved, and her eyes followed him
as he sat at the table. "I don't know what you heard
about Regina, but it's none of your business. Close
the door when you leave." Noah went back to his
dinner. Eve was seething. The loud slam let Noah
know she'd left.

CHAPTER 9

*E*ve slammed the car door as well. She slapped the steering wheel, then leaned her head on it. She was fuming, too angry to drive, so she sat there for a moment, trying to collect herself. She was too ashamed to think about what just happened. She tried to clear her mind and think of nothing as she took gradual, deep breaths. Five minutes passed. It seemed like an eternity to Eve when all she wanted to do was get as far away from Noah as possible. Calm enough to drive, Eve started the car and pulled away from the curb. She told herself to concentrate on driving to keep her mind busy, but that didn't work. Noah refused to stay away.

How could I? Eve agonized. How could I make

such a fool of myself? Tears threatened and then rolled down her checks as she punished herself with the memories. She was on autopilot as waves of anger, frustration, and lust battered her body. "It just doesn't make sense," she whispered. "How can I crave his body and want to beat him at the same time?"

Eve was only mildly surprised to find herself at Ebony's shop. Glancing at her watch, she noticed it was past ten o'clock. She'd been driving around for at least a half hour. The door was locked; however, Eve could see Ebony from the window. She knocked on the door and, with a shocked look, Ebony let her in. Eve knew her eyes must be red and swollen; she didn't know if it was that, or the unexpected visit that caused the surprised look on Ebony's face. Ebony was the only stylist in the shop, and it looked like she was almost finished with her sole customer. "Hey, girl. How's it going?" she asked over her shoulder as she walked back to her client.

"All right," Eve answered in a low voice.

"I'll be done in just a minute. Turn around." Eve did. "Oh yeah, you're due for an edging." The shop was silent as Ebony finished. "Okay, Louise, you're done." Although Eve knew Ebony wouldn't mention her condition in front of a customer, she was still grateful. Ebony handed her client the mirror, then she studied Eve as the woman looked at her hair from all angles. Ebony told Eve to sit in her chair as the woman handed the mirror back, and stood to pay for the services.

Eve sat. Nothing was said as Ebony turned the sign to closed, shut the blinds, and relocked the door. She grabbed her tools, put a cape on Eve, and began cleaning up her hairline. She started at the nape of Eve's neck. She used the comb to lift the hair up, then shaped it with clippers.

Ebony waited until she reached the side of Eve's head before she asked, "So, what's up?" Eve sighed. She knew she was here to talk and that she could tell E-bone anything, but she didn't know where to begin. Ebony knew Eve just about as well as she knew herself. "Start at the worst part and get it over with."

That's exactly what Eve did. "Noah made a fool of me and discussed our relationship with Regina."

"Who's Regina?"

"The receptionist at my office. She and Noah got together at some club last weekend."

Ebony stopped cutting and released a long, drawn out, "Ooooohhhhhhh."

"Then I made an ass of myself by going over there to kill him, and I wound up pressed against a wall panting instead." Eve covered her face, so she wouldn't have to look in the large mirror directly across from her.

Ebony swiveled the chair around so Eve faced the wall. "Well, I know you're having a hard time with this, but to be honest that doesn't sound so bad. I can definitely think of worse things than to be caught between a hunk and a hard place." Her comments didn't get the expected chuckle from Eve. Uh oh, Ebony thought.

Eve continued as if Ebony hadn't spoken. "He talked about us, Ebony. I feel humiliated. I will be humiliated if he continues to gossip and this gets around! And that's not all. I went to the Links fashion show tonight and Rico Suave was there, drooling over the models! How could I let him kiss me like that when, not an hour before, he was busting his pants for the babe in the swimsuit? I wonder if he's going to tell her about us."

Now that sounds absolutely ridiculous, Ebony thought. She didn't voice her opinion because she didn't want to upset Eve more, but that didn't sound like Noah. She and Yoshi had been out with Noah several times over the years, and he was way too reserved to openly lust after a woman. His usual style was to sit back and let the women come to him. And like sharks smelling blood, they always came. Ebony couldn't figure out if it was his good looks, aloofness, or some combination that drew them in, but he always seemed to have his pick while expending very little energy. Ebony kept her thoughts to herself and continued to clip Eve's hair while she listened to her vent. After a time, she got tired of Eve fussing about other people. "Eve, who cares what people think. The question is, how do you feel about Noah?"

Eve angled her head back to glare at Ebony. "How can you ask me that, E-bone? I hate him, and I despise being the butt of gossip. How can you expect me to separate my feelings for the man from the fact that he's running his mouth and trying to destroy me?!"

Ebony twirled Eve around to face her. "Oh, Eve, I'm sure he's not trying to destroy you. Now you know you're exaggerating."

"You're right. He's so egotistical, inconsiderate, and selfish that he's probably not thinking about me! He's just out there living up to his reputation. I'm just another notch in his belt! Who cares if my family and I get hurt in the process? Or maybe he's trying to get back at me because I didn't want to go public with this. He's accomplishing two goals at once: shaming me and furthering his reputation."

Eve rattled on without interruption from Ebony. She knew Eve was too incensed to be rational, so she went back to the quiet listening role, and finished Eve's hair as she continued to condemn Noah's character. When Eve's hair was perfectly shaped and faded, she sat in the chair across from her. She listened attentively and nodded her head or chuckled when appropriate while patiently waiting as Eve had her say. Eventually, Eve ran out of air and stopped talking. She splayed out in the chair: head back, throat exposed, arms and legs spread as wide as possible, her bare feet sticking out of the full-length dress. Ebony continued her patient vigil until, with a sigh, Eve sat straight, crossed her legs, and gave her a weary, drained smile. Ebony smiled back, handed her the mirror, and watched as Eve checked her hair from all angles.

"You've done a great job as usual." She gave Ebony the mirror back and slipped into her shoes. Eve didn't attempt to pay Ebony. She had stopped accepting her money years ago.

Admiring her handiwork, Ebony told her, "You need to let me texturize it in a couple weeks."

Eve nodded. "Thanks for listening to me." She stood and bent down to the still-sitting Ebony and kissed her on the cheek.

"Oh, girl, that's what I'm here for. Shoot, you've certainly listened to me enough over the years." She stood and gave her a big hug. "I'm sorry all I could do was listen. I feel like I should have some answers for you."

"Maybe answers elude you because there are

no easy ones or face-saving ones. I have to look to myself. I made a big mistake taking a chance on Noah. Now I have to live with it. The sad thing is that I can't put all the blame on him because I went to him knowing what he's like."

Ebony wondered if Eve really knew what Noah was like. She returned the hug when Eve gave her another.

As Eve walked to the car, she said, "Oh, by the way, your hair looks great."

"Eve, it's in a ponytail."

"I know. It's classic, simple, and it looks good. A nice change from all the curls, updo, and other exotic stuff you do."

Ebony just shook her head at her.

When she reached her Bug, Eve sat down with a heavy sigh. She told herself that she'd ranted and raved, screamed, and vented. Now it was time to settle down and go on. The first step to doing that was going home to face herself. But first, she had to face Beulah. Eve opened the garage door to find her standing there.

Beulah stepped aside, and Eve pulled into the garage. While she reached to grab her purse from the passenger's seat, Beulah opened her door. "Girl, I've been worried sick about you! You said you were coming straight home, and that was hours ago!"

"I'm sorry, Mom."

"I was just about to call all the hospitals and wake up Sean!"

Eve slowly got out of the car, forcing Beulah to move back. She pecked her cheek and apologized again. "I went by the shop to see Ebony. See." She twirled around. "She gave me a trim."

Beulah thought Eve should grow her hair longer than an inch and, at choice times, told her so. "What hair? It's already less than an inch!"

"Oh, Mom, stop fussing at me. I'm sorry I made you worry. I should have called you and let you know what I was doing."

Beulah followed her through the garage, still grumbling. "I don't see why you're going to get a haircut so late at night anyway. It just doesn't make any sense. If I hadn't seen Noah, I would have called the police a long time ago."

Eve passed through the door leading from the garage into the kitchen. She twirled around at the mention of his name. "You saw Noah!"

"Sure. At the end of the evening, when we stood to leave, I saw him across the runway. He was looking at you like you were a martini, and he was Dean Martin. He left before I could say hello. Your being late doesn't have something to do with Noah, does it?"

"Of course not, Mom." Eve hoped her mother

didn't ask if she knew he was there. She didn't want to lie or discuss the situation with Beulah. "I'm beat, Mom, and I'm in the middle of a trial. I'm really sorry I made you worry," she said, kissing her cheek again. "I'm going to turn in." She left Beulah in the kitchen shaking her head.

After Eve left, Noah put down his fork. He stared in space. He disregarded his throbbing body and told himself what he did was for the best. Sex with Eve was phenomenal, but it alone just wasn't enough for him anymore. When he first stood, he had no intentions of kissing her. He saw the pain and wanted to comfort her; wanted to tell her that whatever nonsense she'd heard about him and Regina was a lie. But then she reverted to Ms. Freeze, and something inside of him took over. Damn it! He pushed his food away. She made him lose control, and he didn't like it! He laid his arms on the table and rested his head on them. What to do about Eve? She was driving him crazy!

The more time passed, the angrier he became. He was indignant by the time Dina called about a half hour later. Her four-day trip had been extended to eight. She'd returned home a couple of days ago, but she spent the first day sleeping and reacquainting herself with her fiancé, so she was just now getting around to checking on him. After hearing his hard, short tone, she knew something was wrong. She asked him, and as she expected he said, "Nothing." Knowing how hardheaded he could be, she didn't waste time trying to pry it out of him. Instead, she hopped in her car and drove over to his condo.

Noah heard the bell, and his heart accelerated with the fantasy that it was Eve, returning to apologize. After he graciously accepted her apology, they would go to bed and see who had the most stamina. "Oh, it's you," he said when he saw Dina. "Gee, handsome, don't get so excited. It's been two weeks since you saw me last. Don't you miss me?" Dina said as she hugged him and came into the condo. She made herself comfortable on the couch and looked around, reflecting on how much she liked her brother's place. She and Tim were becoming cramped in their one-bedroom apartment, and as soon as they were married, they would be looking for a new space. Her brother's place wasn't like the stereotypical bachelor's pad. He usually kept it very neat, the décor matched, and it never smelled. The furniture wasn't what she would have picked, but the heavy, plush black leather fit Noah. So did the black lacquer coffee and end tables. An entertainment center, which featured a sixty-inch big-screen TV, dominated the room. There were no pictures decorating the walls. In fact, the only picture in the whole place was in his bedroom. It sat on an oak nightstand that matched the queen-size sleigh bed. It was a happy picture of their family taken about twelve years ago.

Noah grabbed the remote off the top of the TV and began flipping channels. "Yeah, I missed you. How long have you been back?"

"I got in late yesterday. Turn that off and come sit down." She patted the couch.

Noah sat beside her and pushed the off button. "How were your flights?"

"Long and tiring. I'm glad to be home. I spent most of the day catching up on my sleep."

"Oh, that's good. How's Tim doing?"

"Tim's fine."

"How's the planning going?"

"Great. The wedding coordinator is an angel. I would've eloped a long time ago without her."

"Good."

Noah seemed distracted to Dina. "So, what about you? How have you been, handsome?"

"Fine." The pain was too raw, the confrontation too new for him to discuss it rationally with his sister. He just wanted her to go, so he could deal with it in private.

Dina grabbed his hand and squeezed it. "That's not what Mom says. She's fretting about you."

"Why would she be worried?" Noah frowned. "I even went to see her last week. She knows I'm okay."

Dina sat straighter, "Noah. You went to see Mom on a Saturday night. You haven't been in that house on a Saturday night since Dad passed. I thought she was joking when she first told me. That, little brother, is conclusive evidence that something is bothering you."

Noah shrugged his shoulders. "Nothing serious is wrong. I just needed a break from the club scene. I hadn't visited with Mom in a while, so I killed two birds with one stone."

Dina wasn't convinced. He looked tense, and he kept tightening and releasing his right fist. No, this wasn't her easygoing brother. His tone wasn't rude or harsh, but it was clipped, like he was thinking of something else and answering her quickly, so he could get back to his musings. She knew if she pushed, he would get irritated. She touched the back of his hand, rubbed it, and held it gently. He gave her a weird look, and she smiled at him. "Does this have anything to do with Eve?"

He scowled at her, and that was all the answer she needed. "Okay, I won't bug you, but you know you can always talk to me."

"Yeah, I know. Go home, sis. I'm fine." He hugged her and escorted her to the door. He loved his sister, but he couldn't wait to get rid of her. He wanted to be alone with his thoughts. Dina took the hint and turned to leave after kissing his cheek.

He watched her leave and suddenly called her.

"What?" she yelled from her car door. He motioned her over.

"I'm telling you this because I know you'll go home and rack your brain, dreaming up scenarios of what's wrong with me. Then you'll call Mom and the both of you will spend way too much time and energy pondering the mystery. So, I'll tell you this much, and you promise me that you'll tell Mom I'm fine."

Dina nodded.

Noah took a deep breath and spat it out. "I wanted a real relationship with Eve, and she wants something completely different."

"Yeah?" Dina urged him to go on.

"She wants a stud service."

"What?!"

"Wait. I'm not being fair. She wants to see me privately until she decides if I'm good enough to date."

A woman being hesitant was the last thing Dina expected to hear about. Women had been swarming her brother for as long as she could remember. "Okay." Dina nodded, thinking about Noah's words as she leaned against the doorjamb. "You must really care for this woman; otherwise this suggested arrangement wouldn't bother you as long as she was in your bed."

Noah wasn't ready to admit that to himself, much less Dina. "No, Dina, you're wrong. It would bother me under any circumstances." His voice was hard, and he didn't elaborate any further.

"All right." Dina let the issue go. She was beginning to get angry herself with the thought that, if first impressions were correct, her brother had finally met a decent woman that he cared for, and she wanted to play games. "Thanks for letting me know, and I'll tell Mom you're okay." With a small wave, she got in her car and left.

As she was driving, she examined her brother's words. She imagined the twilight zone he must be in. If this weren't the first good woman he'd met in his adult life, Dina would have found the situation very funny. But she knew her brother was more like her than he cared to admit. He wanted a bond, a connection like she'd found with Tim, like her parents found and nurtured for four decades. Her heart ached for her brother, and her loyalty made her take on his anger whether it was justified or not. From the car, she called her mother on the cell phone. "Hi, Mom, it's me."

"Hi, honey. I'm glad your home. How were your flights?"

"They were fine. I talked to Noah." Dina stopped at a red light.

"Good. What's up with him?"

Dina rarely hid things from her mother, but she always kept Noah's secrets. "Actually, he's fine, Mom. I think he's getting tired of the single scene, and that's why he came over. He just wanted to take a break."

"Huh, I could have sworn something was wrong with the boy. Are you sure that's all it is?"

The light turned green, and Dina's foot moved to the gas pedal. "As sure as I can be. He was completely normal when I talked to him a minute ago."

Her mother still sounded skeptical. "Okay, if you say so. Well, if he's getting tired of the playboy scene, maybe he'll be ready to settle down soon. I would really like some grandkids. You and Noah need to get busy."

Dina chuckled. "I am getting married, Mom. I'm taking some steps in the right direction."

"I'm sure that's not the only steps you're taking since the two of you live together."

"Mother!"

"I'm glad you two are becoming legal, and keep an eye on your brother."

Ebony went home that night, hoping that Yoshi knew something about what was happening with

Noah and this Regina person. She knew her hubby liked to stay out of "all that mess" as he called it. He hated gossip and lectured her about how much she engaged in it. She always told him, "I'm a hair-dresser. Gossiping is part of the job responsibilities, and that's why most of the people keep coming to the shop. It's not how well you do the hair, but how much you're entertained." Yoshi would just shake his head as if to say, she's hopeless. As far as Noah's wild reputation, he didn't justify, glorify, or berate. He ignored it, saying that no matter what he did with women, he was an excellent firefighter and a good friend. Sure he liked to tease Noah, in general, but he always said what, whom, and how Noah dated was his own business.

Ebony knew Yoshi's attitude was developed through pain. He was a military brat. His mother was Japanese and his father was a black soldier. The two married and had Yoshi, their only child. His father was stationed in Japan until Yoshi was eleven. Then the family moved to Fort Polk, Louisana. Yoshi and his mother suffered from culture shock. The young mixed-raced Yoshi was teased, harassed, and gossiped about until he showed his martial arts skills and beat up one of his tormentors. After that, he still suffered the effects of cruel classmates with rabid tongues, but he was never physically threatened or loudly talked about in public. Over time, he adjusted to his new world, and the new world adjusted to him, and he even made friends.

Despite his history and his attitude, Ebony was hopeful he would know something because she remembered that Yoshi had recently gone out with Noah, and maybe he'd seen Regina and Noah together.

Ebony had to wait to ask Yoshi because he was extremely amorous when she got home. He answered the door in the buff, and all thoughts of Eve flew from Ebony's head. Yoshi rose early the next morning because he had to report to the station by eight. Ebony was so exhausted, she could only groan when he engaged in a little prework grope. She was too pooped to fondle him back. Rigorous lovemaking and standing on her feet for twelve hours had worn her out. Her first appointment was at eleven, and she planned to stay right where she was, sprawled out in the middle of the bed, until the last possible moment.

Ebony's next opportunity to ask Yoshi didn't occur until Wednesday morning when he came home. She didn't want to bother him at the station, and she didn't want to do it over the phone. Also, she rationalized, the time would give Eve a chance to calm down and possibly be more objective. Yeah right, she told herself. However, when Yoshi got home, he was worn out from fighting a restaurant fire hours before. Yoshi said there was talk that the owner had set it on purpose to get out from under his debt. He planned to use the insurance money to pay his bills. Just the thought infuriated Ebony. Here her husband was risking his life to fight a fire that might have been intentionally set for selfish, greedy reasons? Didn't that idiot know that people got killed in fires? Yoshi usually didn't tell her when he fought a blaze where arson was suspected because she got so upset. But this time Yoshi's friend had been hurt. The burns would leave permanent scarring on his arms and legs, but with time and with extensive therapy, he would get the use of his limbs back. Yoshi had spent two hours at the hospital until he heard that his friend would be all right.

The guys in Yoshi and Noah's unit had to work overtime until the schedule could be rearranged to compensate for their injured coworker. Yoshi volunteered to cover that night. That meant he would be gone by the time Ebony got home from the shop. Considering the circumstances, Ebony didn't want to bother him about Eve. So, she waited until he came home Thursday morning when she turned the tables on him, and met him at the door completely nude. After making slow and leisurely love, Yoshi stayed up to eat brunch with her. Her first client wasn't due until one. When she left for work, he planned to go back to bed.

When she asked, at first Yoshi just gave her that "honey, why are you bothering me with this" look. She reached over the table and rubbed his cheek with hers before kissing it. "Please, babe, it's important."

Yoshi sighed and set down his spoon as he thought. "Regina? Regina? That name sounds familiar. Oh, yeah, I remember," Yoshi said, snapping his fingers. "She's the chick we ran into that night I went out with Noah. Remember when I went out with him to cheer him up?"

"Yes, did he go home with her?" Ebony ate a bite of cereal.

"No. Noah didn't want any parts of her, and believe me many were showing. Not that I was looking," Yoshi quickly added after seeing Ebony's face. "Yeah, she came on to him strong. Noah was polite but he showed no interest."

"Well, that hoochie mama has Eve in an uproar." She brought her husband up to date.

Yoshi had a good laugh. "Well it sounds like she's playing games with Eve, and winning, if Eve believes all that nonsense. Noah never talks about his women, so even if he had gone with Regina, I don't believe he would have talked about Eve."

"Good. My gut was telling me Noah wasn't that

kind of man, but Eve wasn't trying to hear that."

"Yeah, I could see that. Eve's almost as scary as you when she's on the warpath."

Ebony threw her napkin at him and took both of their cereal bowls to the sink. She bent to his kiss and then said, "I have to get to the shop. See ya tonight, tiger."

He growled at her.

Ebony couldn't wait to call Eve. She used her cell phone and dialed Eve's office number from her car. She got her voice mail. She pressed zero, and the receptionist told her Eve was signed out to court until noon. "Damn," Ebony uttered to herself. She returned to voice mail and told Eve she wanted to meet her for lunch because she had important news. She needed to tell her face-to-face that Regina was full of shit.

Eve called her back at 12:30 and reached Ebony's answering machine. She told Ebony she just got out of court, so it was too late for lunch, and if it was real important, to come by the house when she left the shop. Then she asked if Ebony was pregnant. Ebony laughed when she eventually listened to the message. Eve knew Yoshi wanted a baby, yet Ebony wasn't quite ready. Although she'd been working with hair forever, it had always been for other people. A couple of years ago, she and Yoshi scraped enough money together for her to start her own shop. Things were rough the first year, but now it was picking up. She wanted to insure the shop's success before she took the time to have a baby. Yoshi tried his best to be empathetic, but she knew he was disappointed and worried about her age. She kept telling him she was only thirty-four, and women were having babies in their forties these days. This knowledge eased his anxiety a little; however, she knew he wanted to start growing their family.

At 12:45, Eve stared at the open file on her desk. She munched on her turkey sandwich, and acknowledged that the already sour case was becoming rancid. She'd talked to the detective assigned to the case earlier in the day and it wasn't looking any better. It was a vehicular homicide where she needed to prove that the accused was the driver, and that he'd been drunk when he smashed his car into a telephone pole, killing his two passengers. Establishing that he was drunk was the easy part because he had a blood alcohol level of .32, which was four times the legal limit of .08. Showing that he was the driver would be infinitely more difficult. The accused was the sole survivor, and he claimed that one of his deceased friends was the driver. However, everyone who knew the accused claimed he was so proud of his rebuilt '65 Mustang that he would never let another sit behind the wheel. The car was smashed up and badly burned, so it would be hard to get evidence from it. Even so, Eve was hoping that the technicians could find something showing that the accused's injuries were consistent with being in the driver's seat. If this could be confirmed, Eve could file charges against him.

Eve reread the police report, ignoring the loud voices and laughter that she could hear despite her closed door. Her coworkers were deep in the throes of a pizza party in honor of Regina's last day. Eve refused to attend. She didn't care if her absence was noticeable or awkward. Seeing Regina was torture. It didn't bring on anger, but overwhelming jealousy. Imagining the two of them together, visualizing Noah doing to Regina what he'd done to her, made Eve want to kill, and then hide behind the temporary insanity plea because the two of them were driving her crazy.

Eve closed the file in front of her and leaned back in her office chair. The case wasn't going to get any better because she kept staring at it. She stood up and walked to the window. It was a windy, rainy day, and the waters of Puget Sound clashed around like a giant spoon was stirring it up. The water fit Eve's mood, and she felt camaraderie as she watched the angry waves. She didn't have to go to court that afternoon, but she looked at the clock out of habit. Restless, she decided to take a trip to the precinct and talk to the detective in person. Maybe she could tag along if he was going to speak to any of the witnesses.

Regina watched Eve walk past the lunchroom and make her way to the elevator. Every time she saw Eve, her face grew hot with humiliation. Nearly a week had passed, and the feeling was intensifying instead of dwindling. No woman had gotten the best of Regina once she'd decided to challenge her. She wanted to leave Washington State with that record intact. Eve might be stupid enough to think the battle was over and done with, but as far as Regina was concerned, she'd only made a momentary retreat. Regina left the lunchroom and stopped at the corner near the lobby, casually watching Eve's back as she waited for the elevator. She only half replied to the many congratulations thrown her way as a plan began to gurgle to life and take form in her head. She smiled and turned away from the corner when the elevator swallowed Eve inside.

Though Eve and the detective failed to uncover any new evidence, she was pleased that she'd gotten out of the office, and away from Regina for most of the afternoon. It was about 3:30 when she stepped off the elevator, and at first, she didn't notice it. The peculiar stares and odd glances were lost on her as she made her way to her office. Her head was full of her adventures with the detective.

They had spoken to several of the suspect's friends, and all of them claimed that he was incredibly obsessive about his cherry-red classic Mustang. They said, a person had to be special to ride in it; the owner would rip a passenger's head off if he slammed the door; you couldn't eat in it; and he'd curse you for a week if you lit a cigarette in it. No one could picture the suspect letting another touch his keys! That was unheard of. Not even his mother, who bought the muscle car for him, was permitted to do that. One friend put it best when he said, "If someone else was sitting behind the wheel, there must have been a gun pointed at his head." It was circumstantial evidence that the accused was indeed the driver, yet it was still persuasive. It would be even more convincing if the defendant's injuries proved to be consistent with being in the driver's seat, Eve consoled herself as she made her way toward her office.

When she passed the receptionist area, she noticed that the chair was empty, and Regina's personal effects were missing. She took that as a sign that the witch was gone. "Good," she mumbled under her breath. As Eve continued down the hallway, a prosecutor named Jerry started wailing like a wounded animal. He lifted his arm above his head and waved it around in a circle while smiling at Eve.

Jerry was known to be a jokester. Eve stopped walking and looked. His wild dance seemed to be aimed at her. "Jerry, what are you doing?"

Jerry kept grinning and didn't answer her directly. "Don't you know the sound, Eve? I'm a fire engine." Then he started singing some song that Eve didn't recognize about rockets in flight and afternoon delights. Eve giggled at his antics. People came out of their offices and poked their heads around corners. Some joined in and sang with Jerry and others laughed like Eve. She didn't know what to think about the strange behavior. Shaking her head, she slipped into her office.

She immediately noticed the note taped to her computer monitor. There was no title or greeting, just a folded piece of yellow legal paper. Eve picked up the paper more interested in Jerry's weirdness than the note. She had no reason to be apprehensive. Friends or colleagues would often drop by and leave her a message if she was gone. However, this was the first one that had been taped to her monitor. Usually, they left it in her message box or on her office chair. Eve began reading the note with only half a mind; the other half was on Jerry and the drunk driver. As soon as she recognized the handwriting, the slip of paper had her full attention. Because Regina was the receptionist, Eve had been receiving notes from her for about two years now, and only Regina wrote with such large dips and swirls. The writing was beautiful and had a childish quality to it. Eve could feel the pressure start in her chest as she read the short note. She threw it to the floor and quickly turned on her computer. "Hurry up," she whispered as the screen came to life.

"Read your e-mail, Eve," was all that was printed on the paper. She rushed to do so, anxiety making her motions jittery.

"all@seattlelaw.com" was written in small, block letters at the top of the e-mail. This was the first thing Eve noticed because it meant that it was a global e-mail. Everyone in the office network received what Eve was about to read. It started out pleasant enough. Regina wrote:

"Thank you to the entire office for all the good times, and believe me, I have had plenty during my two and a half years here. It's been a great experience working here, and I have learned so much from each and every one of you. I would like to write a special note to each person, but this e-mail would be a hundred pages long. However, I can't leave without thanking one very exceptional person, from whom I've learned so much. That person is Eve Garrett. Eve, I'll always be able to look back and say, you really know how to take advantage of a lunch hour."

Eve stopped reading and closed her eyes to steady herself. Jerry's silliness and the stares were beginning to make sense. She opened her eyes and read on.

"All of us thought you were in your office working when you didn't join us in the lunch room. A red-hot member of the fire department makes me wonder if you are really all work and no play. Eve, do you really know the true meaning of afternoon delight?"

Eve's hand flew to her mouth to stifle the gasp. That bitch! How could she imply such a thing? Eve quickly read the e-mail again, then rubbed her arms vigorously to stop herself from trembling. "Stop it, Eve." She swiveled away from the screen. "You don't have the luxury to fall apart now." She could imagine her coworkers listening at her door to hear her reaction. Regina expected her missile to humiliate Eve, and she'd been successful, but she'd be damned if she let the rest of the office know. She wouldn't give Regina that satisfaction! Eve turned back to the computer, and deleted the e-mail with quick, hard strokes on the keyboard. "I could reply to it," she uttered to the empty office. "But what would I say? Regina's a psycho bitch that just wants to hurt me for some unknown reason." Sighing, Eve decided there was no dignified response she could make. She wouldn't stoop to

Regina's level. She'd keep her head above the fray and hope for the best. The phone rang, interrupting her thoughts. She answered it, and then left her office.

CHAPTER 10

The shock wore off by the time Eve reached home that night. Every time she thought of Jerry whooping and waving his arms around, she tensed with embarrassment. It would wash through her, leaving her feeling drained. When she wasn't feeling mortified, she felt angry. She wanted to find Regina and relocate her mouth for her. Maybe break off each of her fingers and shove them in a meat grinder so she'd never be able to type again. After she did all of this, she would ask her, why? That was the most puzzling thing. Was she attacking her because of Noah? Was she trying to scare away what she perceived as competition? If she was so wrapped up in Noah, why was she leaving the state? The whole thing just didn't make sense.

The doorbell rang, and Eve sat up in her bed. She had gone to her room as soon as she got home. So far, no one had disturbed her, but the doorbell reminded her that she'd told Ebony to come over. She hoped it was one of Sean's friends because the last thing she felt like doing was being sociable.

"Mom, Mrs. Beaumont is here!" Sean yelled as loud as he could.

Eve got up and headed downstairs. At the bottom, Ebony greeted her with a big hug. Eve asked, "What was that for?"

"Because I'm happy."

Ebony was practically glowing. "What, are you having a baby? I knew you'd be happy about it if it really happened!" Eve did her best to muster up some excitement.

Apparently, Ebony was fooled. "Down, girl, down. No, I'm not pregnant. I'm just happy. Can't a black girl just be happy?"

"No, not you, E-bone. You're more than a black girl; you're one with a devilish look in her eye and that scares me. What are you up too? I just know you're not trying to match-make after the Noah disaster."

"Hey, I was innocent there! He was only supposed to be your domino partner." She hurriedly continued before Eve could interrupt. "Anyway, that's not why I'm here. Well, it sort of is. I'm here to tell you the truth about Noah."

Eve looked puzzled and frustrated. "E-bone, to say I've had a bad day would be a gross understatement. The last thing I want to talk about is Noah."

Eve's comments did absolutely nothing to dent Ebony's enthusiasm. In fact, they encouraged her to make Eve understand. "Girl, you'll want to hear what I have to say. I guarantee it!"

Eve surrendered, figuring it would be easier to let Ebony have her say, and then get rid of her. "Okay, let's sit down so you can tell me about it." They both sat on the living room couch.

Ebony got comfortable, and then she began: "I talked to Yoshi about Ms. Thang; you know, Regina?"

Eve nodded. Before Ebony could continue, Sean came hobbling through. "Hey, Mom. Hi again, Mrs. Beaumont." He plopped down on the couch and used the remote to turn on the TV. Soon he was jamming to Rap City on BET.

"Uh, Sean, we were having a discussion. Can't you watch that in your room?"

He didn't take his eyes off the show, "Ahh, Mom, this TV's bigger, the reception is better, and the bass is boomin'. I need to watch the raps on this TV."

They both stared at Sean as he bopped around on the couch right next to them. Eve rolled her eyes as she motioned Ebony to the kitchen. Inside, Beulah was putting the finishing touches on her fried pork chops, potato salad, and mustard greens. "Oh, good, you're here. I wasn't sure because I haven't seen you since you got home from work. Hi, Ebony, it's good to see you. Eat, Ebony, you're getting thin."

"But, Ms. Beulah, thin is the goal. I'm supposed to be skinny."

"See, that's the problem with you youngsters. There's nothing wrong with a little meat on your bones. It gives your man something to hold on to. Eat some food."

Eve and Ebony both started chuckling. "All right, Ms. Beulah, I'll eat," Ebony managed to say. Beulah took off her apron and placed it on the back of a kitchen chair. "Eve, you eat too. I have book club tonight. I'll see you in a couple of hours." She hugged Ebony and kissed Eve on the cheek and left.

Ebony immediately went to the plate of chops and picked one up. Eve tried to resist, but ended up grabbing a plate. "God, I'm going to gain a hundred pounds if that woman keeps cooking like this."

"I thought you had her trained." Ebony took the plate Eve offered and started spooning up mustard greens. "No one makes greens like Beulah."

"I thought I had her trained too. She cooks healthy for a few weeks, then she reverts to this. Comfort food she calls it." Both women sat at the small dinette table and began eating. "So, what did you have to tell me?"

Ebony finished her bite before answering. "It just doesn't seem important compared to all this food."

Eve gave her an irritated look.

"Okay. Yoshi was there that night when Regina saw Noah in the club. He said Noah definitely wasn't interested in her, and he's positive Noah didn't discuss your relationship with her."

Eve put her fork down. "How does he know?"

"Earth to Eve. He knows because he was there."

Eve's heart began to pound, a captured bird within her chest. "I know he was there. You know what I meant, Ebony. How does he know what they talked about?"

Ebony kept eating, unperturbed by Eve's doubt. Finishing her greens, she started on the pork chop. "Eve, Yoshi was there with Noah," she said in between bites. "I'm sure he didn't eavesdrop, but he's intelligent enough to get the gist of what's going on. He said Regina was coming on to Noah all night. Noah kept her at arm's length, and he definitely didn't go home with her. What do you want? A videotape?"

Yes that would be nice, Eve thought.

Ebony got up and helped herself to a Coke from the refrigerator, and then she sat back down. "Come on, Eve, use your common sense. Yoshi and I both believe that Noah just isn't the type to spread his business to every hoochie mama he meets. Also, he cares for you, or he wouldn't give a damn about when and where you want to see him. This chick was trying to get under your skin, and you're letting her." Ebony took a long drink and looked quite satisfied with herself.

"You're being silly, and do you know why you're being silly?"

"No, but I'm sure you'll enlighten me." Eve crossed her arms.

"It's obvious! Because you like the guy, maybe even more than like huh? Your emotions are bouncing around like jumping beans, and they're scrambling the electrodes to your brain, so you're not thinking clearly. That's why you need me to think for you." Before Eve could respond, Ebony said, "You need to apologize and reconsider this secrecy thing."

Eve was quiet. "Come on, girl. I've seen you around him. I know you loved Todd, but you never lit up around him like you do with Noah." Eve glared at her. "Oh, shit. I said too much. Good thing I'm done eating. Don't get mad. I just love you, girl, and I want to see you happy, really happy." Eve watched as Ebony threw away her scraps and washed her plate. On her way to the kitchen door, Ebony stopped and ran a gentle hand over Eve's springy curls, "I'm going to go, and I'm asking you to think about the fact that the man's not a gossip or a liar." She kissed the top of Eve's head and began to leave.

"Ebony, wait a minute." She stopped at the door. "I had a really ugly day at work, and I'm aggravated about that more than I'm mad at you. Let me tell you what that, that, chicken head, Regina did!"

Ebony sat back down. "Chicken head! Eve, where did you learn such language?"

"E-bone, you forget I have a teenage son."

"Girl, I think some of this has to do with Noah. You meet him and you're doing booty calls and using slang."

"Ebony!" Eve was indignant.

"Don't, Ebony, me. My man, Noah, has loosened you up in a good way!"

Eve sat back in her chair. "Ebony, you sure know how to make me not want to tell you a thing."

Ebony lowered her eyes and tried to look contrite. "I'm sorry. Tell me what the chicken head did."

Eve smiled at Ebony's silly expression: downcast eyes with a big grin. She wasn't remorseful at all. Regardless, she was glad that she'd stopped Ebony from leaving. She wasn't quite ready to face what Ebony had told her about Noah, and sharing with Ebony would probably help her get beyond the shame she still felt about the e-mail. By the end of the tale, Eve's smile had melted into tight lips and a furrowed brow. "And that's not all, Ebony. I was called into my boss's office." Ebony grabbed her hand and squeezed. "I was so scared and feeling stupid for being afraid because I hadn't done anything."

"That's what I've been trying to tell you, Eve," Ebony interrupted. "You need to stop worrying about others so much because you have no control over them. All you can rule are your own actions."

"E-bone, do you want to preach or listen to what I have to say?"

Ebony sat back and listened. "As I was saying, Mark called me into his office. He was sitting behind his desk, and he twisted his computer around to face me. I recognized the e-mail. Then, he said, 'What's happening between you and Regina? Why would she write such nonsense?'"

"So, he didn't believe it?"

"No, thank goodness. Apparently, most of the office didn't believe it, but it certainly didn't stop all the questions and jokes. I told Mark, and everyone else that asked, that I had no idea why Regina did it. Although I'm sure she did because of Noah, she's attacking the competition."

"Oh, Eve, you can't blame Noah for this one. That chick is crazy, and you know it!"

"Ebony," Eve said putting her elbows on the table and leaning forward to make her point, "if I hadn't met Noah, I wouldn't be in this predicament. Do you know how embarrassed I was at work today?"

Ebony leaned back in her chair and crossed her arms. "Eve, you forget who you're talking to. I know exactly how you feel, and I can tell you that the little bit of embarrassment you faced today is nothing compared to having your ass kicked at work! Remember how we were reunited? You called me because I was a victim in a police report. That fool chased me around a crowded shop and knocked me out, Eve. I had to go back to work with bruises on my face. I wanted to quit so bad, but I couldn't because I needed the money. I cried every night and sometimes during the day in the bathroom. I wanted to just curl up and die. Be happy they're just teasing you at work. That's a hell of a lot better than everybody looking at you with pity in their eyes and a bunch of whispering that always stops when you enter a room or look their way. I

had problems with Yoshi at first because I thought
he pitied me more than he liked me. I couldn't
understand how he could really like a woman who
was stupid enough to get involved with a loser like
Ronny. And you know what? Ronny happened
years ago, I was even in a different shop, and still,
every once in a while, I catch someone talking
about it. How's that for shame and humiliation?"
Ebony had tears in her eyes.

"Oh, E-bone, I'm sorry. You're right. What happened to you is ten times worse, and I have nothing
to complain about." She grabbed her hand across
the table, and held it.

Ebony used her other hand and dabbed at her
eyes with a napkin. Skillfully, she avoided smearing
her mascara. "No, Eve. You have plenty to fuss
about, but put the blame where it should go, on
Regina, not Noah." There was too much going on
in Eve's head for her to admit the truth of Ebony's
words. She needed time to think and sort things
out. She smiled wearily at Ebony. Ebony got up
and pulled Eve to her feet. She hugged her hard
and said, "Just think about it, girl, okay?"

"All right," Eve said and sat back down as
Ebony left. Ebony's words about Ronny had hum-
bled her. True, Regina had done a mean, malicious
thing; however, she was gone, and it was time to
move on. People at work would get tired of teasing

her, especially if she rolled with the punches and acted like the whole situation didn't bother her.

Eve continued to sit, unable to avoid thinking about it any longer. The repercussions of Ebony's words about Noah washed over her. Some unreasonable part of her still wanted to be angry and continue to believe that Noah had a wagging tongue. Her psyche couldn't muster up the feeling. Despite herself, Eve felt lighter as if the birds in her chest had escaped, broken through her breastbone, and flown free. As the flock left, they took the twenty-pound weights off her shoulders. Noah didn't discuss me with Regina, she joyously repeated to herself. But why did Regina write the e-mail? The question still remained. Eve remembered what Beulah told her when her bike was stolen when she was eight. "Eve, some people are just mean. There's no explaining it; they're just mean." It was easy to believe that Regina was such a person.

"Forget Regina," she told herself. "She's gone, and the man didn't talk about you." Again she felt exhilarated. Her lightheartedness was short-lived. "Oh, God." She covered her face with her hands, and tried to rub the hotness away, which was caused by the acid-like embarrassment dripping through her system. Eve's mind was on playback as she relived how she slapped him. "How could I?" she whispered. She'd been a self-righteous fool to attack him the way she did without giving him a chance to explain, or even know what she was upset about. "He probably hates me," she said to an empty kitchen. Tears threatened. Her impulse was to call him. Humiliation stopped her. Sean's loud singing in the next room reminded her that she wasn't alone. She had to pass through the living room to get to the sanctuary of her room. BET had Sean so entertained, he didn't notice or even look in her direction when she passed behind him. It was one time in Eve's life when she was happy to be ignored.

🌼🌼🌼

Hours later, sleep refused to come. She tossed, turned, and pounded her pillow as she agonized over what she should do. The analysis wasn't made easier by the memory of how Noah looked at the model. She remembered that and wanted to take the easy way out and do nothing. Time would take care of everything, and they could both forget about each other. This option forced her to think about and face what she really wanted. Did she really want Noah out of her life? Three weeks ago, she would have answered with a resounding yes! Now the answer wasn't as clear. Well, if she was being absolutely honest, the answer was no she wanted him in her life. There was no denying that the man made her feel. He electrified her senses and not just in the bedroom. His conversation stimulated her; his wit kept her on her toes, and made her think. She was used to being able to verbally dominate others at will, but not so with Noah. When he chose to, he left her speechless, and she had to admit, this made him maddeningly attractive. Todd could stand his ground, especially when it came to overworking, but he couldn't verbally stump her. Noah could, and this ability drew her to him and gained her respect.

Then he had his soft side. He was so sweet with his sister, and so tender with children as he showed with the child at the Sonic game and her son. God, she just couldn't face how much she wanted to be with that man, so she hid behind the thought that she wasn't sure what she wanted to happen. She knew that the next move was hers. She had bombarded and pummeled him with misconceptions and accusations that were unjustified. It was up to her to try and make it right, but the fear of rejection made her tremble. What if he didn't want her anymore? As the Links Fashion Show provided, he wasn't sitting around pining away for her. But heck, if the tables were turned and he was constantly misjudging her, maybe she'd be drooling over runway models too. Her stomach cramped and rolled. She got up and went to the bathroom. Her attempts to use it were unsuccessful, so she swallowed a bunch of Tums to calm her belly, then she took a sip of Benadryl to escape her thoughts and help her sleep.

Twenty minutes later, Eve was still tossing and turning as she lay dreaming. Her dream was vivid and life-like. Later, she would reflect on how weird it was watching herself and being herself at the time. In the dream, she stood perfectly still behind a tree, waiting. She could feel the cool night air against her skin. Her flesh pimpled, but she didn't know if it was the air or anxiety that was causing it to do so. She knew the men were coming her way because the scouts told her so. Closing her eyes, she concentrated on the songs of the forest, not for enjoyment but for the disruption. She knew any interruption of the joyous melody meant that the enemy was near. Breathing deeply to help calm herself, she smelled the familiar heavy pine smell that hung in the air. She opened her eyes and focused on a nearby elk, foraging freely under the safety of darkness. She continued to listen and watch the animal, taking advantage of its keener senses. Suddenly, the elk raised its head, frozen in time, and then, within the span of a twitch, it was gone. Eve's fingers itched on her sword as she listened to the night rhythm change. Branches

groaned, twigs creaked, and leaves rustled as ani-
mals scurried away. Danger wove its way into the
night air, creeping up like a dense heavy smog
smothering the forest. The sleeping Eve's eyes
moved frantically beneath her eyelids as her limbs
twitched unnaturally.

Warrior Eve was a statue. The others were
already in position, and Eve knew they were as
aware of the approaching enemy as she. They all
waited in absolute stillness. And then they came.
Darkened forms crept through the trees, trying to
sneak up on their prey. But they were all well aware
of their presence and their intentions. The men
thought to take the women warriors by surprise.
They thought their attack was a secret, and they
planned to hide under the cover of darkness.
Unbeknownst to them, the women had spies and
allies everywhere. Eve felt fear and an incredible
sense of urgency. It chilled her, but she'd seen battle before, and she took the fear and put it in a hidden place deep within her.

Patiently, the women waited until the men had
slithered into the right position. All of a sudden,
there was a flurry of movement, and the men were
surrounded. Eve signaled the counterattack with a
blood-curdling scream. She handled her sword with
brutal determination, delivering blow after deadly
blow. Eve was not sure what she was fighting for,

but she knew she had to fight to the death. Blood was everywhere; its rusty scent filled her nostrils and she swung harder. The moans and groans of the dying filled her ears as she faced enemy after enemy. Soon, she faced an opponent who seemed mightier than the rest. The others faded and the two of them become larger than life. Eve knew that this was the battle that counted. Whoever won would be the victor, and this knowledge made her swing harder, thrust faster, giving her fighting a desperate edge. Her foe's face was invisible in the darkness, but instinctively she knew he was familiar to her. Their fight seemed endless because they both anticipated each other's moves. Eve was near the point of exhaustion when fate stepped in, and her enemy fell over a rock. Without hesitation, Eve ran her sword through his heart. He clutched the blade and struggled to pull it out. Eve stepped back and watched. Mysteriously, his face became clearer as his life force left him. Eve's heart began to pound when she realized it was Todd. She rushed to pull the sword out to save her husband's life. Her hand was on the hilt when the features suddenly change to Noah. She quivered with indecision. Should she pull it out or twist it further? Before she can decide, he died.

"No!" The shouted word startled her awake. Her legs were imprisoned in the sheets and she fought desperately to free them as tears streamed down her face. She was shaken, frightened, and disoriented. She wiped away water that had dripped in her eyes and she brushed her hair. Her hand came away wet, and she stared at it in confusion. Looking down, she realized that she was drenched, and her T-shirt was soaked. She shivered in the cool air. Finally, she managed to free her legs. She stumbled to the bathroom where she flipped the switch and squinted in the light's harsh glare. Eve was not prepared for what the mirror revealed: wide, troubled eyes; puffy lids; tears glistening on her face.

She heard a concerned "Mom?" coming from the bedroom doorway. Eve knew the bathroom door blocked Sean's view of her.

Taking a deep breath, she spoke as calmly as possible. "Honey, I'm fine. I just stubbed my toe on the way to the bathroom. I'm sorry I woke you." She hoped and prayed he would think the hoarseness in her voice came from sleepiness.

"Okay." She could hear him yawning, "Do you need help?"

She just wanted Sean to go back to bed, but his sweetness touched her and made her want to hug him. Glancing in the mirror, she knew her appearance would bring questions she wasn't prepared to handle. "No, baby, there's no blood. It's just sore.

263

Go on back to bed."

"Night," he mumbled as he shuffled back to his room.

Not being able to stand the sight of herself anymore, Eve fumbled around until she managed to turn off the light, then splashed water on her face. She stood with her arms and hands braced against the sink, head down, trying to gather herself. When she felt like she could walk without shaking, she made her way back to bed. Once there, she stripped off her wet clothes and climbed in naked. She pulled the comforter over her body and tried to make sense of what she now knew was a dream turned nightmare. She burrowed into the mattress and curled her legs into the fetal position, shivering from the cold inside and outside of her body.

The dream shook her to the core. She knew it would take her a while to analyze it fully, to figure out all of the nuances, but one message was resoundingly clear: Noah was in her, under her skin, running through her veins the way no one had before. The knowing popped into her head. Eve could no longer deny that there was some kind of unexplainable link between her and Noah. She could ignore him, pretend they had never been intimate, and he and the connection still wouldn't go away. She was addicted to him. Was Noah bad for her? Was that's what all this craziness was about?

This man had gotten to her like no other, and she was scared. When she looked into her heart of hearts, she was terrified of the way Noah made her feel. The thought of losing control horrified her and made her want to run from him and herself. However, she couldn't run far from Eve and maintain her sanity. Noah had his hooks, and other things in Eve, so she had to deal with him. Plain and simple, no way around it, she had to face Noah, or her unresolved feelings would pound her to death.

She knew that was only part of the nocturnal message. She had to deal with Todd. Common sense dictated that any romantic relationship would make her feel some guilt about her late husband, but her feelings for Noah were so much stronger than what she experienced with Todd.

She was first attracted to Todd because he was such a change from what she was used to. Track and the books had consumed her life at college. Consequently, most of the men she associated with were athletes. She quickly learned to keep them at arm's length because none of them seemed sincere, at least not about her, and there were too many groupies willing to do just about anything to be the girl for the month, week, or even the day. Todd was a breath of fresh air, so different from her norm. He was polite, considerate, studious, monogamous, handsome, and to top it off, he was crazy about her. Eve felt like she'd stumbled upon the jewel of the university. He was someone she could talk to. Someone who wanted the same things out of life: a good job and a family. She'd truly loved Todd in a quiet, comfortable sort of way. She felt content and secure in his presence.

At least that's how she felt until a few years before his death. Those years had been filled with a growing resentment of how much time Todd spent away from the family. Sean's craving for his father's attention made her realize just how much Todd worked, and it also made her reflect on how little time she spent with her husband. In college, they wanted to spend every spare minute together, even if they couldn't. Their lovemaking was not always frequent, but it was satisfying and something they both encouraged and looked forward to. Somehow, they floated even farther apart once Eve started working, then going to school. Their time together evaporated while they both strove for success. Sean's birth made Eve realize there was more to life, but it had the opposite effect on Todd. He insisted he had to work more for the betterment of his family. Eve resented that she honestly couldn't remember the last time she'd made love to her husband before the accident. She vividly recalled that she was looking forward to a weekend of catching up. Also, she resented that sometimes she felt like mother and father to Sean, and neither she nor Sean thought she was an adequate substitute at the time. She remembered Sean complaining because she took him to T-ball practice. No matter what answer she gave, he kept asking, "Why can't Dad take me? You don't even know how to catch." She didn't bother to tell him that his father probably couldn't catch either.

The memories were still painful, and now that she had a taste of Noah, she knew the passion with Todd was lukewarm at best. Noah had awakened her to how much she'd been missing. Noah proved that a man could be good, honest, and still make her burn up with lust and fire. In college, she didn't think she had that choice. She'd settled and loved a good man and sacrificed the excitement. Although in retrospect, she didn't know what she was missing until she exploded in Noah's arms. She squirmed at the memory.

What to do? She agonized over the question. Nothing wasn't a viable option. She had to face Noah and see if he still wanted to give it a try with her. She'd never been a wimp, and she wasn't about to start being one now. But where and how? She decided she would give herself time to plan a

267

strategy. But first, she had to make something right. She would do it at her earliest opportunity. Eve lay on her stomach and hugged her pillow hard. Sleep came easier now that she had accepted her feelings.

CHAPTER 11

Damn he was tired. Absolutely exhausted. But he had to admit that's how he preferred it. "God, what a day," he muttered, lying on his bunk, staring at the ceiling. It was Wednesday, and he wasn't scheduled to work that day or the next, but it was his turn to cover for Billy, the injured firefighter. He'd gone to see Billy soon after he'd been hurt. All firefighters knew there was a chance that they could be injured. Most ignored that possibility or else they wouldn't be able to perform their job. However, going into the sterile environment of a hospital to visit an injured coworker made the reality crushingly clear. When Noah glanced into Billy's room, he was asleep. He stood by Billy's bed and reflected on how precious life was, not something to be played with. He became

269

angry at the thought that the fire where Billy was injured could have been the result of arson. He thought it would be poetic justice if all arsonists suffered their own crime. They could just be burned out of existence.

A nurse entered quietly and disturbed his musings. Noah nodded and didn't speak; he didn't want to disturb Billy. The nurse saw that Billy was asleep, and she turned to leave. Noah dropped off the magazines he'd brought, quickly wrote a note, and followed her. After he asked, the nurse assured him that Billy was doing fine, and he would recover the full use of his arms and legs.

Billy would be out for a while, and they were getting a new person to take his position in their unit. The new person would start next week. Noah didn't mind the extra shifts. The more he worked, the less he thought about Eve. Or at least that's what he told himself, as he bunched up his pillow and turned on his side. It was the wee hours of the morning when Noah's weary eyes finally shut. Despite this, he was full of energy the next day.

The day started out early with breakfast, and then an equipment check. Noah was the first to climb on the trucks. He switched on lights and sirens, making sure they were working. He checked breathing apparatus and flashlights to see if there were enough on each truck. He lifted the hood and checked oil and coolant levels, and he looked at the gas gauge.

When he and his coworkers were done checking the gear, he volunteered to clean the kitchen and the bathroom, even though it wasn't his turn on the duty roster. Most firefighter hated housework, and the others happily agreed to let him do their chores. They teased him and asked if he was temporarily insane or just nuts, wanting to do the "shit" work as they affectionately called it. Noah only laughed and told them it was an early Christmas present. He didn't tell them how close they were to the truth. Eve was making him batty. So, he worked hard to keep himself fatigued because it was a lot easier not to think when he was brain dead. Thinking meant remembering--remembering the fire in Eve's eyes as she addressed the jury and the students. Remembering how good Eve's face felt tucked into his neck, her breath sending tremors through his body. Remembering how good she smelled when she came to him that morning.

Instead, he filled his nose with the smell of bleach, hoping it would cleanse him of Eve. As he scrubbed the shower, he intentionally focused on how undignified it was to expect a firefighter to scour toilets and wash windows. Even maids didn't have to do windows! He could tolerate washing dishes and sweeping floors, but cleaning the toilet seemed like a rotten thing to make a firefighter do. It seemed unfair to expect him to risk his life, and then come back to the station and disinfect the bathroom. Once, he asked his pop why.

His dad shrugged his shoulders and said, "Tradition. Firefighters have been doing housework for a hundred years, and I imagine they'll do it for a hundred more." As Noah stuck his gloved hand into the toilet bowl, he thought, to hell with tradition. It was time for the fire department to start hiring maids.

Noah finished cleaning and joined the others for the daily drill period where training was performed. Between fires, Noah though, the firefighter's job was rather tedious: an endless cycle of inspections, chores, training, and downtime. The joke around the stationhouse was that they couldn't have a fire because it would mess up the schedule. It was almost four o'clock, when free time would start, and Noah was wondering how he would keep himself busy. The piercing wail of the alarm cleared his mind of everything but the need to get ready.

Riding in the screaming fire truck, he learned that it was a house fire in the Central District. The area's name had been shortened to the CD, and many referred to it as the Colored District because of the large number of blacks that lived there. Over the years, the inner-city area had fallen into disrepair. However the CD was an area of change. Gentrification hit when suburbanites, both black and white, got tired of commuting, and realized that the CD was right next to downtown and the business district. The result was a very eclectic district where the culture of a neighborhood changed by the block. The house the firefighters were rushing to wasn't on one of the better streets.

A reporter for a small community paper once asked Noah how it felt to be serving some of the poorest sections of the city. Noah told him the only effect it had was to make him and the others he worked with more dedicated. He asked the reporter if he'd ever seen a kitchen fire in an affluent neighborhood? The family went to a nice hotel for a few weeks, and then they came back to an even better house. They had new draperies, new curtains, new wallpaper, new Formica countertops, new kitchen gadgets, new everything. He told the reporter to imagine that same fire in a poor neighborhood. When a firefighter looked at the burned-out hulk, he or she knew people were probably going to be sleeping in that house that night, or someplace even less desirable. So, Noah told the reporter that he and the others worked even harder, were more diligent when they fought a blaze in a less affluent area of town.

When the truck arrived, they were greeted by

the next-door neighbor who told them that he saw the entire family leave about a half hour before the flames started. The crew blew a collective sigh of relief. Three things raced through a firefighter's mind when he or she approached a fire: Is there anybody inside, how bad is the fire, and what's the immediate thing to do? All Seattle firefighters were trained as Emergency Response Technicians, but that didn't mean they enjoyed using their skills. The fire had consumed one small bedroom and was moving to the second. Noah and the team worked quickly. The strategy was to move from the unin-volved area to the involved area. This meant that they entered the house at places that weren't burn-ing, and then they surrounded the fire and put it out. Later, they learned an electric blanket was the cul-prit. Someone forgot to turn it off, it malfunctioned, and it ignited the fire.

Noah was performing a routine secondary search and security check when he found a small black puppy underneath the living room couch. It appeared as if smoke had overcome the pooch, rendering it unconscious. Noah picked up the dog and rushed outside the smoky house as he checked its vital signs. Nothing. He was so focused on the animal, he didn't notice that a news crew had arrived. Unbeknownst to Noah, he was being filmed. He ripped off his head gear, and immediately began CPR. His mouth covered the small puppy's nose and mouth while two fingers gently pumped its chest. Noah worked feverishly. Sweat formed on his forehead and dripped into his eyes, distracting him until he felt a twitch. He worked even harder as the twitch developed into a full-fledged tremor. The pooch wiggled with life. Noah looked up, wanting to shout to the heavens, I did it! The cameraman cheered and clapped his hands. Noah looked at him in confusion.

"I got it on tape," the man said as he gave Noah the thumbs up.

A white woman in a blue suit asked Noah if he could answer a few questions. Noah didn't want to answer anything. "Come on," she coaxed. "You just saved a puppy, and we got it on tape. This is a wonderful human-interest story."

Noah and the reporter turned when a car pulled up to the curb. A man, who Noah assumed was the father, got out of the driver's side of the car, looked at the house, and then turned to Noah with a confused, disbelieving look on his face. The woman got out of the front passenger's seat and leaned against the car as if she couldn't support herself, then began crying. The man circled the car and gathered her in his arms.

A boy, who looked to be about seven, ran to Noah jumping up and down. "Sparky's okay,

Sparky's okay." Noah gave the boy the dog, and Sparky began licking his face.

Both parents looked at Noah. He and the boy walked over to the couple. The woman clung to the man and both of their faces wore the same shocked, lost expressions that Noah had seen many times before.

"Look, Dad, he's fine." The boy held up the puppy.

His father managed to smile faintly, and he rubbed his son's head. Looking at Noah, he said, "Today's his birthday. Sparky, here," the man said pointing his chin toward the dog, "was his birthday present."

Before Noah could respond, the reporter was shoving the microphone in everyone's face. "Hi, I'm Cindy Emerson from Channel Five News. Did I hear you say that today's your son's birthday?" Noah hated being involved with the media. He understood that they had a job to do; he just didn't want to be part of it. He slipped away while the reporter was preoccupied.

🍎🍎🍎

"Mom, Mom, come here quick!"

"What does that boy want?" Eve muttered. She was in the kitchen fixing a salad.

"Mom, hurry up! You'll miss it." Eve put the lettuce down and went to see what Sean was fussing about.

He was in the living room, sitting on the couch with his broken ankle propped on the coffee table. He pointed to the TV. "I just saw the fireman. He's coming on next. I think he's a hero, Mom!"

Eve's stomach lurched. She forgot her dinner and rushed to sit by Sean. Her son had said he might be a hero, but that didn't mean he wasn't hurt. The commercials were agonizingly slow. Two minutes seemed like two hours. Then, the anchorman teased her by telling her that coming up was a story about a local fire, but first they were going to take a look at the weather. She groaned, and Sean looked at her funny.

She ignored the look. "Sean, did they say if anyone was hurt?"

"No, but they flashed a picture of the fireman holding a dog, so I'm pretty sure he's okay. You all right, Mom?"

Eve slumped as she relaxed. "Yes, I'm fine, Sean, and his name is Noah Russell. Mr. Russell to you, not the fireman."

"Okay." Sean was still gazing at her with a slightly puzzled look on his face. Then he smiled like he knew something.

The conversation at the Sonic game was still

fresh in Eve's mind. She wasn't ready for round two with the hip-hop-wise Sean. She wanted to resolve some issues with Noah first.

The story came on, and both were riveted to the TV screen. The reporter went through the details of the story while pictures flashed, showing the partially burned house. There were no casualties thanks to the valiant efforts of one fireman. Noah's image filled the screen and Eve's heart. He was cradling a small animal in his left arm while his right hand appeared to be massaging the dog. His mouth covered the animal's mouth.

"Yuck!" Sean sat back on the couch, obviously repulsed.

Eve glanced at him, "Sean, he's saving the dog. That's what firemen do."

"Mom, that's going well beyond the call of duty when you have to kiss a dog."

Eve forgot about Sean when the camera switched to a closeup of a small, brown-skinned boy. "He saved my dog. I'm so happy because today's my birthday, and Sparky was my present." Eve's heart melted.

"See, Sean," Eve said pointing at the TV. "He revived that boy's puppy."

Sean was beaming at her. "Yes, Mom, your fireman is quite a guy."

Eve gasped. Despite her shock, she found herself thinking, He's not mine yet, but maybe he will be. Sean laughed. Eve stammered, trying to contradict her son.

"Wait, Mom. They're talking to him."

The reporter was speaking. "Our hero was very reluctant to talk to us, but we did manage to catch him before the firefighters returned to the station." Noah was sitting in the truck, and the reporter had a microphone jammed into his face.

Noah dug in his pocket and pulled something out. He spoke, "I can't tell you how happy I was to save the puppy for the kid, but if you really want to help this family, why don't you start a fund to help them rebuild the house that burned on their son's birthday." Noah handed the woman a bill. "I'm donating the first twenty bucks."

The reporter turned and spoke to the viewers. "What an excellent idea." The camera closed for a tight shot of the reporter waving the money. "Back to you, Bob so you can tell folks out there how they can help this boy and his family." The picture switched to the newsroom where the anchorman gave information on where to send money.

"Let's donate, Mom. I've got some money." Sean hobbled quickly to his room.

Eve memorized the number flashing on the screen. She rushed to get pen and paper to write it down. Beulah came in from running errands, and an excited Sean told her about the terrific fireman. Beulah looked at Eve. Her beaming smile and head nod said, "See, Eve, I told you he was a good man." Between the three of them, they donated two hundred dollars.

Back at the station, everyone sat or stood at attention as they watched the news story. Noah was proud of himself, and he knew his coworkers were proud of him also. They switched between praise and good-natured ribbing. He wondered if Eve saw the story. His mother and sister and a few others had called to congratulate him. Would Eve call? He remembered their last encounter; how she'd slapped him. Anger sizzled through his chest. She wasn't going to call, and even if she did, he didn't want to talk to her.

CHAPTER 12

$\int$ aturday arrived, and Eve rose early. It was time to make things right, time to visit the graveyard. While Sean and Beulah slept, she dressed with care. She wore a simple navy blue dress with a high scoop neckline. Before heading to the car, she grabbed the vase of flowers that she'd purchased the night before from her dresser. In the car, she took extra care placing the colorful arrangement on the floor of the passenger seat. As she drove, she paid particular attention to the speed limit and her speed odometer to insure they were in sync. At the cemetery, she was equally careful as she parked and took the flowers out of the car.

Seattle was a beautiful city, even in the winter. Eve admired the deep green trees and lawn of the cemetery grounds. Once out of the car, she raised

her umbrella to protect her from the shower and lifted her face to enjoy the fresh scent riding on the
raindrops.

Eve had the cemetery to herself. On autopilot,
her low heels clicked along the cement until she cut
across the lawn to Todd's well-tended grave.
TODD DOUGLAS GARRETT read the massive
gray headstone. After she placed the flowers
beneath the stone, she traced the letters of his
name. She was surprised she didn't feel the least
bit angry. Usually, when she visited Todd, she
always felt varying degrees of frustration and irritation, mixed with a sense of love and guilt. This time
she just felt sadness.

Then, Eve did something completely out of
character for her. She sat down, cross-legged, on
the wet grass. She stared at Todd's name and said,
"What do you think about this mess, honey?"
Despite fierce concentration, Todd was silent.
"You're not going to help me, are you, Todd?" She
hung her head and studied her hands, which held
the umbrella handle. "You know, I loved you, and in
my own way I always will." She looked at his name
again. "I'm sorry I've been pissed at you for all
these years, but I can truly say I'm not angry anymore. Like Mom says, what happened was God's
wish and not for us mere mortals to understand.
Well, she didn't put it quite like that, but you get the

gist."

She smiled. "You'd be so proud of Sean. He's turned into a fabulous adolescent. He's a joy to be around, full of teenage fire that keeps me on my toes, and he's smart, absolutely brilliant in math, just like his daddy." After a short pause, Eve continued her monologue. "I don't know if you'd like him, Todd. He's so different from you, but he's a good man, and to use one of Mom's phrases, 'he'd do right by Sean.' Now I realize that both of us need a man in our lives, and I really like him." Eve took one hand off the handle, rested her elbow on her knee, and used her hand to support her lowered head. "No, Todd, I more than like him; I love him. Is that wrong?"

She studied his name once more, and then looked to the sky. Her heart filled with a sudden happiness, which she attributed to admitting her love. She dropped the umbrella, then clasped her hands to her chest and started giggling uncontrollable. Ignoring the wet grass and the rain, she laid back and laughed, shouting to the sky. "Is this your answer, Todd?" Arms and legs spread, she wiggled in the grass like she was trying to make a snow angel. She knew her clothes would be ruined, but she didn't care.

A movement to her left caught her eye. She glanced over and saw a worried groundkeeper. Oh, shit. I wonder how long he's been watching. He probably saw my underwear, and he thinks I'm nuts. She got up and waved to him. He leaned on his rake and nodded back. Heck, he's as crazy as me raking leaves in the rain, Eve thought. Disregarding the groundkeeper, she walked as close to Todd's headstone as she possibly could. It was too big for her to put her arms around, so she just spread them out as far as possible. She laid her cheek upon the cold, wet stone and breathed deeply. "Thanks, honey." She kissed the stone, picked up her umbrella, and headed back to the car without a second glance. She would still visit Todd's grave, but more as a friend than as a wife.

She was practically skipping by the time she reached the car even though she was soaked. She tried to brush off before she got in and found that it was futile. Wet grass clung to her hair, dress, stockings, and shoes, and she was shivering. She got in the seat, not caring as she turned up the heat full blast and drove home. This new sense of freedom, of rightness was well worth the price of a new dress and a car detail. She drove with her hands at the top of the steering wheel. The large diamond twinkled at her from the third finger on her left hand. Without a flicker to her new lightheartedness, she slipped the ring from her finger and put it in her purse.

When she opened the front door, Beulah poked her head out of the kitchen, spatula in hand. After staring at Eve a full thirty seconds, she asked, "Where in the world have you been, and what have you been doing?"

Eve laughed. Beulah continued to stare as Eve spun around, and she got a full view of her daughter. "I went to visit Todd, and we came to an understanding while I twirled around in the grass." Eve danced her way to her room, leaving a wet trail. Beulah shook her head and let the kitchen door swing closed. As she flipped pancakes, she muttered, "Either she's going crazy, or she's in love. Hey, maybe I'll be able to move out of this house soon."

Beulah loved her family; however, she sorely missed her independence. She stayed at her daughter's house because she felt like Eve and Sean needed her. They were both full of so much resentment and pain when Todd first died. Sean got better, but Eve reminded her too much of herself to leave. She didn't want her daughter to isolate herself out of companionship. Beulah was a realist, and she knew that this thing with Noah might not work out, but Noah had gotten the ball rolling. He woke up Eve's dormant emotions, so she'd have a chance of enjoying a fulfilling relationship with somebody. Just the thought made Beulah whistle and smile.

In her room, Eve retrieved the ring from her purse. She put it in her jewelry box, intending to save it for Sean. Closing the lid symbolized letting go of the past, and heading into the future with a renewed spirit.

All morning, Eve soared with the newfound sense of freedom. She'd released her past and given herself permission to feel and love again. Yet, she still had the dilemma of how to approach Noah. Every time she thought of something, she recalled her past temper tantrums and cringed with embarrassment. She knew her strength was directness-- at least it always worked for her in her professional career--but Noah wasn't court, and she wasn't in love with court like she was with Noah. Eve groaned. It all came down to the fact that she was scared. Terrified that Noah would laugh and say, "Well, you're too late, baby. I thought you were special, and now I know that you're too immature. I need a real woman, not one who comes ranting and raving to me over every little bit of gossip." God, Eve felt herself dying inside just imagining it. However, this limbo crap was killing her. She had to face Noah, apologize, and tell him how she felt. Then, she could start dealing with the aftermath.

That afternoon, Eve tried to reach Noah. He wasn't at home, and she was too anxious to leave a message. She called the fire station, pretending that Noah was a witness, and she needed to talk to him about a case going that week. She disregarded the guilt she felt about the teeny-weeny lie, but boy would Sean and her mother tease her if they knew. She was a stickler for honesty, and they'd get a big kick knowing she fibbed to find out "the fireman's" whereabouts. Her trickery was successful. She learned he was checking equipment, and he was scheduled to be off at eight the next morning. Eve told the person not to disturb him, and she would call back later. She was extremely hesitant to approach him while he was on duty, so she decided to gut out the wait.

One o' clock. Eve had the rest of the day to fill. She went to find Sean. He had a telephone connected to his ear. She piddled around while she waited patiently for him to get off. It took a half hour. Eve was on him the minute he hung up. "Sean, do you want to go hang out? We could go see a movie."

"Sorry, Mom. That was Susan, and she needs my help with geometry. I'm about to head over there."

"Uh huh, I'm sure that's your only reason for going there," she said sarcastically, "I've seen Susan. She's the pretty cheerleader."

Sean gave a mile-wide grin. "Yeah, that's the

one. Good thing I'm good at math. We're in the same class, and she's struggling."

Eve chuckled and playfully punched Sean's shoulder. "That's my boy, always willing to lend a helping hand, especially when there's an attractive girl involved."

"Yup." Sean's chest puffed out. "Just like Dad. Didn't he make the moves on you while he was your math tutor?"

"Yes, that he did, Sean. You're a chip off the old block. You're getting to be just as tall and handsome as he was. And I bet you thought it would be your basketball skills, and not your brains, that got you dates."

"Well, Mom, she noticed me because of my magical moves on the court. I think the math thing was secondary." Sean hobbled out the room with that comment. In a couple more weeks, the cast could come off.

Eve yelled, "Sean, how are you getting there?" He turned. "You're taking me, Mom."

"Oh, no problem. Thanks for asking first. It's not like I have anything to do today," Eve grumbled good-naturedly.

Eve wandered into the living room where Beulah was reading. "Hi, Mom. Do you want to go shopping or see a movie?" Beulah was so engrossed in her book, Eve had to ask her twice.

"Oh sorry, Eve. This is a really good book. I have to finish it by tomorrow for my book club. What did you ask me?"

Eve sighed and grabbed her car keys. "Nothing, Mom. I just wanted to let you know Sean and I are leaving. I'm taking him over to a friend's house."

Eve dashed to her room, and quickly changed her jeans for sweatpants and pulled on tube socks and running shoes. She left on her Sonics T-shirt. She met Sean at the car and told him she was going running after she dropped him off. She instructed him to call Beulah if he wanted to come home before the hour it would take her to run.

Sean looked at her like she was crazy and assured her that it would take much more than an hour to make sure Susan understood all of the finer points of geometry.

Eve guffawed at that.

Eve parked and grabbed her hooded windbreaker from the trunk. The rain had stopped, and a weak sun was making an appearance. Looking at the sky, Eve noticed a few dark clouds. "Better to be safe than sorry," she whispered to herself as she pulled on the light jacket. She looked around as she did her warm-up exercises. Seward Park was fairly crowded. Eve liked the park because it was close to her house, and it had two paths to choose.

Edwina Martin-Arnold

One that went through the park, and the other that went around the circumference.

Eve preferred the one that circled the park because it was longer--more than three miles--and it ran partially along the lake. Also, the wide trail was absolutely beautiful. Large majestic trees lined the path at the beginning. Eve had no idea what type of trees they were, but looking up at them always helped her put her problems in perspective. After about a mile, the trees opened up and revealed a breathtaking view of Lake Washington. On sunny days, the water sparkled so delightfully that regardless of her troubles, Eve always smiled. "There," Eve murmured. She'd spotted her mark. Competition always made Eve's workout more productive so, when she could, she would follow a routine that created a sense of rivalry. She would pick someone she thought was a strong runner and try to stay within a hundred yards of that person; then the last quarter mile, she would run all out and try to win. Usually, she picked men because they tended to be stronger runners and gave her more of a challenge.

The mark she picked today would be hard to beat. Eve stripped off her jacket. She was about to run fast enough to keep warm in a blizzard. She knew this because she'd picked this mark before and had yet to win. He was tall--at least six feet--

and his stride devoured the pavement. He wore a tight, long sleeve nylon top and shorts, revealing what Eve already knew he possessed, a tone body that shouted "I'm a serious runner." But the last clue was the most telling, his shoes. He wore Etonic. Eve considered Etonic to be the top running shoes, and they were expensive enough that only a running nut would buy them. Eve wore the same brand.

As Eve watched her rival, a woman on a bike stopped beside him and pecked his cheek before continuing her ride. A few more stretches and her rival started at a quick pace. Eve was right behind him. She had to run at about seventy-five percent to keep up with him, which was a real tax to her system. He always started out fast, and when he reached the water, he slowed a bit. Eve didn't know if he was taking a break, or enjoying the view. He picked up the pace when there was about a mile left to go. In the past, Eve's mistake was letting him get too far ahead of her. A hundred yards was too much space for her to close the distance at the end. She didn't have enough kick to catch him. This time she hoped to stay closer, if she didn't die from the pace, and maybe, sheer will would give her the stamina and speed to get him at the end.

Eve was so absorbed in her goal, she didn't notice the female bike rider who passed them several times. Each time she passed Eve's rival, they would blow kisses at each other. However, Dina almost fell off her bike when she recognized Eve. "That's where I know her from," she exclaimed to no one in particular. Now her feelings at lunch with her brother and Eve made sense. Eve was familiar because she'd seen her running at the park.

Dina's fiancé, Tim, went to Seward Park at least three times a week, regardless of the weather, to run. Dina joined him during the spring and summer, if the weather was good. Dina thought the weather was borderline yucky today, but she agreed to come to Seward Park because Tim insisted it would help relieve tension. They were getting married the next day, and both were feeling the strain of endless wedding plans. About an hour earlier, Tim threw up his hands and said, "Come running with me, Dina. I need to run before rehearsal dinner, or I'll go crazy."

So, they went to Seward Park. Dina usually rode her bike or sat in the sun and read while Tim ran. She hated running, and even if she liked it, she wouldn't run with Tim. He was much too serious, and he ran too fast. He'd be done before Dina ran ten feet. That's why she noticed Eve. She could keep up with her dynamo, and her body was the envy of any flight attendant who had trouble making the weight restrictions imposed by the airlines.

Dina remembered thinking, if I had a body like that I could eat anything I wanted. Dina disregarded the fact that Eve probably had that body because she didn't eat everything she wanted, and she was obviously into exercise. Dina enjoyed bike riding, at a leisurely pace, and that was about it.

Dina parked her bike, sat on the seat, and watched Eve and Tim as they ran the last half mile. Tim wore a bright purple shirt and was easy to see. Eve's short hair and form made her recognizable. As the two drew closer, it appeared as if they were racing. Eve caught up to Tim, and Dina could see surprise, then the strain on his face as he fought not to let her pass him. Although Dina wasn't a runner, she listened to Tim and his friends enough to know that Eve had good form. Her head was straight and didn't move from side to side, or up and down. She kicked her knees up high, and her arms pumped hard and straight, not crossing her body. She had a determined look on her face as she ran harder.

As Dina watched the struggle, she felt anger building in her belly and spreading throughout her body. Who was this Amazon? Who was she to doubt her brother's worth? Dina was well aware of her brother's outrageous reputation, and it did nothing to ease her growing wrath. She'd always wished she'd had a chance to give Noah's college flake a piece of her mind. It seemed reasonable to

Dina that she confront Eve.

Eve was slightly ahead when the two breezed past Dina. She was still ahead when they reached the place where they'd started. Eve stopped running and put her hands on her knees. Dina could hear her harsh breathing as she grabbed the water bottle attached to her bike, and walked toward them. The bottle numbed her hand it was so cold. She liked it that way, so she had filled it with ice before they left the house.

As she approached, she noticed that Tim was breathing hard, but he didn't look like he was about to die. Dina was worried that Eve wouldn't survive long enough for her to tell her off. She could see that Tim was concerned about her health too. She heard him tell Eve to walk it off. Eve straightened slowly and put her hands on top of her head while trying to shuffle her feet. "That's it," she heard Tim say as he walked slowly beside her.

Dina caught up with them and squirted cold water on Eve's head. Tim shouted, "Dina?" Eve jumped, then doubled over coughing and sputtering. Knees bent, she braced herself with a hand on the ground while the other clutched her stomach. She knew she was close to hyperventilating, and she tried desperately to calm herself so she could catch her breath.

Disbelief and confusion marred Tim's face as he

stared at her while lightly tapping Eve's back. After a time, Eve managed to stand and supported herself while she slowly recovered. Water dripped from her hair into her eyes, causing her to blink rapidly. Tim asked Dina to get a towel. Their car was parked close by. Dina quickly returned and handed Eve the towel. She watched Eve struggle to wipe her face and felt a twinge of guilt. She dredged up the memory of her brother's face the last time she saw him and used that to blot out the pangs.

Eve wiped her face and rubbed her head with the towel. She peeked at Dina and felt dizzy her mind reeling as recognition slammed into her. Her physical pain kept her focused. Each breath was cut short by a stabbing ache in her chest. She hurt so badly, she wanted to cry, but she refused to completely break down in front of this woman. Tim stayed by her until she stopped swaying.

When Tim was sure Eve wouldn't collapse, he walked over to Dina. Once again, Eve observed Dina while she was focused on Tim. God, she looked just like Noah, a female version without the muscles and the height. She had the same beautifully smooth mocha-colored skin, and the same long, straight nose. Her long, black hair was pulled back into a ponytail, and it sparkled in the afternoon sun. Earlier, she'd worn a bicycle helmet and Eve assumed that's why she didn't recognize her.

Tim reached Dina and asked, "What's going on?" Tim's arms were outstretched, and his body blocked Dina from Eve's view. He leaned down, and Dina spoke rapidly in his ear. Eve couldn't hear what was being said, but she imagined it wasn't complimentary. Tim turned back, and they both looked at her for a moment. Heat coursed through Eve's exhausted body. No one can accuse me of being a coward, she thought as she stared back defiantly. Tim smiled and nodded his head at Eve. Turning to Dina, he whispered, "Your brother may have met his match." Then, he left to go sit in the car, so the two women could have some privacy.

Eve stood with her hands on her hips and the towel slung over one shoulder. She was still breathing heavily. Dina walked up to her, and Eve handed her the towel. "Thanks."

"No problem." Dina took it. The two women held each other's gaze. Unsure of Dina's motives, Eve thought it best to be silent and let Dina speak first. Her wait was short.

"You know, I love my brother, and you may claim my opinion is biased, but it really isn't. He's a great guy. Not only is he handsome, he's morally sound and extremely loyal. He's a hero, you know. He saves puppies for little boys on their birthdays." Eve hid her smile. Dina was warming to the subject. "Now, I wouldn't presume to claim that my brother is perfect. He does have one fault that's incredibly irritating. He has lousy taste in women, and I use the term, women, loosely."

Eve took a deep breath, squared her shoulders, and stood a little straighter. Dina took note and continued as if Eve hadn't reacted. "At least he did until he met you. I was so pleased to meet you that my heart jumped for joy. I thought to myself, okay all of my preaching has finally sunk in, and my brother is infatuated with a real woman. I'm a good judge of character, and I knew you could be a fabulous partner for Noah. Someone he could depend on, and not just have the strength sucked from him with nothing in return. In other words, you were independent, and you had substance combined with self-respect. Plus, you two looked marvelous together."

Dina stopped to breathe, and Eve caught herself before she said thank you. "And then you had to..." Dina seemed to be at a loss for words. She looked at Eve; she knew Noah would kill her if she revealed how much he told her. "Actually, I don't know exactly what you did, but I do know my brother cares a great deal for you, and you've hurt him. I just don't get it. I have friends like you. I see women like you on the talk shows, in movies like *Waiting to Exhale*. All of you say that all you want is a good man, and when you find one, you abuse him, try to use him, and trash his feelings like they're nasty socks."

Eve had to laugh at that. Dina looked murderous. Before she could speak, Eve butted in, "You're right!" Dina still looked angry. "No, Dina, you're right!" She took a chance and touched her shoulder. Dina didn't slap it off, so Eve left it there. "Your brother's a wonderful person, and he has been since we were first introduced. I'm the one who's been suspicious, unreasonable, and plain meanspirited. I feel horrible about it. I was so stupid with Noah. I'm scared to go and say I'm sorry. I think he's going to tell me to get lost."

Astonishment silenced Dina.

"I was going to apologize today, but he's at work until tomorrow morning. I thought running would take my mind off it, and I run into you. Is there some hidden message in that?" Eve chuckled. "Really, it's kind of funny when you think about it." Dina found herself chuckling as well. Soon the two were laughing hysterically. A weak Eve staggered over to a nearby bench and sat down. Dina followed and handed her the bottle as a peace offering. Eve took small sips and handed the bottle back. "You know, you almost killed me when you dumped that water on my head?"

Dina looked mischievous with her shoulders hunched and a big grin. "I know," and she started laughing again. The giggling was infectious, and Tim found them slumped against the bench holding their sides.

"Wow, Eve, you have to teach me that trick. She stays mad at me for days."

"Well, honey, Eve has the right idea; she just agrees with me. It kind of takes all the wind out of my sails."

"Well, forget that. I'll just disagree with you, and keep my feisty woman." He bent down and kissed her. Eve turned her head to give them privacy.

Dina stood. "Eve, I'm glad we had this conversation. It's been very enlightening. I have a wonderful idea about how you can apologize, are you doing anything tomorrow?"

"Nothing special."

"Come to my car, I'll give you my number, and we can discuss my plan."

Eve grabbed her jacket and slipped it on. The air was crisp, and she was soaked for the second time that day.

On the way to the car, Tim looked at Eve and asked, "Why were you racing me?" Eve explained her running game.

Dina looked at her sideways. "You're weird."

Tim supported Eve. "No, she isn't. I understand exactly what she's talking about, but you know, if I knew what you were doing from the start, you would've lost."

"Is that so? Sounds like a challenge to me. Which car is yours? I'll race you." Eve knew she was all talk and no action. She was so tired, it was a struggle to walk straight.

Dina saved her. "Oh, no. You two have done enough racing for one day."

🪻🪻🪻

That night, both Eve and Noah struggled with sleep. Noah lay in his bunk at the fire station. He wondered how Dina's wedding rehearsal and dinner went. At first, he'd felt guilty because he had to miss the festivities, but now, he felt relieved. He didn't want to be around all of those happy people when he felt so miserable. Tomorrow would be a challenge. Rest, he needed to get some, because tomorrow was his sister's wedding. If he looked like something was wrong with him, he'd distract her, and that's the last thing he wanted on her big day. But he wasn't sleepy. Noah got up and went down to the TV room. He watched some mindless program with the rest of the crew. It had a dulling effect, and he dozed off. Someone pushed his shoulder and told him to go to bed. He slowly got up and did so.

At her house, Eve wasn't having an easy night

either, and like Noah, she anesthetized herself with the boob tube. Dina's plan was simple, still, it did require her to take a big chance in public, not something she relished. She was well aware that her apology might be too little too late, and he could say thanks but no thanks. Nevertheless, she'd been a real witch to Noah, and this was a test she needed to take and pass. Not only for Noah, but also for her own self-respect.

The sun rose and defeated the clouds the morning of Dina's winter wedding. The day started with light drizzle and overcast skies. By two o'clock, it was still chilly, but the sun had blazed through and created a clear, lovely day. Feeling anxious and giddy, Eve intentionally arrived late. She had yet to go to a wedding that started on time, and the thought of facing Noah before she could apologize made her wince. She and Dina agreed that it would be better to approach him after the ceremony just in case things didn't go well. Dina told her she'd invited more than three hundred guests; Eve thought it would be easy to get lost in the crowd.

Noah spotted her as soon as she stepped in the church. What the hell is she doing here? The question thundered through his brain. Irritation burned in him when he felt his lower body react to the vision of her in long, smooth lines of dark red satin. He swore he saw heatwaves radiating from her when she moved. Looking around, he noticed he wasn't the only one paying attention to the vision in red as she slipped past the usher and quickly sat in a pew at the back of the elegant old church. Noah was third in the line of four groomsmen. The bridesmaids were lined up in a similar fashion on the other side of the aisle. Tim stood with his back to the altar, waiting for Dina to appear. Noah looked up at the vaulted and elaborately decorated ceiling and asked the angels painted there, why? He didn't have long to ponder the question because the wedding march began, and Dina and his uncle began walking toward them. His eyes shifted between his beloved sister and Eve.

Eve was unaware of Noah's reaction to her. She thought she'd slipped in undetected. When she saw him standing up front, her breath caught. He glowed in his black tux. Tears came to her eyes when she saw Dina walking down the aisle. She was absolutely gorgeous in a mound of silk and lace. When Noah was present, Eve's gaze didn't stray from him long. She shifted, looking back to the front of the church, and her heart stopped when he pinned her with his eyes. The unwavering glare was cold and questioning. Eve met it without flinching. Ten seconds seemed like an eternity, but that's how long it took for the eyes to release her and return to Dina. Eve felt like a deflated balloon. She took long, deep breaths trying to fill herself back up. The beautiful ceremony ended with applause, and a deep kiss exchanged between the bride and groom. The wedding party stayed in the church for pictures as the crowd slowly migrated through the huge wooden doors for the short walk across the lawn to the banquet room where the reception was being held. Eve waved and spoke to several people she knew from the fire department, police department, and others she'd met from working in the legal community. Dina warned her there would be people there she knew, and that's why it was so important that she be there, to put action behind her atonement. If nothing else, Noah would know she was past the point of worrying about other's opinions.

As she walked across the lawn, a voice behind her said, "So, how many brothers did you send to the gallows this week?"

"Yoshi!" Eve gave him and Ebony heartfelt hugs. She had been so wrapped up in her own drama, it didn't dawn on her that the two of them would probably be there.

People walked around them as they stopped and spoke. "Girl, why didn't you tell me you were coming?" Ebony scolded. Her long hair framed her face with beautiful ringlets.

"I didn't know it myself until yesterday. I ran into Dina at the park, and she invited me. I came to tell Noah I'm sorry."

Yoshi didn't comment, and Ebony said, "Good," and hugged her again, a warm, solid hug that let Eve know that Ebony was proud of her. She squeezed back, glad that her friends were here. If Noah turned a cold shoulder or gave her a tongue lashing, she'd need their support to get out of there.

The reception began when the bride, groom, and the rest of the wedding party entered the hall among loud claps and cheers. Noah spotted Eve immediately, and more than a few heads turned as he made a beeline for her with long, sure strides. Ebony sat next to her. Underneath the table, she took Eve's hand and squeezed. He reached her, and without a word or glance to Ebony and Yoshi, he said, "We need to talk." He held his hand out. His manner was rough and intimidating, but Eve looked at his large, callused hand and felt a shudder remembering the things it could do to her. She didn't hesitate and placed her left hand in his. The first thing he noticed was that her wedding ring was gone. He caressed the finger where the ring used to be and led her out of the hall, then back to the empty church.

Eve missed the warmth when he released her

hand and took up a posture that said "you have some explaining to do." She looked at him, so stiff and angry with his legs wide and his arms crossed at the chest. She could see the outline of his thigh as he flexed and released the muscle, waiting for her to speak.

Eve always found directness to be the best way. She took a deep breath that made her breasts rise, teasing the red silk, causing Noah to clench his jaw. Would there ever come a day when his body didn't react to her like he was sailor on shore leave?

"Noah, it isn't easy for me to explain myself…" There was a pregnant pause. Eve was at a loss for words. She practiced and analyzed her apology, and now that the moment was at hand, she was speechless. Frustration made her movements jerky. A rush of words flowed from her mouth. "Noah, I'm sorry. I'm really sorry for being so stupid from the minute we met." She spoke with her hands moving quickly to accent each sorry. "I'm sorry I listened to rumors instead of getting to know you for myself. I'm sorry I put restrictions on our being together. I'm sorry we've wasted time we could have spent together. I'm sorry if you think all I want to do is sleep with you." Eve looked at his chest as she listed her sins. Now she shyly looked into his eyes. "I'm not sorry we slept together. That was wonderful, and I'll never regret it."

A rock in Noah's chest crumbled, then vaporized. His eyes were unreadable. Eve's gaze returned to his chest. "I'm also sorry for slap..." He interrupted her.

"Shhh." He put his index finger to his lips. "Shhh, apology accepted." Her eyes lifted and were treated to a wonderful view of his strong throat and underneath his chin as his arms engulfed her in a tight embrace. She wrapped her arms around his middle, and even though her fingertips barely touched, she managed to crush him to her. She breathed deeply and opened her lips against his neck. God, it felt so right being mashed against this wall of a man, nuzzling and nipping at his neck. Noah buried his nose and mouth in her springy curls and enjoyed her fresh, clean scent; just a hint of what he thought was vanilla, his favorite ice cream. Her nips graduated to sucking. Noah knew he would take her here if they didn't stop soon. He wondered if it was sacrilegious to make love in a church. He pulled back a little, and Eve looked up. She surprised both of them by whispering, "I love you." The soft look in Noah's eyes became a simmer. Their lips met in a burning kiss as each tried to devour the other. Noah was gone and threatening to burst through his zipper when Eve pulled back. She leaned her forehead upon his chest, and breathed like a severe asthmatic. Without lifting her head she said, "Noah, I'm dying here, but we can't in a church." They were motionless, still embraced as they waited for the world to right itself on its axis. "Let's head back so I can get the formalities over with, and we can get out of here."

"Wait! I have a question first." Eve felt awkward asking him, but she had to know the answer. She hesitated.

Noah lifted her chin with a forefinger. "Eve, where you're concerned, my life is an open book. Ask me anything, and I'll answer as honestly as I can."

"What about the swimsuit model?"

Noah threw back his head, and his laughter bounced off the high ceilings. "Oh, honey," he said engulfing her in his arms. "If only you knew how lost I am in you. I didn't even look at that woman's face."

"I know that!" Eve interrupted. Her arms were wrapped around his middle, and she playfully pinched his back.

He wiggled suggestively and then became serious. He placed each large hand on the sides of Eve's face and stared into her eyes. "Honey, I'm so full of you, there's no room for anyone else. I saw that woman's body, and all of those sleek muscles reminded me of you. Suddenly, I was back in my condo, sitting on the bed, and you were sauntering over to me." He kissed her long and deep. "I wanted you so bad, my mind was creating your image wherever I looked." He said the words against her lips. Eve's hands clutched his jacket. With a groan, Noah separated their lips, "Come on, baby, or my mother and sister will send a posse out to look for me."

They entered the reception hand and hand. Ebony gasped and kissed Yoshi on his cheek. "Look, they're together, and Eve's holding his hand in public." Yoshi looked, and he and Noah nodded at each other. He was happy for his friend.

Noah bent to Eve. "I have to go join the shake-hands-and-nod-forever line. I'll be back as soon as I can." He gave her a quick peck; Eve clutched his neck and kissed him fully.

A few people hooted and whistled at their public display. Someone shouted, "Where's the minister? I think these two are next."

Their kiss ended, and Noah whispered, "You won't regret trusting me, babe."

Eve was rooted to the spot as she watched Noah join his family. Her tunnel vision kept her from seeing Dina's beaming grin until Noah leaned down to hug Dina. Eve returned her thumbs-up sign. Ebony was jumping up and down by the time Eve reached her. They embraced tightly and Ebony whispered in her ear, "I'm so happy for you, girl!"

A smirking Yoshi said, "I guess this means we can restart domino night. I know you two have been avoiding me, and you have no excuses now."

All three of them laughed. "Yes, Yoshi, I believe we can start playing again," Eve answered.

Yoshi left to get them all something to drink.

Eve turned to her friend. "E-bone." Eve's serious tone surprised Ebony. She gave Eve her full attention. "How do you cope with Yoshi's job being so dangerous?"

Ebony sighed. "I won't lie, Eve. It's not always easy. I tell myself that Yoshi is extremely well-trained, and he knows what he's doing. Also, I know my husband is very cautious. He's not a showboat at his job." Ebony looked Eve in the eyes. "Yoshi tells me that Noah is the same way. I know that Yoshi's not taking unnecessary chances, and that gives me a lot of comfort." Ebony smiled and hugged Eve, whispering words meant for her ears only. "The loving is well worth dealing with the stress of his job, girl. Go for it!"

Eve laughed and hugged Ebony back. "That's why I love you, Ebony. You're so earthy. You go right to the root of the issue and tell it like it is."

"Earthy?" Yoshi returned and handed the ladies their drinks. "Eve said I'm earthy, honey. I think I like that."

Yoshi laughed. "She's right. You're the salt of

the earth, babe." He pecked his wife's lips.

Eve and Noah's separation wasn't as brief as they both wanted it. Noah found himself swept away by family responsibilities, which included meeting numerous relatives he barely remembered. His body was at war, divided between getting to Eve and making sure he didn't mess up his sister's day. He looked at Eve longingly as he waited beside his mother. She returned his look. His mother tugged on his arm. "Let's join them now." Dina and Tim were enjoying their first dance when Noah led his mother out on the dance floor. Tim's parents joined them.

Noah looked down at his mother as he waltzed her around the floor. She looked beautiful. The thin mother of his youth had rounded into the stately matron he now held in his arms. She lifted her steel-gray hair and looked at him with warm brown eyes. He knew Dina's nuptials made her world fill with joy. She smiled radiantly as he hugged her close. His mother deserved to be happy. She hugged him back and teased. "It's your turn now. When are you going to bring me a daughter-in-law?"

Noah chuckled, thinking it may be sooner than you think. He remembered Eve's whispered, "I love you." She loves me. He wanted to shout the news to the world. He twirled his mother around and dipped her.

"Whoa, Noah, you're going to have to save that for Dina because these hips are too old."

"Mom, time only makes you better." He twirled her again, and then he glanced at Eve. She smiled and wiggled her fingers at him. He nodded back at her. "Mom, there's someone I want you to meet. Don't mention wedding bells because you'll scare both of us off."

"Who? Where is she? I didn't know you brought someone."

"Unfortunately, she didn't come with me, Mom, but now I have to dance with the lovely bride. I'll introduce you when I have a chance." Noah kissed his mother's cheek and turned to Dina. "Hey, sis, I'm so proud of you." The two embraced warmly and then separated slightly to dance.

Watching them, Eve appreciated their deep love for each other. She was an only child, and happy to be so until she witnessed Noah and Dina together. She wondered, what it would be like to have your best friend in your family. When they were teenagers, they could have had soul-searching conversation without leaving the house. Even though Eve had explored her heart, the risk she was taking still scared her. Looking at them made her wonder if Dina was the mold Noah would expect her to fit into? Catching herself, she realized how silly she was being. Noah had more reason to be concerned that she would pit him against Todd's memory. Although she'd explored her heart and decided to risk a relationship with Noah, she still felt nervous and insecure. Emotionally, this was one of the greatest gambles of her life, but, oh, the rewards would be so sweet. Eve slightly straightened and relaxed as a small shiver went through her body.

On the floor, Dina beamed at Noah. "I see you and Eve have reconciled."

"Well, I guess you could say we're working our way to an understanding."

Dina leaned away from him and ducked her head a little to the side. "Oh, you're working on it, huh?"

"Yes, we are, and it may require overtime to smooth all the rough edges."

Dina burst into laughter. "Well, brother, from what I hear, you're pretty good at this line of work. I don't imagine you'll have to stay long after hours."
"But, Dina, the entire job will be performed after hours."

Dina missed a step. "Stop, Noah. I can't keep a rhythm if you keep making me laugh. You're making my side hurt." She pressed a hand to her side. "Uh oh, look over there. It looks like some uninformed person is trying to make a move on Eve. You'd better go help her out."

By this time, the dance floor was crowded. No matter because Noah felt as if he and Eve were connected by some invisible wire. He spotted her shiny curls immediately. His view was suddenly blocked by some jerk in an expensive suit who was leaning down talking to Eve. Noah wanted to run over and claim his territory, but Eve scooted her chair back, poked her head around, and smiled at him. He relaxed, knowing she could more than handle herself. The poor guy probably needed more rescuing than Eve. He finished the dance with his sister.

At the song's end, Noah strode across the floor to Eve once more. The suit looked like a vampire bat hovering over Eve. He was so enamored that he didn't notice Noah until Noah leaned over Eve's free side and gave her a peck on the cheek.

"Hi." She smiled brightly, looking like she was thankful Noah was there. "Sit down." Noah was already pulling out the empty chair beside her. The suit stopped leaning over Eve and stood up. "Noah, have you met Robert? He's a friend of some friend, I forget exactly why he's here."

Noah put his arm around Eve's shoulder, and she placed a hand on his thigh, openly caressing it. "No, I haven't met Robert. It's nice to met you." Noah caught Robert's hand in a tight, quick grip. "Would you like to join us? Eve, is there an extra seat?"

"Actually, no, Ebony and Yoshi are dancing, so these two seats are taken."

The suit was already backing away. "Thank you, but I'm already sitting at another table." He turned and disappeared into the crowd.

Eve turned to Noah. "I saw you on TV. You make a wonderful hero." Her eyes were smoldering, and her voice was husky. Noah was so aroused, he was beginning to perspire. He was about to throw his eternal soul to the wind, and suggest that they return to the church and devour each other when Yoshi and Ebony arrived. Eve leaned over and her lips touched his cheek. For his ears only, she said, "Later, love. We'll have all night to do what you're thinking. Mom doesn't expect me back until tomorrow after work."

Eve floated through the rest of the reception. She was so happy, everything seemed surreal. She sobered a bit when Noah introduced her to his mother. His mother's brown eyes twinkled happily as she ignored Eve's hand and wrapped her in a strong embrace. Eve liked her immediately. It was too crowded for meaningful conversation, so before they parted, Noah's mother hugged her again and said, "Have Noah bring you by the house so we can really talk."

A pleasant fog surrounded the rest of the

evening as erotic tension slowly spiraled around the two of them. Indecision no longer hammered Eve's brain, and she enjoyed being steeped in desire. Both of them were sure of the purity of each other's motives, and this allowed the hunger to grow unchecked. They were ready for each other long before the festivities ended.

CHAPTER 13

Noah's front door shut, and they were enclosed in darkness and privacy. Neither of them thought of the bed as Noah pressed Eve against the front door. Eve quivered as Noah seared her with his lips.

He came up for air while leaning his upper body back and thrusting his hips forward, making sure he kept their lower bodies connected and in motion. In the car, he'd removed his jacket and rolled up his shirtsleeves. His arms were on both sides of Eve's head, and she turned to the right and licked his wrist, causing him to draw in his breath. He spoke with difficulty in a low, husky voice, "My sister says I've become a poet since I've met you. I think she's right." Eve stopped sucking his forearm and looked at his face. A sliver of moonlight stole through the curtains, helping her adjust to the dark and allowing her to see him. "How do I love thee? Let me kiss the ways. I love you." His lips caressed her forehead. "I love you." He kissed her ear and darted a tongue inside. Eve's pelvis involuntarily jerked against him, briefly interrupting their rhythm. "I love you." His teeth and tongue tantalized her neck. "I love you." His tongue toyed with the hollow at the base of her throat. "I love you." He licked the vee between her breasts.

His declarations burned through Eve and manifested as a deep moan. Hands trembled and grasped at his waist, then slipped down to his buttocks where they kneaded and shaped the firm flesh. She changed the tempo to a slow, hard grind.

Despite a harsh, ragged voice, Noah continued his proclamations. His hands smoothed the red satin up her legs until it was bunched at her waist and her legs were free. He hoisted Eve up as he straightened his knees and stood upright. Eve wrapped her legs around his upper thighs, and her hands clutched his broad shoulders. Their rhythm continued. Eve was an electrical storm with currents jumping all around, incinerating her insides. Heart stopping vibrations flowed through her, stirring her up so much, she could no longer understand Noah's actual words. But she felt them, murmured against her skin, firing down her belly, tingling in the area just between her thighs, and settling there. Noah's hands gripped Eve's buttocks, holding her firmly in place. His pants and her underwear were in the way of his ultimate desire, but he knew Eve was too close to stop now. Noah was drawn to the hard pebble beneath the scarlet silk that draped her breast. He began sucking and nipping, making her groan in such a way that Noah almost came.

Eve was striving for what Noah was avoiding, and she was close. Her world narrowed down to one last stroke, one more hip twist. She was at the precipice, poised, and anticipating. When Noah delivered, she went completely still and silent. His eyes shifted to her face. He smiled at the grimace; her eyes were squeezed shut as she began to pant. Then Eve began a quiver that had Noah struggling to hold her. Noah ground through the earthquake, gradually reducing the pressure until Eve went limp, dangling across his body.

"God, I needed that." She rubbed her open mouth on his shoulder. "I've been fantasizing about this since that morning." Her softly spoken words nearly caused his undoing. He held her, fighting for control.

After a time, he moved. Eve wasn't even aware

that he was carrying her to the bed until he gently laid her down. In a daze, she watched him strip and join her. God, she would never get tired of watching him undress. She compared it to unwrapping a Hershey kiss.

Noah saw her tongue and asked, "For me?"

Eve remembered the fajitas. "Oh, yes," she cooed. "It's definitely for you this time."

Passion lowered Noah's eyes to half-mast as he gently rolled her to the side and unzipped her dress. Soon bare flesh was pressed against bare flesh. Eve knew he was about to enter her, and she had other plans. "Wait a minute. Not so fast." Eve nudged him to his back, grabbed his hands, and put them high above his head. "Stay! It's my turn to have some fun, and when you touch me, I get too distracted, so stay!"

Eve straddled him. Noah felt her wetness pool against his stomach and wanted to disobey. With graceful fingers, she touched him. Tenderly, she traced his majestic features, pausing at his long, straight nose. She brushed her lips across it, traveled up and down its length, and treated the tip to a kiss. Her fingers danced over his proud cheekbones and traced the shape of his strong jaw. She lingered at his lips. Slowly, she moved her fingers over the top and then the bottom. The tip of her tongue replaced her fingers as she toyed with the plump flesh. Noah couldn't resist opening his mouth and teasing back. Eve allowed this minor rule violation. Noah mumbled inarticulately when Eve pulled away and slipped down his body. She reverently touched the hard chest, smoothing down the few hairs that covered it. Noah twitched and moaned beneath her, but his hands and arms were still. Growing hunger made Eve quicken the pace. Unable to resist, she bathed his chest with her tongue, flicking his nipples often.

Anticipation, anticipation, I'm building anticipation, she repeated over and over in her mind. She wanted to savor him; relish the taste and feel of him. She breathed deeply through her nose as she rubbed her cheeks on his chest, smoothed her forehead across his ribs, and then she followed a thin line of hair downward until she came to the tip of him. After spreading his legs, she settled between them. Without touching his penis, she used her tongue to trace the outline of it as it lay ramrod straight against his stomach. Noah couldn't stand it. He moved his arms, so he could lean on his elbows to see what she was doing. Eve looked directly at him and blew gently on his penis. Noah sucked in his breath and held it. Her mouth hovered over him at a pace that seemed excruciatingly slow to Noah, then she licked his length from bottom to top. At the top, she engulfed the head and moved her tongue around it. Noah flopped back on the bed with a long, harsh groan. Eve paid close attention to Noah as she worked her magic. If it looked like he was getting too close, she eased up. Eve played this game until Noah growled and trembled in frustration. Smiling, Eve took the hint, and Noah withered as moist kisses ascended his body. Noah pointed to the nightstand. Understanding immediately, Eve reached into the drawer and took one of the many packets she found there. Ripping it open, she slowly rolled it down over him while she licked here and there.

"Stop toying with me," Noah growled.

"Okay." Eve put his hands back above his head, positioned herself, and eased down on him. When he filled her completely, she rocked gently to and fro, reveling in the sensation. As her excitement grew, she reflected that she could definitely get used to this multiple orgasm thing. Leaning forward, she balanced herself by bracing her hands against his upper arms. She showered his face with kisses as she began to move up and down while Noah dug his heels into the bed, so he could thrust his hips forward, matching each stroke perfectly.

Eve leaned up a bit as she quickened the pace. His arms were trapped, but his mouth was free, and he used it to kiss and lick her breasts whenever they were near. Their movements became more frantic. Eve's upper body was rigid with excitement, but her hips felt liquid as she rode him like a sea-soned jockey. Her body ached with sensation, mak-ing it difficult to maintain the rhythm. Suddenly, Eve released his arms. Noah took this as a sign that there were no more rules, and he didn't hesitate to grab her hips and flip her over. He kissed her. His mouth was hard and hungry. His thick, hot tongue plunged in, filling her completely. She wanted it and accepted it greedily as her hands grabbed the back of his head and pulled. Noah thrust his hips, and she was there to meet him halfway. The pace increased again, and her ears filled with the sound of her roaring pulse and his ragged breaths. Feeling him sliding inside her, joining with him in this way, was a mind blower for Eve.

Noah knew he was close. He inhaled the soft, secret scent hidden in her neck. He tasted the sweetness and nuzzled in the warmth. His hips had a mind of their own, and continued the fierce pace, despite his desire to prolong the lovemaking. "Oh, Noah, I love you." She licked in his ear. Then her head fell back as she came long and hard, scream-ing his name through tight lips. Listening to her was maddening. The thought that he loved this woman coming apart beneath him, and she loved him back meant everything to him at that moment. With a primal yell, his climax ripped through him and poured into his protection, threatening its durability. Neither of them had the ability or the desire to move. Noah had collapsed on Eve, and after a time, she whimpered and nibbled at his chest. He got the message and managed to roll so Eve lay on top of him. Labored breathing was all that could be heard while they recovered.

Later, the sheets were a tangled mess and the sweat had long since dried on their bodies when Eve stirred slightly and said with a husky voice, "I loved my husband."

"I understand." No, he didn't. His heart beat faster, and his body tensed because he was unsure where she was going with this. He contemplated that this love thing was for the birds. The highs were tremendous but the lows were horrendous. If Eve started treating his feelings like a yo-yo again, that she could toss up and down, he was done. He'd pick her up and put her outside. Eve moved, adjusting herself and then snuggled back into him. To hell with it, Noah thought as he wrapped his arms around her and held her firmly against him. He'd fight her, the dead husband, and anyone else he had to fight to keep her. The minute she started saying "I'm sorry" she was his.

Eve continued as if there hadn't been a pause in the conversation. "That's why this has been so confusing and difficult for me. I thought what I felt for Todd was the best that love had to offer, and also, I was very mad about how he died. But now I've let go of that anger, and I've truly said good-bye to Todd." Her after-sex voice was just as raspy and sexy to Noah as it was the first time they made love. Noah spoke from his heart. "You know, Eve, you don't have to love him any less. I just want a place of my own somewhere in there--a big place."

She lifted herself just enough so their eyes could meet. "You have more than a small corner. When I met you, I discovered that love could burn you up and blow you away. Before I met you, I thought love songs were silly and overrated." Her eyes smoldered into Noah's, raising his heat level considerably. "Now I think I could write one." Her fingers began to leisurely stroke his chest. "Todd was comfortable, a good friend that I shared a bed with. You..." Eve searched for words to make Noah understand the depth of her feelings. "Noah, you scare me because you're not only here," she said, pointing to her heart. "You're all through me. You consume me as no one else has. You, you complete me. You're my soul mate. I feel whole with you, and I actually get giddy when you walk into a room. It's embarrassing and thrilling at the same time."

Noah laughed and rolled until they were both on

their sides, and he could see her face better. He gently kissed her lips and stroked her face. Eve continued to explain herself. "I fought my feelings for you, and it was hard, damn hard, to fight against something I wanted with every fiber of my body." She rubbed against him. "It feels so right being in your arms like this, surrounded by the smell and feel of our recent adventures." She smiled into his eyes. "I don't ever want to leave." Eve had other words she wanted to say, but none seemed important when her lips met Noah's.

Much later, they lay spoon fashion with her back to his stomach. She was exhausted and about to fall asleep when Noah murmured into her hair. "So, when do we get married?"

"What?" Wide-awake she turned around to face him.

"We've been horrible at dating, so why don't we just take this to the next level and get married."

Eve was incredulous and stared at him. Finally, she said, "Are you serious?"

"I'm serious about my love for you. I feel the same as you. I want you here with me."

"Noah, I have responsibilities, a son to consider."

"Shush." His lips touched hers briefly. "I know the answer would be no right now, but I want you to understand that I do love you, and I'm making a commitment to you that I've never made to another woman. When you're ready, I want to put a ring on your finger, and officially make you mine, and tell the rest of the world that I'm yours.

Eve had tears in her eyes. Noah kissed them away as they spilled over her lids. "Don't cry, baby." "It's okay to cry when they're happy tears. How can I refuse such a beautiful proposal from the man of my dreams? Yes, I'll marry you when the time is right. Also," she said, looking in his eyes, "I want your children."

Noah was shocked. "Are you sure?"

"Yes, I've always wanted more kids, and I know you'll be a wonderful father. It would be an honor to share a little one with you."

Now Noah was the one with tears in his eyes. "Oh, God, I love you, baby." Children. He was surprised the thought hadn't entered his mind. His kid growing in her belly was blowing his mind. He realized he wanted kids with her badly. Noah was too emotional to put his joy into words, so he gathered her into his arms, and kissed and stroked her reverently. Then, he fell into a deep sleep. Eve looked up at the strong jaw, the smooth cheek, the delectable lips, and struggled to keep her eyes open, wanting to savor every minute she was with him.

The lights were off, and a streetlight played with a crack in the curtains. Eve imagined it was the glow of their love surrounding them. She never wanted it to go out.

EPILOGUE

E ve's eyes flew open. She shifted her backside; managing to rub it against the back of the solid, warm presence lying next to her. Turning over, she wrapped her right arm around Noah's side. He moaned, deep in sleep, and shifted, trapping her arm against his middle. Eve nuzzled her face between his shoulder blades, and breathed deeply. Oh, the sweet smell of a warm man next to her. She licked the slightly salty skin, savoring the taste that tantalized the tip of her tongue. Progressing upward, Eve placed small kisses along Noah's upper spine and shoulders.

He rolled into her embrace and pulled her into his sleep-warm body. "What, baby? Is the princess awake?"

God, Eve thought, I'll never get tired of this.

After she got done burying her nose in his chest, she answered his question. "No, sexy, she's been sleeping through the night for a month or so now, remember?"

"Oh, yeah." He stretched and yawned. Eve felt every inch of his six-foot-two frame move against her, and her nipples pimpled in response. His body was just stirring awake, but his adjusting thrust her senses into overdrive. "What's wrong, babe? Can't sleep?"

Eve didn't answer with words. She peppered his chest and neck with slow, deliberate pecks and strokes of her tongue.

"Ohhhh!" Noah's voice was a deep, sexy rumble, still heavy with sleep. "The queen is hungry, not the princess!" he teased.

"Famished," Eve admitted in between bites.

Noah moaned and cradled her head as she gyrated against him. "I think the six weeks was harder on you than me."

Eve chuckled at that. "After being with you, I have to confess that I'm not a fan of abstinence."

"Good, as long as you only indulge with me!" Noah tilted her head for a kiss. As they enjoyed each other's bodies, Noah thanked the Lord for the love he shared with this woman. While his hand fondled her baby-enlarged breast, Noah was amazed that his love hadn't diminished one iota. If anything, it was stronger after two years of marriage. Eve groaned, drawing in Noah so he gave her his complete attention. Sometime later, she yelled loudly as pleasure drained every muscle in her body. Noah's telling hiss wasn't far behind.

"Mmmmmm. Just the thing to satisfy a hungry girl."

Noah chuckled. "I can't have my babe starving, but you know, Eve, you're going to have to stop yelling. I'm surprised Sean hasn't burst in here to see what's going on."

Eve lay sprawled across his stomach. She suspected that her savvy, seventeen-year-old son knew exactly what was happening when and if he heard noises coming from their room. She preferred not to think about it as she ran a lazy hand down Noah's stomach, over his groin, across his thigh. "I can't help it. It's your fault anyway, Dr. Feelgood. The prescription you prescribed for me was so good that I have to have it often, and when I have it, I have to shout for joy!"

"I don't think Sean and Noelle Evelyn will interpret it that way. They're going to think I'm killing you."

Oh, but you are killing me, Noah. Softly and sweetly almost every night, I die at least once, most of the time twice. La petite mort, the French call it.

The little death." She reached up and kissed him.

"Keep killing me softly, or sometimes not so softly, eh." She settled back down on his chest and lightly pulled at his chest hairs.

Noah chuckled. "You do have a way with words, my little prosecutor. I love you so much." He squeezed her tight. Eve hugged him back.

Waaaaaaaaaah.

"See, babe. You did wake her up!"

Eve looked at the clock. "Honey, it's six o'clock. It's almost time for her to wake up anyway."

"Ummmm." Noah rubbed his nose in her hair.

"I'll get her. Is there milk in the fridge?"

Eve rolled off him and stretched. Noah ran a hand down her taut body. "Don't start that, the child will never be fed." Noah continued stroking as if she hadn't spoken. She grabbed his hand and kissed the palm. "Yes, there's milk. I pressed some for her earlier." Noelle was breastfed; a fact that would have to change because Eve was scheduled to go back to work in two weeks.

Noah laughed and dragged himself away from his wife.

Eve watched him pull boxers over his nakedness and leave the room. She stretched again, absolutely and completely satisfied in all aspects of her life. She and Noah got married exactly one year after Dina and Tim's wedding. Dina got a kick out of the fact that they shared an anniversary.

Sean was less than thrilled about having a step-father. He was very hesitant about "the whole mar-riage thing" as he called it, but Noah was great with him. The two had bonded soon after she and Noah started officially dating. Her poor son just needed time to make the mental adjustment that his mom was really marrying someone else. Surprisingly, having another baby sealed it for Sean. He adored his little five-month-old sister, and showed her off to all his homeys. He even took her to the park every once in a while, claiming she was an even better chick magnet than the cast. She and Noah got a big laugh out of that. Sean was a senior and would be gone after another year. Eve hated to think about it.

Eve also hated to think about leaving her princess to return to work. Beulah and Noah's mom were going to take turns watching the baby, and Eve was sure they would appreciate it if Noelle did-n't scream for her mother's breast. She really had to start weaning the child. Eve smiled when she thought of her mother. She'd moved out as soon as the engagement was announced. She lived less than two minutes away from the new house she and Noah purchased soon after they were wed. Both of them wanted to start their marriage in a fresh place that only had their stamp on it.

Noah returned with Noelle. "I thought you wouldn't mind since you were up already."

"No, honey, I don't mind."

Noah fitted the baby between them and began feeding her with the bottle. He smiled at his child, and then looked up at Eve. "Thank you," he said.

"For what?"

"For being the woman I love."

They kissed over the baby, and Eve said, "You're most welcome."

INDIGO
Winter, Spring & Summer 2001

❧ January

Ambrosia	T. T. Henderson	$8.95

❧ February

The Reluctant Captive	Joyce Jackson	$8.95
Rendezvous with Fate	Jeanne Sumerix	$8.95
Indigo After Dark Vol. I	Angelique/Nia Dixon	$10.95
In Between the Night	Angelique	
Midnight Erotic Fantasies	Nia Dixon	

❧ March

Eve's Prescription	Edwina Martin-Arnold	$8.95
Intimate Intentions	Angie Daniels	$8.95

❧ April

Sweet Tomorrows	Kimberly White	$8.95
Past Promises	Jahmel West	$8.95
Indigo After Dark Vol. II	Dolores Bundy/Cole Riley	$10.95
The Forbidden Art of Desire	Cole Riley	
Erotic Short Stories	Dolores Bundy	

May

Your Precious Love	Sinclair LeBeau	$8.95
After the Vows	Leslie Esdaile	$10.95
(Summer Anthology)	T. T. Henderson	
	Jacquelin Thomas	

June

Subtle Secrets	Wanda Y. Thomas	$8.95
Indigo After Dark Vol. III	Montana Blue/Coco Morena	$10.95
Impulse	Montana Blue	
Erotic Short Stories	Coco Morena	

Indigo Backlist

A Dangerous Love	J.M. Jefferies	$8.95
Again My Love	Kayla Perrin	$10.95
A Lighter Shade of Brown	Vicki Andrews	$8.95
All I Ask	Barbara Keaton	$8.95
A Love to Cherish (Hardcover)	Beverly Clark	$15.95
A Love to Cherish (Paperback)	Beverly Clark	$8.95
And Then Came You	Dorothy Love	$8.95
Best of Friends	Natalie Dunbar	$8.95
Bound by Love	Beverly Clark	$8.95
Breeze	Robin Hampton	$10.95
Cajun Heat	Charlene Berry	$8.95
Careless Whispers	Rochelle Alers	$8.95
Caught in a Trap	Andree Michele	$8.95
Chances	Pamela Leigh Star	$8.95
Cypress Wisperings	Phyllis Hamilton	$8.95
Dark Embrace	Crystal Wilson Harris	$8.95
Dark Storm Rising	Chinelu Moore	$10.95
Everlastin' Love	Gay G. Gunn	*$10.95*
Forever Love	Wanda Y. Thomas	$8.95
Gentle Yearning	Rochelle Alers	$10.95
Glory of Love	Sinclair LeBeau	$10.95
Indiscretions	Donna Hill	$8.95
Interlude	Donna Hill	$8.95
Kiss or Keep	Debra Phillips	$8.95
Love Always	Mildred E. Kelly	$10.95
Love Unveiled	Gloria Green	$10.95
Love's Deception	Charlene Berry	$10.95
Mae's Promise	Melody Walcott	$8.95
Midnight Clear	Leslie Esdaile	
(Anthology)	Gwynne Forster	
	Carmen Green	
	Monica Jackson	$10.95

Midnight Magic	Gwynne Forster	$8.95
Midnight Peril	Vicki Andrews	$10.95
Naked Soul (Hardcover)	Gwynee Forster	$15.95
Naked Soul (Paperback)	Gwynne Forster	$8.95
No Regrets (Hardcover)	Mildred E. Riley	$15.95
No Regrets (Paperback)	Mildred E. Riley	$8.95
Nowhere to Run	Gay G. Gunn	$10.95
Passion	T.T. Henderson	$10.95
Path of Fire	T.T. Henderson	$8.95
Picture Perfect	Reon Carter	$8.95
Pride & Joi (Hardcover)	Gay G. Gunn	$15.95
Pride & Joi (Paperback)	Gay G. Gunn	$8.95
Quiet Storm	Donna Hill	$10.95
Reckless Surrender	Rochelle Alers	*$8.95*
Rooms of the Heart	Donna Hill	$8.95
Shades of Desire	Monica White	$8.95
Sin	Crystal Rhodes	$8.95
So Amazing	Sinclair LeBeau	$8.95
Somebody's Someone	Beverly Clark	$8.95
Soul to Soul	Donna Hill	$8.95
The Price of Love	Sinclair LeBeau	$8.95
The Missing Link	Charlyne Dickerson	$8.95
Truly Inseparable (Hardcover)	Wanda Y. Thomas	$15.95
Truly Inseparable (Paperback)	Wanda Y. Thomas	$8.95
Unconditional Love	Alicia Wiggins	$8.95
Whispers in the Night	Dorothy Love	$8.95
Whispers in the Sand	LaFlorya Gauthier	$10.95
Yesterday is Gone	Beverly Clark	*$10.95*

All books are sold in paperback form, unless otherwise noted.

You may order on-line at www.genesis-press.com, by phone at 1-888-463-4461, or mail the order-form in the back of this book.

Shipping Charges:

$3.00 for 1 or 2 books
$4.00 for 3 or 4 books, etc.

Mississippi residents add 7% sales tax.

Love Spectrum Romance

Romance across the culture lines

Forbidden Quest	Dar Tomlinson	$10.95
Designer Passion	Dar Tomlinson	$8.95
Fate	Pamela Leigh Star	$8.95
Against the Wind	Gwynne Forster	$8.95
From the Ashes	Kathleen Suzanne	
	and Jeanne Sumerix	$8.95
Heartbeat	Stephanie Bedwell-Grime	$8.95
My Buffalo Soldier	Barbara B., K. Reeves	$8.95
Meant to Be	Jeanne Sumerix	$8.95
A Risk of Rain	Dar Tomlinson	$8.95

Tango 2 Romance

Love Stories with a Latino Touch

Hearts Remember	M. Louise Quesada	$15.9
Rocky Mountain Romance	Kathleen Suzanne	$8.9
Love's Destiny	M. Louise Quesada	$8.9
Playing for Keeps	Stephanie Salinas	$8.9
Finding Isabella	A. J. Garrotto	$8.9
Ties That Bind	Kathleen Suzanna	$8.9
Eden's Garden	Elizabeth Rose	$8.9

RED SLIPPER

Romance with an Asian Flair

Words of the Pitcher	Kei Swanson	$8.9
Daughter of the Wind	Joan Xain	$8.9

ORDER FORM

Mail to: Genesis Press, Inc.
315 3rd Avenue North
Columbus, MS 39701

Name _____

Address _____

City/State _____ Zip _____

Telephone _____

Ship to (if different from above)

Name _____

Address _____

City/State _____ Zip _____

Telephone _____

Qty.	Author	Title	Price	Total

Use this order
form, or call
1-888-INDIGO-1

Total for books _____

Shipping and handling:
  $3 first book, $1 each
  additional book _____

Total S & H _____

Total amount enclosed _____

MS residents add 7% sales tax

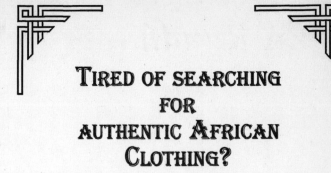
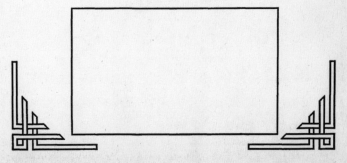